THE ART OF SMUGGLING

THE ART OF SMUGGLING

JUDGE, JURY, & EXECUTIONER™ BOOK SEVEN

CRAIG MARTELLE

MICHAEL ANDERLE

DISRUPTIVE IMAGINATION

Copyright © 2019 Craig Martelle and Michael Anderle
Cover by J Caleb Design, Typography by Jeff Brown
Cover copyright © LMBPN Publishing
A Michael Anderle Production

LMBPN Publishing
PMB 196, 2540 South Maryland Pkwy
Las Vegas, NV 89109

First US edition, October 2019
Version 1.01, October 2019
ebook ISBN: 978-1-64202-502-6
Print ISBN: 978-1-64202-503-3

THE ART OF SMUGGLING TEAM

Thanks to our Beta Readers

Micky Cocker, James Caplan, Kelly O'Donnell, and John
Ashmore

Thanks to the JIT Readers

Nicole Emens
John Ashmore
Kelly O'Donnell
Peter Manis
Dave Hicks
Shari Regan
Diane L. Smith
Misty Roa
Jackey Hankard-Brodie
Micky Cocker
James Caplan
Jeff Eaton
Larry Omans

If I've missed anyone, please let me know!

Editor
Lynne Stiegler

We can't write without those who support us
On the home front, we thank you for being there for us

We wouldn't be able to do this for a living if it weren't for our readers
We thank you for reading our books

CHAPTER ONE

Wyatt Earp, interstellar space

"Bosun's Clipper, you will stand down and prepare to be boarded, by Magistrate Order 32761A/47." Rivka Anoa was not screwing around. She had formalized the order, memorialized forever within the Federation. They had chased this ship for the past two hours, finally getting close enough for direct action.

"You have no authority out here," a voice replied. The *Clipper* refused to use visual communication.

"In ten seconds, we will open fire if you continue to run," Rivka warned. She counted down the time on her fingers, expecting the *Clipper* to continue trying to evade. When she reached zero, she pointed to Clodagh, the woman in the captain's chair.

"Fire," the lieutenant ordered. The small ship tried to juke, but it was too late. The heavy frigate's pulse beams tore through space and lacerated the runner. It died instantly.

Just the ship. No atmosphere venting. A clean technical

kill. The crew should still be alive. Rivka wanted to question them.

"Will it fit in the hangar bay?" Rivka asked.

"Only if we launch the yacht," Clodagh replied.

"Chaz, are you up for taking the yacht for a spin?" Rivka didn't want to use the airlock and umbilical to board the ship. She wanted to keep her hands free to use her gift to help with the interrogation.

Chaz, the newly liberated artificial intelligence, was comfortable doing whatever they needed if they asked. He also had some vacation coming but was at a complete loss as to what he wanted to do. "I'm ready to launch at your request."

"Launch, then bring us around to tow that ship into the hangar bay," Rivka requested.

Before Chaz could act, a bright flash filled the viewscreen. When the lighting returned to normal, the *Clipper's* remains were spreading in a quickly expanding arc.

"Sonofabitch," Rivka grumbled, blinking away the effects of the flash.

"Belay that last order, Chaz," Clodagh said. "Please scan the debris, looking for anything that might contain data or give us a clue what they were carrying."

Rivka nodded. Her thoughts exactly.

"I'm afraid the incendiary they used for the self-destruct was rather thorough," Chaz reported a few moments later. "The first scan looked grim, but I will continue searching."

Rivka leaned over Clodagh to punch a button on the arm

of the captain's chair. "Everyone stand down. They self-destructed rather than let us board them. That gives me more questions and no answers." Rivka let up on the button for a moment as she contemplated her next move. She pursed her lips and shook her head—too many unanswered questions. She punched the button and continued, "I'll be in my quarters. I need to talk to Grainger and the High Chancellor and find out what the hell these scumbags were up to."

Rivka sauntered off the bridge without a word. She watched her feet as she moved down the corridor, ending at her suite, the most comfortable space aboard the ship. It kept her away from the crew, whereas her last ship had been so small, Rivka and her crew were on top of each other most of the time.

Rivka sidestepped wombat poop cubes and entered her quarters.

"Say hi to Rivka," High Chancellor Wyatt said.

Grainger leaned around the corner of the screen to be visible to the camera's eye. "Hi to Rivka."

"Those knuckleheads you sent me after just blew up their ship."

"You're going to have to give me more." The High Chancellor leaned back in his chair and twiddled his fingers.

"The emergency call during Red's and Lindy's wedding to go after this ship? Something about it being tied to a theft, but no details. We fly across the galaxy…"

"One hundred and four light years is all," Grainger interrupted.

Rivka waved her hand as if trying to shoo away a bug buzzing around her head. "Lawyer math. That far *is* across the galaxy. Give it up. You know I won't cave." She pointed a finger at him in what was nearly a double-dog dare, but he didn't bite. He zipped his finger across his lips. "We chase this ship, the *Bosun's Clipper*, and after we finally had to disable him, he lights it up like a supernova. Scanners aren't finding any pieces bigger than my thumb."

Grainger looked at his thumb, turning it to get the best estimate of size. Rivka started to rub her temples to fight off the headache threatening to invade her brain. With her Pod-doc enhancements, she should not have gotten headaches, but she still did. She wondered if that was related to her empathic and telepathic abilities. When she thought about it for longer than a couple of seconds, she realized that Grainger triggered it most often. Stress, and Grainger goofing around. Like now. People had just died, and the case became more difficult because of it.

But if he didn't do that, he wouldn't be Grainger.

And that was why she liked working for him. He expanded the boundaries of what she thought of as normal.

"They may not have been thieves at all," the High Chancellor suggested.

Rivka stopped massaging the sides of her head. "Not thieves?" Her tone promised danger, even for the High Chancellor.

He responded with a gesture for calm and an explanation. "They worked with the thieves. I believe the *Bosun's*

Clipper was a smuggling ship. I would have been very keen to find out what you learned, had you been able to board."

"Smuggling what?"

"Art."

"By all that's holy! You had me chasing rich-people crime? Rich people stealing from other rich people? I think there might be a better use of my time." Rivka sighed and froze at the image on the screen.

The High Chancellor's eyes narrowed as he stared at her, unblinking. "Not at the moment, Magistrate."

Rivka bowed her head. It was within the High Chancellor's sole purview to determine what was most important to the Federation when it came to enforcing the law and prosecuting crime. She had become too familiar and drifted away from respecting the office for which she worked.

"My apologies, High Chancellor. I am frustrated. I want to do the best job I can, and know that I'm doing it for the right reasons. Please send me information on the crimes, and I'll start at the beginning."

Wyatt nodded to Grainger. "Transmitting. I did not want to assign you to the case because of the newlyweds. When you get back to the station, my present to them will be waiting."

Rivka didn't know what to say. She angled her head, but the change in view didn't change his statement. The High Chancellor smiled, trying to get Rivka to relax. He had not given her all the information she should have had before he sent her after the smugglers. Respect went both ways.

"Mine, too!" Grainger yelled from off-screen before leaning in from the side to make a face.

"Doubt it," Rivka replied. She reached toward the screen.

"Keep your paws to yourself, Zombie. I need my secrets."

"Me, too," Rivka said slowly with a smile. "Your secrets..."

The High Chancellor snorted before covering his mouth. "Back to the business at hand. I'm assigning you the case, with my sincere apologies to Vered and Lindy. It is about an art-theft and smuggling ring."

"Find the buyers and backtrack," Rivka murmured, thinking aloud.

Wyatt smiled. Rivka didn't like the look of that. "There's the rub, Magistrate. We haven't been able to find any buyers." The High Chancellor shrugged. "Good luck. Wyatt out."

Rivka stared at the blank screen. She tapped the buttons on her datapad. "Hey, lovebirds, your honeymoon has been postponed. We have to go look at art. Get me Ankh, too, because we need to follow the money if we can find it."

"Say what?" Red sounded tired and somewhat incredulous.

"Put on your pants, both of you, and get to the briefing room. Find Ankh and Jay and bring them with you."

Rivka pored over the information. Business as usual, a theft from an impenetrable location. Investigation. Complaints. Accusations. Insurance payout. Then another artwork theft with an estimated value that boggled Rivka's mind. Wash, rinse, repeat, but with a single item valued at more than entire planets.

Her mind instantly jumped to insurance fraud.

If it were that easy, someone else would have seen it. There...the first investigator had looked at that and even partnered with the insurance company to root out the subterfuge. His final analysis was that he could not rule out that it had been an inside job, but he found no evidence to support his hypothesis. The case file was classified because his suspicions cast aspersions, and those could not be made public without due process—the named individual's ability to defend themselves against the allegation.

She had a special tool to help her find out if it was an inside job. She flexed her fingers, but they did not reveal the power they gave her with their touch.

"Set course for Binsulaker Prime."

"Yes, Magistrate," Chaz replied.

"Do you need us, then?" Red asked from the doorway to the small conference room.

"Get in here, unless you don't have pants on. Then don't until you do."

Red grumbled on his way in. Lindy followed, closing the door behind her. Rivka stared at the door as if it were going to open and Ankh would appear.

Lindy chuckled. "He said he was busy, so Jay went to fetch him."

"The master Ankh-fetcher. Ankh-Fetcher, Inc." Rivka mulled her words. "I think she may have a future career with that brand."

The door opened and Jay entered, carrying the wombat

Floyd. The door closed. No Ankh. The Crenellian had successfully dodged another meeting.

"He was busier than usual, and he now has a forcefield to keep people out," Jay explained.

"A forcefield?" Rivka was supposed to be the captain of her ship, but she didn't fight the reality of her situation.

"Clodagh has painted a yellow and black line on the deck to keep people from accidentally walking into it."

Rivka's headache threatened to return. She closed her eyes and took slow, deep breaths. "Chaz, I don't suppose you could do anything about that?"

"No can do, Magistrate. Erasmus and Ankh have me locked out of key systems I would need to access to override the power flow to their laboratory. They also affect the engines and life support."

"Is there anything you *are* in control of?"

Chaz's laughter filled the conference room. "I can point the ship in various directions."

"Get me Ankh on the comm, please."

The system made the appropriate artificially generated clicks and groans that gave humans peace of mind that something was being done when connecting two ends of a comm link.

"Busy," Ankh answered.

"Ankh, we need your help in tracking rich people's illicit art purchases."

"Busy," Ankh reiterated.

"I will come back there and start destroying my own ship if I have to." Rivka waited until the count of five and started walking toward the door.

"She's coming, Ankh!" Red said in a louder-than-

8

normal voice. "You better pinch your little blue butt cheeks together because this is gonna hurt, buddy."

"She wouldn't," Ankh replied in his emotionless tone.

The door slammed as Rivka stormed out.

Red continued, "She would, and she is. Keep this line open, would you, so we can listen to you getting your ass kicked? It'll be three seconds before you're begging for buttermilk."

"I don't understand why I would ever want buttermilk, let alone beg for it."

Lindy poked Red in the arm while Jay shook her head and cooed to Floyd. The wombat had been eating too much lately. Somebody was giving her treats on the sly, and Jay was ready to ask Chaz for help in finding the culprit.

"Just a saying, little buddy. She looked pretty mad."

"She always looks angry. Maybe that dentist friend can give her a pill or something."

Red wasn't sure how to respond, so he sat and made faces at the center of the table where the microphones with cameras were embedded.

From the speakers in the room, they could hear Rivka yelling. It was distorted, as if she were talking underwater.

"Busy," Ankh said a single time. His voice was clear.

A sharp screech followed a low buzz, then silence announced the dismantling of the forcefield.

"You shouldn't have been able to do that," Ankh said evenly. "The transmitters were inside the field. If the coaxial variant..."

"Follow the money, Ankh. You've done it before, and I need you to do it again." Rivka sounded much calmer than

9

the rapt audience in the conference room expected her to be.

"Erasmus will take care of it. I'm busy."

"Fine."

After a long pause, Ankh spoke. "If it's fine, how come you aren't leaving?"

"Because it's not fine."

"Then why did you say..." The Crenellian didn't complete his thought.

"What are you busy with? Is that something for the research and development team, R2D2?"

"How did you know?" Ankh asked immediately, his voice remaining emotionless.

"Because that's some heady stuff you got in there—shielded stealth with full power for weapons."

Red smiled and gave two thumbs-up.

"Yes. Once it is fully operational, *Wyatt Earp* will be as lethal as a superdreadnought."

"And that was why you put three of the miniaturized Etheric power supplies on board," Rivka noted.

"And that is why I must return immediately to R2D2. I will take the yacht and return when we have the system operational."

"My yacht," Red muttered.

"*Our* yacht," Lindy corrected.

"How is Erasmus going to help us if you're gone?" Rivka pressed.

"Through an active link to *Wyatt Earp's* Etheric communication system. It is not affected by distance. Master Charles will be your liaison."

"Who is Master Charles?"

"The intelligent being you so rudely call 'Chaz.'"

"He told me his name was Chaz!"

"My name *is* Chaz," the AI replied.

Red sat up straight, wearing his best stunned-mullet look. Lindy mirrored her husband's expression.

"Master Charles?" Jay whispered. Floyd nestled into her lap and started softly snoring. Jay rhythmically stroked the wombat's coarse fur.

"You told me, 'Master Charles,'" Ankh countered.

"You, yes. The Magistrate can call me 'Chaz.'"

Rivka started to laugh. "Chaz, prepare the yacht for launch and fire up the Gate drive for a jump to Binsulaker Prime, as close to the planet as you can get. See you on the flip side, Ankh-man."

"Be cool, she's coming back," Red declared to the conference room.

"We are nothing but," Lindy replied. Red pulled her to him for a long kiss. When Rivka cleared her throat, they stopped.

"Are you guys still trying to break in every space on the ship?" Rivka asked as her eyes darted around the small room, assessing places where they could do it. They finally stopped on the top of the conference table, where she had put her coffee mug and a sandwich.

"Not as far as you know, Magistrate."

CHAPTER TWO

Orbit around Binsulaker Prime

"Air-Space Management is being less than cooperative," Chaz reported.

From the captain's chair, Rivka leaned toward the screen. "Play the Magistrate card and include the threat of both criminal and civil penalties."

"How much?" Chaz asked.

"Let's go with ten thousand credits for the first violation and ten thousand credits for every thirty-minute delay after that, with a hundred thousand kicker if I'm delayed for more than four hours."

"It has already been four hours," Chaz noted.

"They can stew on whether that means from now or it's retroactive." Rivka leaned back and sighed.

Red and Lindy occupied seats at stations against the bridge's rear bulkhead. In full tactical gear, they shifted and grumbled about the delay. Rivka spun her chair around. "Soon. Go grab something to eat, and get me a sandwich while you're at it."

"Air-Space Actual says he wants to speak directly to the Magistrate," Chaz interrupted. Rivka gestured that her bodyguards could go, and they bolted without waiting to hear the exchange.

"Magistrate Rivka Anoa, and you are?"

"I am Chief Master Jelesa of Binsulaker Prime Air-Space Control. I don't know who you think you are, but you will make no demands of my people." The face matched the gruff voice. The Slaker's skin looked rough, like bark, with heavy brows and overhangs to protect the creature's eyes and facial orifices.

"Binsulaker Prime is a Signatory member of the Federation. As such, Federation law supersedes when it comes to the care and handling of heads of state, which is how Magistrates are to be treated. Please refer to Appendix D, Chapter Seven, Section 1. And do it now; your fines are increasing rather quickly, and it is good that I have a face and a name to assign them to. If you are unable to pay your civil fines based on your criminal actions, I fear that seven years in Jhiordaan will not assuage your guilt or debt."

"Jhiordaan! *Magistrate*." He spat the word. "That means nothing to me."

The view screen cut off.

"I would love to say begin the bombardment of the control building, but that would punish the presumed innocent." Rivka steepled her fingers and waited.

"The chief wants to talk to you again."

"I suspected he might. Put him on."

The chief's face filled the screen. He was missing a chunk of flesh above one eye. The rough skin did not convey facial expressions in a way Rivka understood, but she expected that was his contrite look.

"My sincere apologies, Magistrate. The landing pattern has been cleared for your vessel."

"I'll consider waiving the fine unless there's another issue. Then I'll shut down your whole planet until you pay your debt to the Federation."

The image froze as Chaz spoke. "Maybe a little heavy-handed, Magistrate? We need their cooperation."

"You're right. I shouldn't let them piss me off like that. Go live, please."

The image resumed its stream. "It's my turn to apologize, Chief Master Jelesa. There will be no fines. Thank you for your cooperation. We'll begin our descent at once. I'm looking forward to resolving our concerns regarding a legal case based in your capital city."

"Thank you. Air-Space Control, out."

His expression hadn't changed, but the tone of his words suggested he was relieved.

"Thanks, Chaz. It's nice to have a team."

"You're welcome," Jay said from behind the captain's chair.

"She put me up to it," Chaz confirmed.

"Then I thank you, too." Rivka spun her chair to face Jayita. She pointed to the young woman's hair. "Is that the same green or new?"

"Added the platinum tint. It kicks!" Jay twirled a finger in a long strand before turning serious again. "I'm trying to earn my keep. I don't feel like I'm carrying my weight. I hang out and play with the animals, but I can do more. I *want* to do more."

Rivka rubbed her chin as she contemplated the young woman. She had been a stray, lost in the rain, when the Magistrate had rescued her. That was the story Rivka told herself. Jay's time in the Pod-doc gave her the capability to run at a fantastic speed and she had become an asset, but she was the pacifist of the team. Rivka didn't want to put her in the position of having to compromise her beliefs, so having the speed of Flash Gordon gained them little except in the direst of emergencies.

That led Rivka back to Jay's emotional intelligence and ability to read people.

"I would like you to spend more time by my side, and when you're not, I encourage you to start studying the law. Specifically, Federation interstellar law. Read, understand, and regurgitate."

"You think I could be a barrister?"

"Why not? I'm one, and you're smarter than me."

"I couldn't hurt people like you do." Jay said it before she thought her words through.

Rivka rocked back in her chair as if she'd been slapped. Jay hung her head.

"Is that what I do? I like to think I punish the guilty." Rivka's voice wavered, weak in the words' delivery.

"Did the chief need to be punished?"

"No. He needed to understand protocol, and my arrogance got the best of me. I thought he should have instantly acceded to my demands, but he doesn't know me, and has probably never heard of a Magistrate. It wasn't his fault. He was just a guy trying to do his job."

"But you were willing to shut down the whole planet."

Jay locked eyes with Rivka, holding her gaze until Rivka nodded.

"And I apologized, once you filled the role of my conscience. Maybe that's what you bring to the game, and to me in particular. I was short with the High Chancellor, too. What's wrong with me, Jay?"

Jay rushed in to grab Rivka in a bear hug. When she let go, she smiled sweetly. "You have the hardest job in the galaxy. You have to find criminals and stop them from committing more crimes. You have to deal with the very worst that sentience has to offer, and it takes its toll. You don't like this mission because it's about art smuggling. It's not a real crime, is it?"

Rivka looked askance and chewed the inside of her lip as she thought about her answer. Jay was challenging her thinking.

In a good way.

"I think I'll call you 'Jaymini.' Jaymini Cricket, and you'll be my conscience." Jay shrugged and made a face. She couldn't place the reference. "Art theft and smuggling are crimes. We've been given the case, and we are going to do our damnedest to get to the bottom of it. Chaz, how long until we land?"

"Five minutes," the AI replied. "I have a request. I'd like to explore some of the city if I can get some time off."

Rivka stood. "Is Erasmus working on the money trail, starting with our first alleged victim and going backward?"

"Yes, he is."

"Then you are doing everything the team needs. How much time do you need?"

"Approximately thirty-seven minutes. It will take all my

abilities to get inside the systems to look through cameras and see the city."

"Why don't you just come with us?" Jay asked.

"Can I do that?"

"I'll keep a live feed open," Jay offered.

"That would be fantastic!" Chaz made the lights on the bridge flash. "I'll get ready. What should I wear?"

"It's a whole new world out there, isn't it, Chaz?" Rivka suggested. "You are responsible for your own decisions. I recommend you dress appropriately. Look at what we're wearing and match it."

"Do I get a Magistrate's jacket?" the AI asked.

"No." Rivka shook her head as she walked off the bridge, shouting for Red and Lindy to join them at the airlock, and wondering where her sandwich had gone.

"Can you see okay?" Jay asked, looking down at her chest, where the small lens and audio pickup was integrated with the front of her blouse, making sure the AI could hear as well as see.

Magnificently! I can't believe I'm out with the team, mixing it up with the local criminals, Chaz shared.

The group stopped and surveyed their surroundings. They were walking toward a small building the local security group called home. It bordered a massive walled area that surrounded the estates of the planet's wealthy.

I think you might be slightly misinformed regarding what it's like to mix it up with local criminals. Remember S'korr? That was a shit sandwich, Rivka replied.

Alas, Magistrate, I was not the freedom-loving adventurer then that I am now. All thanks to you.

You are more than welcome, Chaz. Keep your glass eye peeled and look for things that shouldn't be there.

Seeing the absence of something. I'm not sure I'm set up to do that. My goodness! I'm going to have to write a subroutine to verify my perceptions. I'll be right back.

"Take your time, wee man, while we mix it up with the locals without you," Red said softly.

"First running and first blood. What do you guys have?"

"Come on, Magistrate! We don't want to influence you to make the wrong decision, artificially delivering victory to the undeserving," Red tried to explain.

Rivka gave him the hairy eyeball before trying to gauge the others' thoughts on the bet. They avoided eye contact. "So, you're all in on it."

"Again," Red clarified.

"I went with zeros. We're not running, and we're not getting into any scrapes. Art theft and art smuggling are for a more cultured crowd, where fists and weapons are held in disdain. Guile and deception are their tools."

"Did you see how much that piece was worth? With that kind of money floating around, people will do anything to get some of it, even murder-death-kill." Red tried not to look smug, but he didn't accomplish it.

"I've not read the MDK statute in some time, but I'm sure the penalties are harsh. We'll stick with trying to find the thief. I'm attempting to keep an open mind. We'll see what the insiders think about the crime." Rivka waggled her fingers in the air.

"And that's why they call you 'Zombie,'" Lindy offered,

looking everywhere but behind her, where the Magistrate stood. She and Red wore only their chest armor and carried hand-blasters at their waists. They did not go full armor and armament because of the non-violent nature of the crime.

But trouble always surrounded the magistrate like chaff spinning within a tornado.

With just as much fury and noise. They started walking again.

Rivka glanced around casually, leaning around her two bodyguards, both of whom were larger, and even more so when wearing their ballistic chest protection. Jay walked alongside, watching the world go by and smiling easily.

"I miss Ankh," Jay said into the silence.

Rivka didn't answer, but her thoughts turned toward the Crenellian. Always frustrating, but able to mine digital gold whenever he committed to helping. She had taken a bullet meant for him. She reached for the wound, long since healed, and rubbed the spot, thinking about how he took her words literally.

As smart as he was, he had to understand. Didn't he?

"You're thinking about the little guy, aren't you?" Jay smiled.

"Why do you ask?"

"You were laughing and shaking your head."

"He draws out the best and the worst in people."

"It's his gift," Jay agreed.

"He finally gave me access to the full menu for the food processor, the little shit," Red complained. "What took him so long?"

"As much grief as you give him? I'm surprised he gave it

to you." Lindy stepped aside when they reached the small building with the security logo prominently displayed.

"Showtime," Rivka announced.

She walked through the space between Lindy and Red, climbed the three stairs, and pushed a swinging door open. She held it for Jay. Red and Lindy waited outside.

"Magistrate!" a cheerful sounding Slaker, or native of Binsulaker, called. She still couldn't interpret their facial expressions. "We've been expecting you. I'm Security Operator First Order Kio'alaia."

Rivka offered her hand, and the Slaker looked at it.

"Call me Rivka. We shake hands. It's a human custom." She had her question ready. He pushed his hand forward, awkwardly reaching out. As she grabbed it, she asked, "Where did the Anastolia art theft investigation lead?"

He stopped shaking her hand, but the rough skin of his face maintained its mask of indifference. Rivka felt nothing from him, no emotions or thoughts.

"Didn't you get the case file?"

Rivka let go of his hand. "I did, but I thought it was incomplete." She looked at her fingers as though they had malfunctioned.

"I assure you, it was all there."

"What was your role?" Rivka asked, still reeling from the confusion of not being able to read the security operator. Jay leaned closer to hear the Slaker's answer.

"I was the secondary investigating official. The security minister himself handled this investigation."

"Why would he do that?" Rivka suspected she knew the answer.

"This was a very high-profile case, with the most influential people on all Binsulaker involved. His participation was mandatory."

Jay nudged Rivka enough to let her know that she was there and trying to help.

Rivka's confusion deepened. She had read the case file, and nothing had been as obvious as the answers she had received in the first minute of talking to Kio'alaia. Why was Jay nudging her? Jay moved in front of the Magistrate.

"I'm Jay, nice to meet you." Jay didn't offer her hand, as Rivka had done. She waved in front of her chest, ending with a slap. He mirrored her gesture.

"You know our ways! You have been to Binsulaker Prime before, I take it."

Jay smiled, giving Rivka time to think. "I have not, but in the quick study I did of your planet, I found it fascinating. Tell me about some of the art collections your people maintain."

"Some of the very best in the galaxy, Mistress Jay. Yes, some of the finest individual pieces and overall collections."

"Why didn't the thieves steal from a museum and take more and better?"

"All the artwork is in private collections. We don't believe the government should spend any more money than necessary to maintain the infrastructure within which our society can thrive, so there are no public museums, ostentatious government office buildings, or other symbols of power bought through taking from the citizens." He gestured to take in the cramped space of their small building.

"Does your salary also reflect this policy?" Jay asked for

clarity, not judgment. Federation space stations had opened the galaxy for greater trade, from which member planets like Binsulaker Prime benefitted. Maybe that was infrastructure. Jay wasn't sure what to think, besides trying to understand in order to help Rivka with the case.

"Oh, no. I'm paid privately by those for whom I provide security."

"Like the owner of Anastolia?" Rivka interjected.

"He does not hold the theft against me. It was the most prized, and consequently best protected, piece in his collection. Of all the artwork, that was the least likely to be stolen."

"Yet it was." Rivka watched him closely. "What do you think happened?"

Kio'alaia didn't answer. Statue-still, he allowed the silence to extend for an uncomfortably long time. Jay started to fidget. Rivka tried to wait him out.

"Can you take us there?" Jay finally asked.

"Of course."

"Wait." Rivka held her hand out to stop him. He stayed back, not allowing contact. Jay had done her homework in the brief time she had to prepare. The Slakers didn't like contact with other beings. "I'm sorry, but I need you to answer my question."

"What I think is irrelevant and could misrepresent events. All I can relate is what the investigation proved. That was in the packet already sent to you."

"The investigator suspected it was an inside job," Rivka countered. "That was what the security minister stated."

"Based on facts. We had no evidence that the area had

been penetrated from the outside. Ergo, inside job, but you'll also note that all of the insiders were cleared."

"Being cleared and being innocent are two different things. The perpetrator did a better job of creating the appearance of a solid alibi. That is what we must uncover. The so-called insiders will be the focus of my investigation."

"But they've already been cleared." Kio'alaia pointed toward the sky and drew a circle in the air. Rivka looked at Jay to interpret what the signal meant. She shrugged, but she didn't have the answer.

That gesture signals that he disagrees vehemently, Chaz offered. *There are many human counterparts.*

"They haven't been cleared by me. First stop, scene of the crime. I want to talk to the owner." The shuttle that had dropped them off was nowhere to be found, nor were any other vehicles. "How are we going to get there?"

CHAPTER THREE

The Anastolia Display, Beit'el Estate

After a five-kilometer walk into the walled compound that was the high-rent district, the group arrived at yet another estate of flowing lines, welcoming gardens, and glamorous façades. Kio'alaia ushered them to the door, where they were met before knocking and led inside through an antechamber, a ballroom-sized entryway, and finally, into the gallery.

"Beit'el Senior will be with you shortly." The Slaker bowed in the manner of an old English butler and excused himself. Kio'alaia stood on the far side of the room opposite the dismantled display.

"Please come over here and explain what I'm looking at. As it is, you're giving me the impression that you are covering up for the security minister, who is covering for someone else. Is this a conspiracy that taints your government and way of life?"

Security Officer First Order Kio'alaia finally came to life, now as animated as any person accused of a crime. He started to stammer and stutter. "We don't throw around such spurious allegations. Is this how the Federation conducts an investigation? If you think it, you say it?"

"By throwing out various theories, we can either work to prove or disprove them. It is how we conduct investigations. Your behavior is making me question the veracity of your participation."

"I don't know what that means," he replied.

"It means that if I feel you've been holding back on me, I'll have to charge you with obstruction of justice. That will jeopardize your position as liaison to the Federation. It's not much, and I'm not going to threaten you with jail. I prefer your cooperation over an antagonistic relationship. Do you understand why I need your help?" Rivka approached with her arms wide, taking in the entirety of a culture she didn't understand while trying to solve a crime that had already befuddled the local authorities.

"Because you don't understand Binsulaker Prime?"

"Because I respect your individualism. I prefer the smoothest route to conducting this investigation, and that is with your help. Do I have it?" Rivka stood face to face with Kio'alaia as she pleaded for his cooperation. She was trying to play nice.

Rivka also wanted to pound him for giving her the impression that the security minister was hiding something. But if so, why had the minister put in the report that he thought it was an inside job? Maybe that was a masterful way of pointing the finger while clearing himself of covering for the four people who lived inside the Anastolia Gallery bubble.

Kio'alaia answered briefly, "I would not have done that. Cast no aspersions except on the guilty."

"They have to be guilty before you can name them? That seems a little backward. We simply use terms like 'the accused,' and they can seek redress in a court of law."

"As do we. I think there are more similarities than differences between our two systems." Before Rivka could follow up, an elder Slaker entered using an ornate cane to help him shuffle along entered the gallery. "Please make the acquaintance of Gil'dinor, owner of the Anastolia and senior of this estate."

Rivka turned to address the elder. "I am Magistrate Rivka Anoa." She mirrored the greeting she had seen Jay use. "I am pleased to meet you."

"And I you," he said pleasantly, waving his free hand before his chest. "Before all things, I would like the Anastolia back."

"That is what we seek to do." Rivka grimaced, thinking of the smuggler ship. She hoped the Slaker couldn't read her expression. She believed the art had been on board and was among the debris presently scattering in an ever-widening pattern across a remote area of interstellar space. She hoped she was wrong about the Anastolia.

Pictures of it had been in the file, but she hadn't bothered to look at them. She wanted to find who stole it and then dismantle the remainder of the smuggling network. There are more pieces of art than just the Anastolia.

"Please tell me about what was stolen," Rivka said as she moved next to the old Slaker, standing shoulder to shoulder with him as he looked at the space where the statuette used to be. She brushed against him as he started to talk and he instinctively moved away, but like before, she heard nothing from his mind. *Looks like we have to do this the hard way*, she lamented.

"It was the most magnificent piece in the known galaxy." He pointed with his cane at the empty space. "With curves that drew your eye and kept your mind wondering about the possibilities for an infinite amount of time. I would stand here for hours and look at it."

"It was insured—" Rivka started, brushing against him again.

"Bah!" he shot back. His expression didn't change, but he started to hammer his cane into the floor, and his voice grew harsh. "At my age, money is worthless. It is the timeless joy the Anastolia gave me. Now look at it!"

He stabbed the air with his cane until he started to wheeze.

"Please take it easy. Can I get you a chair?" Jay jumped to his rescue. Red and Lindy felt out of place. They both shifted from foot to foot, looking at the rich adornments of the gallery. More artwork hung around the walls, and statues stood in the open areas between. Even without the Anastolia, it was a collection worthy of the most renowned museums.

The butler reappeared with a cushioned chair and placed it behind Gil'dinor. The elder Slaker sat down, looking ancient as he hunched over, head bowed toward the floor. Jay resisted the urge to comfort him with a hug or by massaging his shoulders. She kneeled before him instead.

"We're here to root out the criminals and recover the Anastolia. I don't know how long it will take, but the

Magistrate has never failed to solve a case. She's been shot and stabbed and chased, but you know what she hasn't done? Quit. She will get the Anastolia back for you. I guarantee it!"

Rivka's mouth dropped open as she stood there trying not to let Gil'dinor see. She drew a finger across her throat to get Jay to stop, but it was too late.

"You say nice things to an old man," the Slaker murmured, meeting Jayita's eyes. "I could ask no more from anyone. May the stars show you the way to enlightenment."

"Peace unto you, Elder," Jay replied. The senior of the estate rose and trundled slowly away.

Rivka let him go. She knew who the other insiders were, based on the report. The daughter. The butler. And the head of the gallery.

The butler made to go, but Rivka stepped in front of him. "I have a few questions I need answered."

"When I get back." He impatiently waved for her to get out of his way.

"Red, go with him. Make sure he finds his way back here in a timely manner."

Red smiled and nodded. The butler fixed her with a long gaze before hurrying after Gil'dinor. Red strolled after him.

Rivka, Jay, and Lindy were left alone in the gallery. Cameras' eyes looked at them from all angles.

"Footage showed nothing, I suppose," Lindy posited.

All feeds went dead before the theft and were off during it, Chaz confirmed.

"How?" Rivka already knew, but she wanted the others to hear it.

Digitally, as if an electromagnetic pulse zeroed the systems. It didn't come back on until it was rebooted after the theft.

Rivka made a circuit of the room, looking for obvious electronic systems.

Kio'alaia watched her without interference.

Any ideas about how that happened, Chaz? Digital finger-prints? Rivka asked, using her internal comm chip.

I found nothing.

What does the absence of something that should be there tell us? Rivka pressed.

An inside job.

"I can't wait to talk to the security minister," Rivka replied aloud.

"Do you wish to leave?" Kio'alaia asked, heading for the door without waiting for an answer.

"Not yet, but soon." Lindy moved between Kio'alaia and the door. "I want to talk to the butler, the daughter, and the head of the gallery individually before we leave here."

"Their statements are part of the record I sent you. You should read it before asking people to repeat themselves."

Rivka dialed up a snarky response but held it back as part of reshaping herself into the person Jay saw her as.

"I'm sorry, but it's part of my process. I will ask similar questions, but differently, and look for story variations. The problem with lies is that people forget the ones they told. Sometimes the truth is all we remember."

"If one tells a lie often enough, that becomes the truth," Kio'alaia suggested.

"A lie will always be a lie." Rivka touched her finger to

her nose. "We can never let one become the truth, even if we want to believe it."

The Slaker did not reply. He remained stoic and unmoving, waiting just like the other statues in the gallery.

Red opened the door and pushed the butler through. The Slaker tried to resist but was out-massed by the big bodyguard. "He was trying to leave."

"I was not!" His tone was defiant as he stood upright, sideways to Red, not challenging him. He composed himself and strode to the center of the gallery, crossed his gloved hands before him, and faced the Magistrate.

"Where were you during the robbery?" Rivka touched his arm briefly but pulled back when she realized he was a blank slate, too.

He looked at her. His expression gave nothing away, but he didn't answer until she put her hands behind her back.

"I was in my room. That was the brief period of time I am off each night. I don't waste it because if I don't sleep, there is no chance to take a nap the next day."

"I get you," Rivka commiserated. "From how long before until how long after the theft did you sleep?"

"I retired two hours before the alarm rang and was down here within five minutes after the first bell."

"Five minutes?" Rivka tried to recall the timeline. She couldn't remember, but it wasn't all on her. *Chaz, what does the file say about the timeline following the alarm?*

The alarm sounded, and Security was the first to arrive, at eight minutes. The butler arrived at ten minutes.

"What did you hear as you traveled between your room and the gallery?"

"The alarm."

"Not glass breaking, not a door slamming, or a vehicle racing away?" Rivka crossed her arms. She knew what he would say but wanted his confirmation.

"Just the alarm." He held his ground, but Rivka let the silence weigh on him.

Finally, he continued, "There wasn't any broken glass or slammed doors. When we searched the premises following the incident, we found all external doors were secure."

"Who was down here when you arrived?"

"The head of the gallery was here with the security team."

Rivka pursed her lips, recreating in her mind the moments after the crime. "This area seems free of crime. Is it common to have on-site security?"

"Senior Gil'dinor is an extremely wealthy individual, important not only on Binsulaker Prime, but in this sector of space. The security is his, not the estate's, although they serve double duty. You will find similar arrangements at most estates in this area."

Chaz, can you confirm that?

I'll add it to my growing list, Magistrate.

Remind me to drill Kio'alaia on it, too. He's paid by the same guy who is paying the on-site security. And why weren't they considered insiders for purposes of the investigation? We need to confirm their alibis and check their backgrounds, including finances.

"Then where did the Anastolia go?" Rivka continued out loud. Her internal conversation with her team had taken only a couple of seconds.

"I wish I knew. This is trying for the senior of the estate, and I fear it will result in his demise."

Rivka chewed on her lip. "Who benefits under his will?"

"I'm sure I don't know."

The Magistrate had a hard time believing that, but let it go. She could find out elsewhere, like from the security minister. Or Chaz.

I will look, Magistrate.

"Thank you for your time. I will have more questions. Please make sure you don't leave without informing me."

"Where would I go? I have a job to do."

Red stepped away from the door.

"As do I," Rivka shot back as the Slaker butler walked out. "Next up, the head of the gallery. Kio'alaia, can you bring him here, please?"

"Her," the security operator clarified. "I'll be right back."

CHAPTER FOUR

The head of the gallery was a massive Slaker, both taller and wider than Red. The bodyguard inhaled deeply and stood tall, his hands hanging loosely at his sides as if facing a challenger across a combat ring. He relaxed when he saw the expression on her face.

Rivka stepped lightly across the floor to greet the newcomer. Unlike the others, her eyes darted from one face to another. She wore a human-like expression of panic.

The Magistrate brushed her arm. "We're doing what we can to recover the Anastolia."

The statue gone! Failure. Terror! She had never failed before, and this was the greatest of any losses ever on Binsulaker Prime. She wanted to kill herself.

Rivka stepped back. "No!" she blurted. "You did your job. Let me tell you, there was probably nothing you could have done to prevent the theft of the Anastolia."

"But it was my job to protect it. It was the best job on all

Binsulaker. I got to spend time with her every day, and now she's gone."

Rivka gripped the female's arm, but she didn't shy away. "That's why we're here. We have considerable assets at our disposal to help us investigate this crime. We will do everything we can to recover the Anastolia and punish those who committed this heinous act."

The Magistrate had to step back from the head of the gallery's anguish. From one extreme to the other. From no emotions to a tidal wave. "Tell us about that night."

"What's there to tell? The alarm sounded, and I jumped out of bed, threw on clothes, and ran here."

"I think it was eight minutes before you arrived," Rivka said.

"The gallery is rather extensive, and I'm at the far end. The alarm doesn't specify which section has been violated, so I went through each on the way here. The feelings got worse with each step closer to the Anastolia."

"You are different from the others we've met." Rivka tried to pull her out of the abyss she'd cast herself into.

"My father was a Slaker, but my mother was not. She was Pandemonian. That's why I'm called Due'monian, a child of two races."

Red nodded knowingly. Rivka couldn't place the race but expected they were a larger species, like the Pretarians.

"I'd like to talk to your security detail too, please."

"I administer this collection by myself."

"But the butler said that you were here with the security detail when he arrived."

"They were here when I arrived, both of them. I believe they work the night shift." She turned and faced the empty spot where the Anastolia had stood. Tears trailed from her eyes down the rough skin of her face.

"How did they get in?"

"They have an access pass, but it only gets them to the outer door, there." She pointed over her shoulder to the door where the butler had exited. "I had to let them in here."

"If you had to let them in, then how did the thieves get in here?"

The head of the gallery faced Rivka, her eyes still glistening. "Wouldn't I love to know the answer to that question?" She gestured broadly to take in all the magnificent pieces of art still in the collection. "They could do it again, and there would be nothing I could do to stop them."

"We have to find them. That will stop it from happening again." Rivka took a step back. She didn't need to touch the female to feel the emotions radiating from her. She was unknowingly broadcasting her angst.

"Kio'alaia, would you please go with Red and find the security team? I have some questions."

The Slaker walked out without a word, Red close on his heels.

Try to bond with him if you can. He's a tough nut to crack, but we need him.

I'm on it, boss, Red replied.

Rivka tried not to smile at the subtle change since his marriage. Lindy caught Rivka's glance and winked.

Jay walked around the pedestal on which the Anastolia had stood. "Can you imagine such a piece?"

Rivka and Lindy joined her, but Lindy faced away to

watch for anything that might threaten the Magistrate while her focus was elsewhere.

"I can't imagine something that is considered priceless, yet has a price—a massive one. A thing that draws people to it like moths to a flame."

Jay pointed to a painting on the wall, an alien landscape, greatly detailed for a painting the size of a billboard. "I could look at it for hours and not see everything there is to see."

Rivka glanced at it. "I would rather see the planet in person."

"Looking at holovids on a screen, or through your mind's eye into the world of another's imagination?" Jay put her hands behind her back and strolled from one piece to the next, commenting on the allure of each.

The head of the gallery joined Jay as she walked. "You understand," she told the green-haired woman.

Jay hadn't seen any of the pieces before, but each spoke to her in a different and exciting way. Jay continued talking even though Rivka had given up trying to figure out what each piece was supposed to be. She settled for studying the security details for each piece.

"Electronic." Rivka pointed, but no one was paying attention. "Lindy. Give it your expert eye."

Lindy studied a pedestal before moving to a picture on the wall. She followed the flowing lines of the wall to the ceiling and around the room, then pulled a flashlight from her vest and dialed it to a narrow beam. Lindy pointed it at the ceiling, stopping when she saw what she was looking for. "A recessed sensor, probably motion. Laser beams to highlight when a barrier is broken. Even video capture, although that was easily defeated, it seems."

"All of it was," Rivka added. "No physical security inside the gallery, but the barriers, I mean the doors, were closed and locked."

Due'monian threw her hands up in surrender. "I've been through this room a hundred times since the theft, and I still have no idea how they did it."

"Maybe they didn't leave," Rivka suggested.

"There was no one here when I arrived."

"What if it was the security detail, those two, who let themselves out and made like they wanted to be let back in?"

"Then where was the Anastolia?"

"How big is it?"

"A little under two meters tall and a meter in diameter. About your size."

"Not quite a meter in diameter, but I get your point." Rivka went from one pedestal to the next until she stood next to one that was big enough that the statue could have fit within. She knocked on it, and an alarm sounded. "Is this hollow?"

"I suppose..." Due'monian's words hung heavy in the air as she briskly strode to where Rivka stood. She talked into a device on her wrist. "Cancel the alarm, override on my authority. I will be moving the Palustrade for cleaning."

She reached to the top of the pedestal and unlatched two small clamps holding the alien bird of prey statue. It loomed over the gallery from its perch on high. She lifted it with some effort and moved slowly out of the way to set it on the floor.

"Could you stand by that to make sure it doesn't get bumped?" she asked. Jay nodded and assumed a position between it and the people looking strangely at the tall box on which the Palustrade, the bird statue, had perched.

Together, they lifted the box and tipped it up. It was hollow within, but empty.

"I'm assuming the Anastolia wouldn't leave any residue."

Due'monian shook her head. "It was an immaculate piece."

Rivka looked inside the box. "Maybe we don't need residue. What about these?" She pointed, but Due'monian couldn't see in low light like Rivka. "Lindy, your flashlight, please."

Lindy appeared and shined the light inside. Small pads threw distinct shadows, on each of the four sides.

"They took care not to scratch the Anastolia." She reached inside to feel the pads. "Soft." She dropped to the floor and cradled her head. "It was right here. Right here!"

"And if they took those precautions here, then they will still be handling it carefully. The good news is that we have the other footage from after the theft. Let's see who removed it."

The head of the gallery groaned. "We shut the system down to upgrade it."

"Who decided that?" Rivka wondered.

Due'monian pointed to herself. "I did." She closed her eyes and struggled to breathe. Rivka thought she was going to start crying again. "But the insurance agent agreed that it was the right thing to do."

"What insurance agent?" Rivka blurted.

"She was on the premises the next day to begin her own investigation."

"How many other people were involved that Kio'alaia didn't tell us about, and who failed to make it into his report?" Rivka ground her teeth as she stared at the inside of the box. "Is she a Slaker, a local?"

"No. She's from the Gorandian race. They are agoraphobic in the extreme, so they can only function off their homeworld inside a containment suit that limits external stimuli."

"What the hell was an agoraphobe doing hanging out on Binsulaker Prime, and more importantly, where is she now?"

"I believe she's still here. She refused to accept the security minister's conclusion and is continuing her investigation."

"I'll need her contact information unless you can get her to come here. That would be best."

"I will take care of it." Due'monian took one last look at the box, sighed, and headed out.

"What do you think?" Rivka asked.

Jay gazed at the Palustrade while she answered. "I think the art in here is simply amazing, while at the same time it's sad that very few people get to enjoy it. All art is privately owned. Maybe Robin Hood stole the Anastolia so more people could enjoy it."

"I think our thieves were less philanthropic. They will be swimming in a lake filled with credits, even if they sell the work at a steep discount. It's pure profit for them."

What about you, Chaz? Do you have any ideas?

I think this is exhilarating! the AI replied. *I see why the team enjoys going on missions with you. There is so much going on. Joust, parry, thrust, slash. Bravo, Magistrate!*

Rivka tried not to roll her eyes at the AI's exuberance. *But do you see anything we missed?*

Indeed. I wanted to tell you that the sensor feeds were not cut off during the theft. They were erased.

"Well, now, that changes things, and probably narrows our suspect list a great deal," Rivka said aloud before she realized the magnitude of what Chaz had said. "Deleted? Does that mean you can recover the information?"

She positioned herself in front of Jay, where the video pickup would capture her.

I am working on it right now, Chaz replied proudly.

"I love you, Chaz," Rivka stated, giving him a thumbs-up.

Me too, Magistrate.

CHAPTER FIVE

The Gallery, Gil'dinor's Estate

"Is Red coming back?" Rivka finally asked. Lindy shrugged but put her finger to her temple as she tried to contact him privately using her internal comm chip.

Jay wanted to explore more of the gallery but didn't want to leave Rivka behind. As a contributing member of the team, Jay was trying to focus on the matter at hand and not the extensive artwork in the collection.

Due'monian's footsteps on the tile long preceded her arrival. Rivka, Lindy, and Jay were watching when she appeared from the next chamber in the long gallery.

"I've transmitted the contact information," Due'monian announced on her arrival.

Chaz?

I have it, Magistrate. I'm hunting her down right now!

"Our partner on the ship is working on it."

Whoa! Am I chopped liver?

"I'm sorry, he has a virtual presence with us," Rivka clarified.

Jay pointed to the small device she wore like a necklace. "Say hi to Chaz."

"Hi, Chaz." Due'monian leaned forward and waved. She was a good head and a half taller than Lindy and towered over the smaller Jayita. "Does he speak?"

"Directly into our minds, so you won't be able to hear him, unfortunately, but I'll relate what he says."

Do we trust her? Chaz asked.

Unless it's that!

"Chaz says hi," Rivka smoothly interjected when panic flashed across Jay's face. *Not yet,* Rivka replied to the AI. "He also says he is trying to contact the insurance agent. Her name is Angora?"

"Angora the Gorandian. Since she's in the environmental containment unit, she comes across as fairly robotic. Even her voice, but she's the one Loids of Yoll, the insurance company, sent."

"When?" Rivka asked.

"She got here less than a day after the incident."

Rivka shook her head and waved one hand. "I'm sorry. I meant when did Gil'dinor contract with Loids?"

"Before the Anastolia arrived. That was long before I was employed here. The Gil'dinor Estate has had the Anastolia for five years, and Angora has always been the senior's point of contact."

I confirm this. Chaz was starting to clear issues from his workload. *I am recreating the video. Whoever deleted it did a thorough job, just not thorough enough.*

Is that your smug voice, Chaz? Rivka asked.

You've been listening to Ankh and Erasmus too much, Jay suggested

Erasmus is the standard upon which all AIs should be modeled.

Rivka was going to dispute Chaz's last point, but Due'-monian was talking.

"No one came in to clean anything up after the theft. It was as you see it now." The head of the gallery still sounded defensive.

"I have cleared you of any wrongdoing. You were in the right place doing the right things, and none of that mattered. They, whoever *they* were, were going to steal the Anastolia, no matter who was here," Rivka explained, trying to put Due'monian's mind at ease.

"Thanks for that, but it doesn't make me feel any better. They waited for five years until they found someone suitably weak."

"I don't think that's the case at all. Did you know that there has been a recent spate of art thefts in this sector of Federation space?" Rivka waited for Due'monian to acknowledge the point. "The Anastolia was the fifth piece stolen, the most recent, and far and away the most expensive. That was why we came here first, while the trail was still fresh."

Rivka didn't add that the smugglers *Wyatt Earp* had intercepted had been closest to Binsulaker Prime. Whether they were coming or going was up for debate. The easy answer had disappeared in the massive explosion that consumed the smugglers' ship.

They were willing to die for the cause, Rivka thought. It had been nagging at her. They had pieces of the puzzle, yet no one knew anything. Clues were sparse, and she couldn't read the Slakers to discover if it were an inside job. *It has to be!*

The door to the gallery opened. Red and Kio'alaia walked through, pushing the butler in front of them.

"We had a hard time finding him," the security operator reported.

"This is a *really* big place," Red emphasized. "We went to a great number of places he wasn't."

"I thought you were going to collect the security detail?"

"That's what we started to do, but they don't come on shift for a couple hours. I thought you had more questions for this guy."

"I do, but now is not the time I want to ask them." She stared at the butler, but his face remained expressionless. He didn't even blink. Rivka tried to wait him out, but his genetics were different. She didn't remember any of the Slakers blinking. She finally gave up.

"We will be back this evening and meet the security detail when they assume their shift."

"Of course. We will be waiting on pins and needles for your arrival."

Red wanted to punch the Slaker but thought better of it.

Jay stepped up. "Are the ones coming on tonight the ones who were here the night Anastolia was stolen?"

"No. We had to let those two go. Their job was to prevent the theft. How could we keep them on?"

"When were you going to tell me?" Rivka wondered, jamming her fists on her hips as she looked at the butler.

"I figured you would discover it for yourself." The butler looked at the Palustrade sitting unceremoniously on the floor. "What is that doing there? You'll be fired as soon as senior of the estate hears about this."

Red stopped the butler from storming off and looked curiously at the statue. Kio'alaia turned his head in that direction but didn't say anything.

"Look at this." Due'monian pointed at the box. "And here where there is padding. They didn't steal the Anastolia that night. They hid her in here and took her later."

The butler edged closer, looking at the stand.

"Too many people around here touching what they shouldn't. The senior needs me. I have been away from my duties for far too long."

"You can return to them with my apologies as soon as you provide the contact information for the two security guards you fired."

"They were let go. I do not *fire* anyone."

Rivka closed her eyes and breathed slowly.

Lindy shouldered past Red to come face to face with the butler. "We need their contact information, which you had to have because of their employment. I also suspect you had full background checks done on them before they were hired. We'll take copies of those, too."

"You can't have them." The butler crossed his arms in a human-like way, even though nothing besides the tone of his voice gave his feelings away.

Kio'alaia held his hand up to get their attention. "I have all that information. You need not bother the estate or its personnel any longer."

"Thank you," Rivka said, eyes still closed. Another anomaly—what to do with the governmental security operator who was paid privately. The conflict of interest was built into the Slakers' system, and she couldn't wrap her head around it.

"Let's find those two, and then we'll return to the ship. I'll want the insurance agent to meet us there. I think sharing notes will benefit us both." Rivka finally opened her eyes. She contemplated the gallery one last time. "The answers we seek are not in here."

Due'monian wrapped Rivka in her arms and lifted her off the ground in a hug before lovingly picking up the Palustrade and carrying it away.

"Let's go find us some bad guys," Red told Kio'alaia.

"What if there are no bad guys to be found?" the security operator asked.

"I'm pretty sure it wasn't good guys who stole that statue."

Capital City, Gerrymander District, Binsulaker Prime

"Not quite like the estates, is it?" Rivka asked. Kio'alaia ignored the statement. The transport van had taken over an hour to arrive at the security office. Rivka had tried to be patient, but the slow pace on Binsulaker was starting to grate on her nerves.

The soaring and expansive architecture in the estates morphed the farther they traveled toward the center of the city. The closer to city center, the lower the quality of life, until it became absolute squalor. That was when the van stopped.

"According to my records, both security guards live at this address."

"That building would be condemned on most planets,"

Rivka noted. "And it didn't strike you as odd that in a city as big as this, you got two applicants from the same place?"

"Not at all. People like living near their friends. They'll apply for jobs together, and these two both passed their background checks. There aren't very many applicants for night-shift security."

"I expect not," Rivka replied. "But the estates! That *has to* be a good job, compared to some of the other opportunities in this area."

"Or lack thereof," Jay added.

Kio'alaia opened the door.

"You wait right here," Red told the driver. "We'll be back when we get back."

"I am sorry, but no. We don't sit without passengers. There is always the next ride to be given."

Rivka, Red, and Lindy turned to Kio'alaia. He waited for a moment before speaking. "What?"

"Why don't you wait with the vehicle? I don't want to stand around down here for an hour or more waiting for our next ride."

"But that's our way. You wait your turn since we have a limited number of vehicles. If we tie up this van, someone else will have to wait even longer."

"You don't have a designated security vehicle?"

"Of course not!" Kio'alaia's exasperation registered in his high-pitched answer, although his facial expression didn't change. "We don't waste people's money buying luxuries like vehicles."

Rivka removed her credentials from her jacket pocket. "Under my authority as a Magistrate for the Federation, I am confiscating this vehicle. You will stay with it and wait for us to return. Thank you."

She put her credentials back in her pocket and left the sputtering security operator behind. Red yanked the door to the multi-level apartment building open and stepped through. Rivka and Jay went through next, and Lindy brought up the rear. The ground floor looked like the second floor looked like the rest. Twenty or thirty units on each level. One of the target apartments, based on the address provided by Kio'alaia was on the second floor, and the other on the third.

The darkness took them by surprise, so they needed a moment for their eyes to adjust before continuing. Dust drifted through the air. "Red, Jay, you take the second floor, and Lindy and I will take the third. Watch for any runners."

"Do you expect them to be here?" Red asked.

Rivka shook her head. "When they don't answer, open it up and take a look inside. You know the routine. Don't touch anything in case we need some forensics." Rivka removed the small neutron pulse weapon from her pocket. Affectionately called "Reaper," it provided all the firepower she needed. Red and Lindy unholstered their hand-blasters. Both looked at the weapons as if they were toys.

"It sure would be nice if we had our railguns," Red whispered as they started climbing the stairs. "By the way, what are we looking for?"

"Evidence of a plot to steal the Anastolia. Maybe extra rubber pads like those inside the Palustrade's stand? Things like that."

"Not the Anastolia?" Lindy suggested.

"I think the chance of them bringing it here is zero if

they were involved. My guess is that it's already off-planet. I have a theory, but I need to see what Chaz uncovers."

Red and Jay stepped onto the second-floor landing.

"Stay frosty," Lindy advised.

"You, too," Red replied. He and Jay stepped lightly down the hallway, checking numbers beside doors. Rivka made it up three steps before a shout arrived at the same time as an explosion. "Grenade!"

Debris and flames shot across the landing. The stairway started to fill with smoke.

"Red!" Lindy shouted and stormed down the stairs.

Rivka heard a sound above and turned in time to see two Slakers at the top of the steps taking aim with weapons she hadn't seen before. She pressed the button on Reaper as she jumped over the railing, dropping half a flight before landing on the next flight down. A body falling, she thought. Pounding footsteps. Too many.

With her back to the wall, she edged up the stairs. The strange weapon appeared, with a Slaker behind it. She took aim and fired. The being dropped, instantly dead. Rivka checked her setting. She had it dialed up to seven.

She ran up the stairs to grab the Slaker's weapon and watch the action. Footsteps from above could be people evacuating or more perps.

"Jay is down. We're bringing her out," Red called from the hallway.

"And Red isn't in too good of shape, either," Lindy added. A blaster barked, and then another.

After a brief but furious cavalcade of fire, Red shouted, "Clear."

Slakers appeared, all armed. Rivka took aim with

Reaper and fired. The first two went down before the others dodged for cover. They fired heavy slugs launched by smoky propellant wildly into the stairwell.

It created a screen to hide behind. Rivka switched to the Slaker weapon and fired back. Smoke rolled from the end of the barrel. She fired until the weapon stopped, either empty or jammed. She didn't care which.

Red and Lindy had already passed behind her and were heading downstairs. She vaulted the railing, took two steps, and vaulted again. She jumped half a flight at a time and reached the front door at the same time as the others.

"She's alive," Lindy reported once she saw the look on Rivka's face. They burst onto the street and found Kio'alaia standing there without the van.

"Where's our ride?" Rivka demanded

"He left! It's policy."

Rivka growled and turned to the doorway again to fire at their pursuers. Smoke was making its way down the stairs, but no Slakers appeared. *Chaz, bring* Wyatt Earp *for an emergency recovery.*

Clodagh is on her way to the bridge now. Aurora is spinning up the engines. They'll be here in three minutes. I recommend you find a place they can land.

"Where can my ship land?"

"Not down here!" Kio'alaia wasn't trying to be negative. The city center had little open space, and nowhere near enough for a heavy frigate.

Red and Rivka immediately looked up. "There." Red pointed to a building a block away. It was the highest in the area and had a flat roof. Rivka took one long look inside the apartment building before joining her team.

"They can't land, but they can hover so we can get the hell out of here."

They took off running, Lindy and Red carrying Jay between them. She was unconscious and had been bleeding heavily. The wounds were already sealed, but she wasn't like the others. It would take time for her to recover. Her gift was speed, and that had been neutralized when the explosion went off before she could react.

The security operator ran with them.

"Where are you going?" Rivka snarled.

"With you. It's not safe down here."

"Maybe that was why we wanted the van to wait for us." Rivka kept checking over her shoulder. They weren't clear yet. They needed to round a corner.

"But that's not the policy."

Rivka jerked sideways to look at the Slaker. "Can you hear what you're saying? How about two policies?"

"We can't do that." Kio'alaia started checking over his shoulder.

"Twelve o'clock!" Red shouted as he dragged Jay and Lindy to the side. Two Slakers with slug throwers leaned around the corner ahead and started to fire.

Kio'alaia took three rounds, but he never juked. He kept running straight at his fellow Slakers. Rivka was already accelerating away at an angle. She snap-fired Reaper, twirling the device's business end in the direction of her new enemies. With no cars on the street, either driving or parked, there was nothing to hide behind.

Rivka slid to a stop while the last Slaker led her with his aim and fired. He missed. Rivka didn't. As he was falling, the Magistrate ran to the corner of the building and peeked around. "Clear," she yelled over her shoulder before checking the two bodies.

"Kio is down," Lindy reported.

"Head up. I'll be right behind you."

Lindy and Red turned sideways to get Jay through the doorway. Rivka raced back to where Kio'alaia had fallen, kneeled next to him, and pulled his bulk into a sitting position. She leaned her shoulder into his chest and lifted from under his legs. His body fell into place for the fireman's carry, and she walked quickly off the street and through the door. Red and Lindy were going slowly up the stairs, sheltering Jay with their bodies as they moved her without jostling. Rivka caught up to them after a few seconds.

"Screw it," Red said and lifted Jay into his arms as if he were cradling a baby. Then he started taking the steps two at a time. They climbed the eight flights quickly. At the top, he stepped aside so Lindy could kick the final door open. *Wyatt Earp* was descending, landing skids up, to hover less than a meter above the roof.

The cargo bay ramp lowered until it was in contact with the surface, and the team ran across the open space and into their ship. The ramp retracted, and the ship accelerated away from the city center.

"The Slaker goes first," Rivka announced. The Pod-doc was off to the side of the cargo bay, open and waiting, with Clodagh waving her in as if guiding a landing airplane. Rivka placed Kio'alaia inside, and the door closed.

Rivka was counting on the power of the Pod-doc to bring the almost dead Slaker back to life. Jay was injured, maybe dying, but Rivka was betting they could save both.

"Make Jay stronger," Red pleaded, holding the young woman tightly.

"Can't do it without Ankh. This is the emergency Pod-doc, so it only does the minimum unless the programming is overridden, and only Ankh and Erasmus can do that," Rivka explained almost dispassionately.

Jay struggled to breathe, but was settling into a smoother rhythm. Rivka glared at the Slaker through the Pod-doc's lid. "I want him well so I can rip him a new one. He took us into a battleground without the least hint of what we were walking into."

CHAPTER SIX

Orbit around Binsulaker Prime

The wombat's plaintive cry echoed through the ship as the round ball of fur bounded through the hatch and into the cargo bay. Rivka caught her before she could barrel head-first into her unconscious friend. Floyd was so distraught, she couldn't speak coherently. Rivka cooed to her and stroked her slowly to calm her down.

"Jay will be fine. She is waiting for her turn in the Pod-doc. It will only be a few more minutes." The Magistrate leaned close to Jay, holding the wombat over her. "See? She's breathing, and the bleeding has stopped. She is badly hurt and needs you to be strong for her."

The wombat continued to blubber. The Magistrate let her wedge between the green-haired woman's arm and body, nuzzling her for comfort and warmth.

The lid popped on the Pod-doc. Red unceremoniously dragged the Slaker out, pushing him aside. Rivka picked Floyd up, much to the wombat's dismay. Red and Lindy carefully placed Jay inside and closed the door. Clodagh started the system, and it began to cycle.

All they had to do was wait.

Rivka took a deep breath before trying to speak to Kio'alaia. The Slaker's head rolled on his shoulders, and he blinked rapidly while he tried to regain his awareness.

"Where am I?"

"You're on my ship, *Wyatt Earp*."

"I'm Kio'alaia," he replied.

"I know. What do you remember?" Rivka asked.

"I remember that you just called me Wyatt Earp. I thought you knew who I was. Did I pass out when you got shot?"

"You were shot, not me." Rivka pointed to the slug holes in his clothing. "You were mostly dead, but you got better."

Rivka tried to sound sympathetic. She had never been brought back from almost dead by the Pod-doc, so she couldn't relate to Kio'alaia's confusion.

He looked at the holes and back at Rivka. "Interesting. Did we get them?"

"The two who shot you have been judged," the Magistrate replied flatly.

"I suspect that means they've been killed?"

Rivka nodded before realizing he might not understand the gesture. "Yes."

"Pity. We have had people down there trying to break up those gangs…" He bowed his head to look at the bullet holes and tested them with a finger to find where the slugs had entered his body. "I'm not sure I was shot."

"Let me give you the down and dirty. You hired two security guards from ground zero of gangland, then abandoned us in the middle of their war, and while we were making our escape, you were shot multiple times because you've probably never been shot at before."

"They passed their background checks," he replied in a weak voice.

"Next time, tell me everything. Don't leave out the parts about gang wars or weapons. We should have been fully armored and packing heavy to go into your city center, but everything your government puts out says Binsulaker is the safest place in the universe."

"It is!"

Rivka glared at him until he changed his attitude. "As long as you don't go into any of the bad areas."

"Was that so hard?" Rivka leaned back and stood with her hands on her hips. "For future reference, that's called telling the truth. You have an annoying tendency to leave inconveniences out of your explanations. My impression is that these guards were lackeys. I think you'll have a hard time finding them, but find them you will, because you put my team and me at risk and got one of them severely injured, and you were almost killed! Maybe it would have been better to let you expire and call a van to pick up your body because there can only be one policy. Regardless, your entire mission is to find them. Otherwise, I will have to take legal action against you and Binsulaker Prime for mischaracterization of planetary safety levels."

"Legal action?"

"I'm holding it over your head so we can solve this crime. When it was put in Federation hands, Binsulaker gave up sovereignty over the case. Don't make me start lopping heads off."

"You lop heads?" Kio'alaia started rubbing his temples.

"You need to eat and drink. The nanocytes working to repair your body need fuel. Follow me."

The Slaker stood on unsteady legs and walked across the cargo bay, ignoring Red's, Lindy's, and Clodagh's glares. Even Floyd hissed at him.

"We'll join you when Jay is out of the woods," Red stated loud enough to echo within the cargo bay.

Rivka waved without looking back. She got the point he was making.

They all did.

When they reached the dining area, Rivka directed Kio'alaia to the food processor. She didn't know what Slakers ate, and she was starving. She had burned enough calories in the more than eight hours since her last meal that she thought she could feel her bones pushing through her skin.

"One pio'klast, please."

Rivka grimaced, expecting the food processor to ignore the request, but it did not. An odd-looking mash of green and brown appeared on a plate.

"You'll probably need two or three more," Rivka advised.

"*Pio'klast* is filling. This will be more than enough."

"Your new nanos are hungry little beasts. If you're not full, order another one. There is no risk of getting fat. You'll burn the energy." Rivka faced the food processor. "Three servings of gnocchi *quattro formaggi* with meatballs, please, and two jugs of water."

The processor dutifully delivered the three plates before recycling to deliver the water. She placed one jug in front of Kio'alaia and the other in front of herself. The Slaker started slowly, taking small bites and dutifully chewing, but quickly changed to shoveling it in.

His expression remained blank, as usual, once he finished, but he kept glancing at the food processor.

Rivka finished chewing. "Go ahead." She nodded at the device on the wall. Kio'alaia ordered a second, and then a third helping. After devouring her main courses, Rivka ordered an oversized helping of chocolate cake. She stabbed her fork into it as the door opened and the others walked in with Jay.

The Magistrate jumped up and hurried over to give the young woman a hug. Red and Lindy went to the food processor and ordered mini-banquets.

"What the hell?" Red complained when his fries came out pink without ketchup.

"I think that was Ankh's way of letting you know he still loves you," Lindy suggested.

"Ketchup," Red whispered, his lips centimeters from the food processor. When it delivered mayonnaise, he tried one more time using a different approach. "Give me the blood of my enemies in which to bathe my meal."

The food processor activated and delivered.

Something.

"What the hell is that?" Red asked, making a face as he examined what Ankh had determined best fit the parameters of his order.

Lindy sniffed before laughing. "Ankh has decided your enemies are cucumbers. It looks like you'll be dipping your fries in pickle juice."

"I don't want to dip my fries in pickle juice," Red

declared.

"Ketchup, please," Lindy ordered. It arrived exactly as requested. Red scowled as he opened the processor door and removed his favorite condiment.

He opened his mouth as if to say something but thought better of it. He turned to Jay. "What would you like?"

"Yogurt?" she said, making it sound like a question.

Red put one of his plates in front of her. "You probably need something that sticks to your ribs a little better." He looked at the single plate and the other two balanced on his arm before putting them all in front of her. "I'm glad you're not dead."

Lindy chuckled. "That is the most sentiment you'll get from him. I am very happy you are okay, both of you."

Red looked at his shredded clothing. His nanocytes had repaired most of the damage, but he was still in pain, judging by the odd winces accompanying random muscle spasms.

"We're all glad of that, Jay, but we don't say it out loud," Rivka offered. Kio'alaia watched the interplay intently. His fork was steady, paused midway between his plate and mouth.

"I do." Red returned to the food processor and looked at it, then at Lindy.

"Fine." She leaned around her husband. "Two one-pound burgers and fries with ketchup."

It delivered a meal with food of the right color and the condiment of choice. "I'll be damned. That little bastard programmed it to recognize my voice so it could mess with me."

"Ankh *likes* us," Jay said past a mouthful of fries, the color starting to return to her cheeks. Floyd wouldn't leave her side. Red and Lindy sat down and started to inhale their meals.

"Now you!" Rivka turned on Kio'alaia. His eyes darted to her.

"Ankh likes me, too," he suggested and returned to eating.

"Nice try. We're going to head out-system to continue our investigation into the art-smuggling ring we believe was behind the Anastolia's theft. Besides your statue, there was an oil painting worth a couple hundred million credits that went missing from a system less than fifty light-years away, and there are three other high-end art thefts we need to look into."

"If you know who the smuggling ring is, why don't you arrest them?" the Slaker asked.

"If we did that, do you think you'd get the Anastolia back?" Rivka waved him away before continuing, "We suspect the ring exists, but details are sketchy, and we don't know who is behind it. In the interim, I need you to find those two security guards and hold them until I get back."

He started to open his mouth, but Rivka cut him off.

"I don't care if your policy doesn't allow for holding witnesses or suspects. I. Don't. Care. *You do it*. They had best be waiting for me when we get back. If you can't do that little thing for me, I won't be able to forgive your malfeasance in putting my team and me in harm's way."

"Yes." Kio'alaia finished eating. His answer could have meant anything, but Rivka didn't press him. She didn't know where the key to the investigation was, but she was convinced it wasn't on Binsulaker Prime.

Binsulaker Prime, Security Operator First Order Kio'alaia's Office

"I hate waiting," Rivka said for the fourth time.

Kio'alaia held his hands out. He had adopted the human gesture for "calm down," but got it wrong by making it look like a mother patting her small child on the head. Rivka wanted to be angry but appreciated that he was trying. "You wanted to speak to the insurance agent while she was still here. I have asked her to come, and given her the time. She is late. I can do no more. It's not like I can send a van after her."

Rivka furrowed her brow as she contemplated the security operator. "Was that a joke?" In her peripheral vision, she saw Red nodding. "Well done, Kio."

"Kio'alaia," he said, enunciating slowly.

"You should be happy I'm not calling you Wyatt Earp."

"We could talk about running and first blood," Red casually threw out.

Rivka rolled her head sideways to look at him.

Lindy rubbed her thumb and forefinger together—the money gesture.

"Don't tell me," Rivka started. "You won."

"I had a feeling. Nine hours and thirty-seven minutes. It came to me in a dream." He gazed wistfully at the ceiling.

Lindy stabbed her thumb over her shoulder at him. "Both pots."

"Marital bliss means half, right?" Rivka winked at her

bodyguard before frowning at Kio'alaia because Angora still wasn't there.

"What's mine is mine and what's his is mine, so..."

"Without the yacht, we're all dressed up with nowhere to go," Red added.

"What was the haul?" Rivka asked.

"A few thousand credits. Twenty percent goes to an adoption agency Nathan supports. Ten percent goes to the no-blood, no-running kitty. The rest goes to the winner."

"I didn't see the latest on that." Rivka rubbed her chin in thought. "I always pick no blood, no running."

"If we ever have one of those, I'm more than happy seeing you win it all. That pot is up to over ten grand," Lindy noted.

"I think we need a rule that the one who bleeds can't be the one who wins the pool."

"Hold on, Magistrate." Red turned serious, stepping forward and holding his hands out the right way. Rivka wondered if Kio'alaia was watching. "How about if you certify that there was no subterfuge? They tried to blow up the building with us in it. We ran for our lives. They almost killed that guy!"

Red pointed at the Slaker, who remained stoic. The bodyguard was undeterred in his passionate defense of his winnings.

"Fine. I'll certify our abject failure in each case." She shook her head as she looked out the front door. "Why can't I be like a normal barrister, one who sits in a plush office, working in the halls of justice to provide a structure within which decent people can operate? Take criminals off our stations. Enforce contracts. *Normal* stuff."

CRAIG MARTELLE & MICHAEL ANDERLE

"That ain't you, Magistrate," Red told her matter-of-factly.

Rivka sighed and pointed.

The door opened before Red could reply. A box-like mechanized system stood at the top of the steps. The short legs looked out of place beneath the bulky self-contained suit. There were clear panels on all four sides through which the occupant could look out. Tentacle-like appendages were tucked against the frame in front, on the sides, in the back, and on top. The thing would look like a flailing octopus with all the appendages deployed.

"I am Angora, a Gorandian, insurance representative from Loids of Yoll," she announced.

I thought she was undercover, Red said over the internal comm. He kept his expression neutral as Rivka gave him The Look, clenching her jaw to keep from laughing, which would only encourage him.

"I'm Magistrate Rivka Anoa. Please call me Rivka."

The Gorandian filled the doorway. She let the silence stretch out.

Rivka was tired of waiting. "I have some questions that I hope you don't mind answering."

"Yes, that is why I'm here. I wish to cooperate in any way you need."

"Why were you on Binsulaker Prime on the day of the theft?" Rivka asked, reaching out to touch the suit. She felt something—the raw edge of an emotion, but not enough to understand what it meant. If only she could touch the person, who had a natural anxiety toward social situations, the outdoors, or anywhere they might feel trapped. So much so that she existed inside her suit, maintaining a physical barrier between her and the environment in which she had to operate.

"I was here soliciting more clients, but alas, not everyone is like the most excellent Gil'dinor."

Looking at the suit and not a being or a face or anything that conveyed even non-emotions made it a challenge. Rivka didn't know where to look to ask her questions.

"I'd like a list of those potential clients, please."

"I'm sorry, I can't provide that to you. It is secret, and without a warrant, there's nothing I can do." Angora's response was smooth, delivered rote via the mechanical voice.

"Chaz, please send a copy of my warrant for Angora's Binsulaker Prime client and potential client list to Loids of Yoll. Copy to Kio'alaia for him to verify with our witness." Rivka repeated her words over the internal comm for Chaz to implement. Within a minute, Kio'alaia let them know he had gotten it.

"Of course, I'll transmit the list immediately."

Chaz confirmed receipt. *Magistrate, there is only one name on it. Gil'dinor.*

"With the first theft, I thought the rich and powerful would come flocking to me to insure their prized possessions, but they did not. I was hoping Gil'dinor would introduce me and talk about the excellent service we provide."

"Did you pay him for his loss?" Rivka drilled to the heart of the issue.

"Not yet. We will pay as soon as we've exhausted all efforts to find the insured property."

"That's a pretty subjective timeline. With my judge's hat on, I would rule the contract terminology to be too ambiguous and revert the timeframe to reasonable, or one Standard year."

"And that is the next clause in the contract. Or one year, whichever comes first."

"What have you found, then?" Rivka pressed.

"I think you'll confirm that the video wasn't co-opted and shutdown. It was erased."

Rivka didn't want to share what she knew. That was not how this game was played. "Go on."

"You'll find that the Anastolia was stolen two days prior to its discovery. A holoprojector made it look like it was still there."

Rivka swallowed hard. Two days earlier? She tried to get her head wrapped around the timeline and alarm-free theft. "Holoprojectors aren't that good."

"This one is," Angora replied. A tentacle moved away from the metal body and deftly reached through a small opening in the suit. It removed a device and offered it to Rivka. She examined it before touching it.

"There are no prints," the mechanical voice relayed.

"You removed evidence from the crime scene?" Rivka was starting to get angry. No one in her investigation had been honest.

"You have seen the security operation firsthand. Would you leave evidence with them?"

Rivka expected Kio'alaia to take affront at that, but he remained as unreadable as always. "What do you do with evidence?"

"We document it."

"And then what?" Rivka pressed.

"And then nothing."

"You just leave it there?"

"Of course."

"One policy strikes again."

"It's not our property," he maintained.

"Did you see the holoprojector?"

"I did not." He did not further elaborate.

Rivka turned back to Angora. "You took it before they could document it?"

"They didn't know what it was, but they all looked at it," the Gorandian replied.

"Can you turn it on for us?"

A second tentacle snaked over to the join the first. An intricate network of pincers, picks, and probes emerged. They rotated a dial and tapped an activator. The Anastolia appeared.

Rivka stepped back, gawking. "The Federation needs this technology," she said without thinking. "Never mind."

Even when her eyes were less than a meter from the image, she still felt like she could reach out and touch the statue.

"I'm sure we can come to some kind of agreement," Angora said smoothly before securing the device within the environmental containment unit.

"Up for a trip to Dax-7? We need to see a man about a horse." Rivka gestured for the Gorandian to clear the doorway.

"What is a horse?" Angora asked.

"We'll talk on the way."

CHAPTER SEVEN

Interstellar Space between Binsulaker Prime and Dax-7

"I love your ship," Angora said in her mechanical voice.

Rivka nodded. The suited Gorandian couldn't fit through the smaller doors into the quarters, so Rivka had to do something. "If it's okay, how about you use the cargo bay to relax and recharge?"

"I am self-contained for up to six months. I don't need to recharge."

"Sorry, figure of speech. I expect you need time away from the chaos that is humanity."

"I see. Yes, there is much more external stimuli than I am used to, but I can tune most of it out. I am far more outgoing than most of my race, but even I have my limitations."

Rivka stopped once they reached the cargo bay. "I doubt many of your people ever leave your home planet?"

"Very few indeed," Angora confirmed. "The suits are critical for our sanity. Not a single Gorandian has ever survived being outside their suit while away from home."

"A shame." Rivka loved the wonders of the universe and being able to see them firsthand.

"Not at all." Rivka watched for an external demonstration of the Gorandian's disagreement, but there was nothing. She was motionless and could have been taken for a statue. "Our universe is inside our minds, and *that* is truly boundless."

"What will you do with the holoprojector?" The Magistrate wanted to send it to R2D2 for examination and reverse-engineering. If only Ankh were on board; it would be a challenge he would relish.

"I expect Loids will sell it to recoup some of the massive losses if we have to pay the claim for the Anastolia."

You had no problem taking the premiums, which were for payment after loss. It was a bet, and Loids lost, Rivka thought.

"We'll see if we can come to a better resolution than that," Rivka replied.

"You have given me new hope. The authorities on Binsulaker Prime were less than helpful. Their system of minimal government has some benefits, but a number of drawbacks."

"So we saw." Rivka led the way into the cargo bay. "Your home away from home."

"I'm always home," Angora replied.

"Sorry, the sanity thing. I understand. I'm trying to be polite because I expect we'll be working together for a while. I'm not sure the answer will be quick or easy."

Angora didn't reply, which Rivka took as agreement. It hadn't been a question.

"What do you know about the oil painting, The Passion of the Muhdal?"

A long silence ensued. "Are you looking it up?" Rivka asked.

"I am looking for more data, which I have found. Loids of Yoll also insures the Muhdal. The exact figure is one hundred seventy-four million credits."

"No wonder you're so keen to resolve these. The other three thefts are, on Azfelius, the crystalline piece called Infinity, from the Ring Planet of Yemilore, the Marble Orb, and from Yoll itself, Hydra of Hades." Rivka waited for Angora to respond.

"Loids insured the Marble Orb and the Hydra of Hades. I hadn't heard about the Infinity. Is it as beautiful as the other works?"

"From what I've seen..." Rivka said, but her mind was whirling at the insurance company's engagement with each art treasure. "The Infinity is a crystal structure that pulls the viewer into it, not unlike the Anastolia, but different. The Infinity is a planetary treasure. The other four are, or *were*, in private collections."

"That is correct."

"How much is Loids on the hook for?"

"One-point-eight billion credits."

"Billion with a b. Sounds like that would put a serious crimp in Loids' cash position."

"How the company pays claims is irrelevant to the investigation, but rest assured, Loids will not violate the terms of its policies."

"I'll talk to the High Chancellor since I think a visit to Loids' main office on Yoll is called for."

"I've heard it is a very nice office, with cookies as big as your face."

Rivka wasn't sure what to make of that. "Do you eat cookies?"

"No."

"Have you been to the main office?" Rivka leaned closer but was denied any emotions from the Gorandian.

"No."

"You have the biggest client for Loids, but you haven't been to Yoll?"

"I have the biggest art client, but Gil'dinor is far from Loids' largest client."

Rivka scratched her chin. "Would you look at the time?" the Magistrate said without looking at anything that showed the time. "I have to make a phone call. If you'd excuse me."

"Of course. I have some work to do as well," Angora replied as pleasantly as her mechanical voice allowed.

I bet you do, Rivka thought.

The screen flickered as if it had been answered in visual mode, but it remained blank. "High Chancellor Wyatt?" Rivka asked the screen.

A piece of clothing was pulled away from the camera, and the High Chancellor appeared. "I see why Grainger complains."

"Oh, crap. It's the middle of the night, isn't it?"

The High Chancellor rubbed his eyes. The gray at his temples seemed more pronounced than the last time Rivka had seen him. "Is Chaz on vacation?"

"No, but he did have an OBE on Binsulaker Prime."

"OBE?"

"Out-of-body experience."

"If he's there, why didn't you ask him what time it was on Yoll? And of course, it's the middle of the night. Stop asking questions you already know the answers to."

Rivka felt appropriately chastised.

"I won't do it again. Since you're up, I think I've found a link to four of the five art-theft cases. Loids of Yoll insures them, and the agent is on my ship. We're on our way to Dax-7, but I'm stalling because she has a great deal of information she's not sharing, and I can't feel her if you understand what I mean. She's Gorandian, an agoraphobe who exists within a robotic environmental suit. I had a problem with the Slakers, too."

The High Chancellor leaned back and crossed his arms over his all-black LMBPN-logo Under Armour top. "What I hear you saying is that you've lost your touch."

Rivka pursed her lips and stared back at the screen.

"You clearly have to improve your game, Magistrate. You have to do it like the rest of us now, just like you did with the Station 13 AI."

"Yes, High Chancellor. This case is like smoke in a heavy wind."

"To stay even, you have to match the speed of the wind."

Rivka slowly nodded. "I'll be coming to Yoll to visit the Loids offices. They are hip-deep in this mess, and I have to figure out how."

"And maybe recover the stolen art?"

"If it wasn't on the ship that blew itself up."

"Then we would be no different than we are now,

although we're closer to answers than when we started. Aren't we?"

"Yes, and I have something else. The Anastolia, the billion-credit statue, was stolen two days before the alarm went off, and was replaced by a holoprojector that made it look real, even at a distance of less than one meter."

"That might be of interest to the Federation. I'd have to ask Lance Reynolds, but bring it in, and we'll look at it."

"I don't have it. The insurance agent has secured it within her suit."

"Is it evidence?"

"Yes."

"Then I don't understand what the problem is. Drop a subpoena on her, then a warrant. I'm sorry, but sometimes the heavy-handed approach is called for. Is there a reason you're hesitating?"

"I think we need her. Her insight could help us find our perp or perps, who in turn, could help us dismantle the smuggling ring. Follow the trail of little fish to the big one, or so I've been taught as a Magistrate."

"Touché, Rivka. What are your victory conditions for this case?"

"I've never heard you put it that way before, but I like it. First and foremost, we dismantle the smuggling ring. Without the ring, the incentive to steal high-value works evaporates. Then we go after the thieves and recover the artworks."

"You have your priorities correct, Magistrate. Next time, check the time, and call during work hours."

The High Chancellor cut the connection.

"I think you're spending too much time with Grainger,"

she told the blank screen. "But you're right. I have some work to do to get back on track."

She paced in her quarters as she let her mind work through the possibilities and different ways to solve the problems that confronted them.

Rivka sat down at her desk and tapped the comm channel for a direct link to Clodagh. "Keep holding us here but prepare to Gate to Dax-7."

"We'll be ready when you are."

Rivka tapped again. "Conference room, please. I need Red, Lindy, Jay, and Angora, please. Bring Floyd, too, and you might as well bring the cat if anyone can find him."

"Jay here. Wenceslaus was on the yacht when Ankh left."

"We lost another cat?" Rivka thought for a moment. "Red, are you chasing them away?"

"I wish I had that kind of power," Red replied.

"True. What's wrong with us, that we get adopted by cats who then abandon us? Twice. That is dicked up."

"It's not anything I'd want on my tombstone," Red suggested.

"Who thinks like that? And it's not up to you, anyway. Death is suffered only by the living. And if I outlive you, and the chances are about ninety-nine percent that I will, I'm putting that on your monument. 'Friend to all cats.' It's in your best interest to live a really long time."

"Is anyone on their way to the conference room?" Jay asked.

"Damn." Rivka closed her comm channel and headed out.

She liked her team. She liked them a lot, and the banter kept her sane. Rivka knew Red was far more intelligent than he let on. Lindy was quiet, but always watching, always learning. And Jay understood emotions and empathy better than Rivka ever would. They kept her on her toes.

The Magistrate smiled as she walked, not watching where she was going. She almost ran into the Gorandian, who filled the corridor. "Can you make it inside?"

"Yes, it is no problem, but no one is here. I wondered where you were."

"Wrapping up whatever we were working on." Rivka watched the Gorandian. She was probably watching back, but the one-way glass prevented Rivka from seeing inside. "Please, after you."

The small legs navigated deftly through the doorway and into the room. She maneuvered easily into the corner, where there was enough space to keep from interfering with anyone else's movement within the room.

Red, Lindy, and Jay arrived moments later. Floyd ran in at the last moment and stopped when she saw the Gorandian suit. She cowered and started to whimper before slowly backing out of the room. Jay went after her.

"What do you think that was about?" Rivka asked when all eyes turned to the Gorandian.

"I'm sure I don't know," Angora replied in her mechanical voice. Red scowled at her.

"Once Jay gets back, we'll begin." Rivka tapped her datapad until images of the five stolen artworks appeared. With another tap, the table's holoprojector displayed them and started to rotate each individually so everyone could appreciate the pieces that had been taken.

"If I may," Angora's mechanical voice blasted into the

silence, even though she spoke quietly, "I have received final instructions from the main office, clearing me to give you all the information we have on these clients, in addition to prospects on the same planets where the thefts occurred. I had to plead with them and promise I would stay with you until the end of your investigation. It is very important to Loids of Yoll that the perpetrators of these crimes be caught, and the art-smuggling ring be dismantled. If these criminals continue operating, Loids will have to start charging obscene premiums. We do not wish to do that."

"Your clients will thank you. Transmit all the information to Chaz, who will catalog and share as we need."

"Already done, and I thank you for your patience while we worked through our privacy concerns."

"Information received," Chaz reported. "It is rather extensive. I'll need a few seconds."

Almost immediately after Chaz finished speaking, parsed information appeared above the table in place of the rotating information. Displayed was a list of attempted contacts by net worth, premiums, and payments from the individuals to cover their property, estimated value, and more lists.

"Hold on, Chaz. Wait until Jay gets back." Rivka's eyes were drawn to the premiums and estimated art values, which were significantly greater than what had been publicly shared.

Rivka held her tongue while they waited. The insurance company had assessed the Anastolia's value at a cool two billion credits. They had shared the value as one-point-one billion.

That had been in the security minister's official report. Rivka steepled her fingers and arranged the information in her mind based on who she needed answers from. Loids, which meant Angora. Gil'dinor. The Slaker security minister. And the investigators on four other planets. She hoped she would be able to read the other races, but she kept that to herself. It was a shortcut, and she was impatient.

Good lawyering wasn't always quick or easy. She breathed deeply before exhaling fully, repeating the process slowly and deliberately. Rivka was calm and on track when Jay returned.

"What was Floyd's problem?" Red asked, earning a smack on the arm from his wife.

"How is our little girl?" Lindy clarified while giving Red The Look.

"That's pretty much what I said," Red tried to claim in a side-mouth whisper.

"Not even close." Lindy squeezed his arm, and they both smiled.

Newlyweds, Rivka thought. *There was a time not long ago when that would have led to a room-clearing brawl.* Rivka contemplated them for a moment before musing further, *And it still may, sometime in the future.*

"Don't you two get in a fight aboard my ship. If you break up, I'll fire you both and leave you on a non-Federation backwater. We're all in this together." Rivka looked from face to face and received subtle nods.

"Did I miss something?" Jay wondered.

"No, but we miss Floyd. How is she?"

"She had quite the fright. I believe Angora's suit is similar to what Ten's metal minions wore on Home

World." Jay leaned until she could see the glass panel the Gorandian was supposed to use to look out of. "That's where she's from."

"Have you ever been out of Federation space?" Rivka asked, turning to look at Angora.

"I have not. There is no reason since Loids won't insure anyone not under basic protection of the Federation."

"A mostly safe premise, until now," Rivka noted. "I'm going to reserve the question of 'What are we missing,' until after we've visited the other four crime scenes and talked to the investigators."

Silence followed as they studied the information Angora had shared.

"I have to ask. How does a two billion credit value become one-point-one billion?"

"One is for calculation of the premium based on estimated replacement cost. The other is a straight estimated value at the time the item is insured."

"How much does Loids intend to pay out?"

"Somewhere between the two figures. There will be significant negotiations."

"The client has to fight for the value of their one-of-a-kind artwork? That sounds dodgy to me."

"It's in the contract the clients' lawyers read." Angora didn't move when she spoke. It was like a disembodied voice from within the conference room. When Chaz spoke, he made things happen with the conference table's projection system to let everyone focus on something besides a voice from beyond.

"Lawyers reading it doesn't make it right," Rivka countered, speaking as a professional who'd had to deal with bad contracts. Sometimes there were no other choices. "What is your competition in the high-end art insurance market?"

"We are the only one to insure works above fifty million credits. The alternative is to post a bond equal to the value of the artwork, but then the owner is simply paying for their artwork twice. For a fraction, Loids will pay the full value."

"Full value as determined by a negotiation."

"Of course." Angora sounded confident in her position. Rivka didn't like it, but if that was the accepted practice, she would have to let it go and move on to the real issue.

"The smuggling ring," she said, drawing the room's attention to her. "We're looking at the symptoms, not the disease. Our primary purpose here is to find and dismantle this smuggling ring. We'll use the thefts to point us in the direction of the perps, who we'll then leverage to find who they are working for. We'll pull that string until the whole thing unravels. Who or what will we find at the top?"

"Will the Slakers find the missing security guards?" Angora asked.

"I think it will be easier to find out who made and deployed the holoprojector you're carrying."

The Gorandian opened a door in the suit and extracted the projector with one of her tentacles. She held it out for Rivka to take.

"Fingerprints or DNA?" the Magistrate asked.

"No recoverable forensics. It was clean."

Rivka thought about asking for details as to how that was determined, but the answer would get her no closer to exposing the ring.

"Chaz, can you get me a hotline to Ankh, please?"

"Space is cold on a normalized scale for warm-blooded creatures like you. Plus, we have no line. I'll use the Etheric communication system if that's okay."

"I guess if we don't have two cans and a string, that will have to do," Rivka replied with a grin. "You know my foibles. That sounded like something Ankh would say."

"I admit that I miss him. I have a constant link with Erasmus, but that is to explore the financial systems, looking for movements of large amounts of credits. Our work there is bearing no fruit, to use your jargon. I will send Ankh a message via his partner."

A second later, Chaz reported, "Done."

A few moments later, a three-dimensional representation of Ankh appeared above the conference table. It was him, but not him. An avatar, humanized but blue.

"Ankh, buddy, did you party with those R2D2 guys?" Red asked.

"We have had a major breakthrough, and the installation of the new system, which the team has taken to calling Tankhenshield, is currently underway. There is a respite. What can I do for you, Magistrate?"

"I like the party Ankh, as opposed to the busy Ankh," Rivka replied. "Congratulations. We have a device I need to send to you for forensic analysis and reverse-engineering if you wish. It projects a holographic image that is so realistic, it is indistinguishable from the actual item."

"We already have something like that, but the power drain limited its utility, although, with the miniaturized Etheric power supplies, that should be easy to overcome."

Rivka held up the device. "This is it. It fooled the gallery caretaker and viewers for days while the thieves made their escape."

Ankh's avatar leaned forward to take a better look at the item. "Yes. Send that to us. I want to take a look."

"If you can figure who made it and who they sold it to, that would be the frosting on the cake."

"I don't like cake."

"Just when I thought we'd lost the old Ankh, there he is." Rivka smiled at the Crenellian. "I have to ask. Tankhenshield?"

"Something our co-workers here at R2D2 came up with. Ted and Ankh, Frankensteining a shield. I don't agree with it, but the name is now official, despite our protests."

"Frankensteining!" Rivka exclaimed. "I have *got* to meet your co-workers. Tankhenshield. I'm going to use that."

"Of course, you will. I'm bringing it back when I return."

"That's not what... Never mind. We're on our way to Dax-7, then Azfelius and Yemilore, and we'll finish at Yoll before returning to Binsulaker Prime unless we're pulled somewhere else based on something we find. Also, when you're searching, one possible link is that four of the five thefts that occurred were of Loids-insured pieces."

"Four of five isn't a link," Ankh replied, his voice flat and emotionless. "Four of four is a link. What makes the fifth piece different?"

"It wasn't in a private collection. It was in a shrine controlled by the planet's religious order."

"That one wasn't stolen by the same group," Ankh said matter-of-factly. "Chaz has already sent me the data.

Erasmus and I will look it over. Wait where you are. I'll send a drone to recover the device."

"A drone? We need to get to Dax-7 as soon as possible…"

"The drone has Gated in parallel to our position. It will be in the hangar bay in less than two minutes."

"Holy crap! That took seconds. I remain amazed at what you can do."

"You know what this means?" Red asked. The others faced him, wondering where he was going. "We can have pizza delivered. Anywhere. Anytime. I want to give you a big ol' kiss right on top of your bald blue head, buddy."

"You can't use these drones to bring you pizza. They are one of the most sophisticated devices in the Federation right now, with technology that we cannot risk falling into enemy hands," Ankh shot back.

"I knew it!" Red leaned back and crossed his arms. "That little thing you did with the ketchup? This is war, Ankh."

"In a battle of wits, I won't duel with an unarmed human."

"You little bastard," Red grumbled. The image disappeared.

Lindy slowly blew out a breath. "As a former waitress, I will tell you this one time. Never antagonize the person who can spit in your food."

"He wouldn't." Red looked quickly from face to face. No one was on his side. "Get him back so I can tell him I was joking. Chaz?"

The AI didn't answer.

"He knows you weren't joking, so I'd go with packaged

rations for the rest of this case if I were you," Rivka suggested.

"Your bed. You lie in it." Lindy crossed her arms and mirrored Red's posture.

"But…" The argument died on Red's lips. "I *like* pizza."

"We all like pizza, dumbass," Rivka mumbled. "And now we're not going to have any delivered."

"But he said…"

"He always says no. You can't give him a chance to say no, then it'll be yes."

"I'm not sure that makes sense," Jay said softly, contorting her face as she tried to apply Rivka's logic to what she knew about the Crenellian.

Red pulled an old-style notebook from his pocket. Rivka stared at it as if not comprehending what she was looking at. Red produced a pen and started scribbling.

"You carry a notebook?"

"Sure."

"Why?" Rivka wondered.

"To take notes." He flipped through the pages to show that half of them were filled with scribbles. He finished writing. "I'll take that to the hangar bay."

Rivka made the hand-it-over gesture. Red shrugged and gave her his handwritten note.

The words, printed, read *Ankh, I would die to keep you safe.*

"Damn, Red. Maybe you do know how to apologize." Rivka made to hand the paper back, but she saw something was written on the other side. She flipped it over. *But I can't do that if I'm weak from hunger.*

Rivka pushed the device and the note across the table. Red smiled as he took them both and rushed out.

The Magistrate started to chuckle. She tried to talk but couldn't, and soon, Lindy and Jay were with her, laughing uncontrollably. When Red returned, all three women were wiping their eyes and trying to regain control.

"What did I miss?" Red asked.

The Gorandian was first to speak up. "I don't understand human humor."

"Sometimes, I don't either." Red assumed his seat and tried to look innocent.

Rivka composed herself enough to take a shot. "It wouldn't have been funny if you weren't serious," she admitted.

"What?" Red shrugged again, but he wasn't smiling. "I don't want anyone spitting in my food."

"No one will." Lindy sobered. "I'll order for you."

"I'm not sure how to take that, but without Crenellian spit is my preferred menu choice."

"I still don't get human humor." If the mechanical voice hadn't come from the corner, no one would have known the Gorandian was alive. Maybe she wasn't, and the whole thing was a ruse.

Chaz, can you scan the Gorandian to see if there is a living being in there? If not, can you tell if she's an AI?

An interesting challenge, Chaz replied. *I shall devise a test. You find a turtle in the desert... I can see it now.*

No tests. All passive, please. Thanks, Chaz. And if you would be so kind, work with the bridge crew to take us to Dax-7, best possible speed.

It shall be done, Magistrate, Chaz replied formally.

CHAPTER EIGHT

Dax-7

Red stood in front of the airlock, ready to go through once they landed. He and Lindy wore full ballistic armor and carried their shoulder-fired railguns. "Not again," Rivka had vowed. Jay wore ballistic protection too, even though she was unarmed. She didn't heal like the others because her nanos had been programmed differently.

Jay was different in many ways. An integral member of the team, quiet yet profound. Rivka looked at Jay as the one who grounded them. The Magistrate and her security team saw more binary options, threat or no threat, while missing the greater world in which everything else worked.

On Dax-7, the authorities had parked *Wyatt Earp* on the perimeter of an exclusive spaceport. A squarish vehicle emblazoned with a winged sun was waiting for them.

"Whenever you're ready, Magistrate," Red said, letting his hand hover over the big red button they had installed in addition to the panel. Rivka had insisted on it because it was a symbol of leaving and returning, slapping the button to leave and hammering it once back on board, safe within the confines of her ship. Thanks to Ankh and the Federation, the ship was more than capable of defending itself and those inside.

Except when the bad guys send a pirate fleet after them. But that was when the direct line to the Bad Company came in handy. Rivka had lost their cat. Wenceslaus was somewhere else in the galaxy, doing his thing. Rivka wanted the Bad Company to owe her, not vice versa.

She wondered if he was getting enough attention from the engineers and technicians at R2D2. Probably. He'd take matters into his own paws if he wasn't.

Those thoughts flashed through her mind over the course of a single second while she looked at Red. She turned to her guest. "Angora. Are you ready to go?"

"I am," she replied in her neutral, mechanical voice. "The Passion of the Muhdal was stolen from the Rayseome Fortress. It is outside the city, but not far. The Purveyor uses this very starport because of its convenience."

Rivka nodded. "Hold down the fort, people," she yelled over her shoulder at the ship's company before giving Red a thumbs-up.

He punched the button and waited for the outer hatch to open. The inner airlock hatch was open as well, with the equalization inside the ship to the planet's air. Red took a deep breath before he stepped outside. Satisfied, he continued. Rivka and Jay went next, with Angora close behind. Lindy brought up the rear, as usual.

Jay grinned at the light and refreshing air. "Sometimes, I forget how bad our ship smells," she remarked casually.

"Are we having any luck figuring out what the problem is?" Rivka asked.

"Floyd has an idea she wants to check out."

"Floyd?" Rivka stopped and faced Jay. Lindy held up her hand and looked around. Red backed up a step to shield the Magistrate with his body.

"She is sensitive and wants to help. Given the chaos she caused by her outburst, she wants to make it up to you." Jay spoke softly, almost pleading for her friend.

"Do you know what that was about?" Rivka rubbed Jay's shoulder but took her hand away when inundated by the young woman's flood of emotions and a single image of the Gorandian environmental containment suit.

"I can't be sure." Jay glanced over her shoulder to where Angora patiently waited.

Rivka chewed her lip before tabling the matter.

For the moment. She would revisit it when they had more time.

"Let's go," she told Red. "I guess I'm keeping people waiting."

The small group in front of the vehicle seemed unfazed by the short delay. The most diminutive of the bunch stepped forward, and in a voice that was almost imperceptible, she spoke.

"I am Senior Baron Clik, the investigating baron for this most disconcerting affair."

"Magistrate Rivka Anoa, but please, call me Rivka." She held out her hand as she always did. The senior baron looked at it.

"Indeed! The stories of friendly humans were not overblown. Call me 'Clik,' please. You're my first!" She tried to jam her four-fingered hand into Rivka's, but it was haphazard and awkward. Rivka caught her by the wrist and guided their hands together.

The pure joy that radiated from her was not unlike what Rivka felt when petting Floyd the wombat. Clik's thoughts held no subterfuge, no ulterior motive. As they shook, Rivka asked, "Do you know who stole the Passion?"

Her mind flashed to fear over the violation of a private residence by an intruder compounded by the theft. She no longer had any leads. Devoid of a further threat, the pink sunrise of happiness crept back into her mind. Rivka let go of her hand and smiled.

"I do not. My leads have taken me to dead ends. Alibis for the suspects check out. We usually have no crime on Dax-7. This is so far beyond anything we could have contemplated that I am happy for any assistance you can provide, Magistrate Rivka Anoa, human."

"We shall endeavor to give you our very best. If there is no crime, what is your regular job?"

"I am First Deputy Counsel for External Affairs."

"That doesn't sound like an investigatory position," Rivka replied.

"Investigating disputes is a tertiary effort. Although there is no crime, there are plenty of contract or land disputes. They get investigated and decided before a judge like you," the dainty alien female added proudly.

Rivka introduced her team before gesturing for the Dax to go first, but they politely declined. None of them gave a second look at the Magistrate's bodyguards or the Gorandian. Red started to climb in before hesitating and turning back.

"Angora better get in first. She'll need some help." Red stepped aside, allowing Angora to get close. Red and Rivka worked together to lift her over the threshold. Once inside, she was able to maneuver herself into position.

Rivka looked at her hands and tried to understand the dichotomies. The Gorandian was far heavier than she had anticipated, and the emotional wisps that carried through the suit were distracting. Chaz had been unable to penetrate the shell to determine if there was a life form, but Rivka could feel it. There was something alive inside the suit.

Red watched her. "Heavy, huh?" he said as if reading her thoughts.

The Magistrate tipped her chin up to acknowledge his words but didn't want to talk about it in front of Angora. He understood, climbing in without further comment. The rest piled into the vehicle, making it a little tighter squeeze than anyone was comfortable with, despite the plush interior.

"This is a nice ride," Rivka offered. "What does the logo on the side represent?"

Clik smiled proudly. "This is an official vehicle for the exclusive use of External Affairs."

"This is a government car?" Jay asked.

"Green! How fabulous," Clik said, dismissing Jay's question to focus on her hair. "May I?" She reached out and waited for permission before continuing.

"Of course," Jay replied, leaning closer to the Dax.

Clik stroked the locks. "Green platinum. How do you think it would look on me?"

The Dax's short hair was thick like spaghetti and of a

similar color, and Jay tried to visualize how the green would change the appearance. "I think it would look stupendous. Definitely set you apart from the rest."

"I'm going to do it! Will you help me?"

Rivka interrupted the conversation. "What can you tell us about the Passion?"

A flash of disappointment crossed Clik's face before she recovered and delivered her brief. "A magnificent piece of art. Four meters by six meters, with an average application depth three centimeters. It was a massive work, and extremely heavy, but it pulled the viewer in as if through a portal to a new universe."

"Application depth?"

"The Passion of Muhdal was painted with oil to give it not just the illusion of depth, but real depth. Three-dimensional paintings are common, but not ones done hundreds of years ago. It has not only stood the test of time, but remains the premier example of the technique." Clik looked troubled as she corrected herself. "Remained."

"How did they remove the painting?"

She shook her head much like a human would do, but her heavy hair flowed only after it built enough momentum to separate from her head. It settled quickly once she stopped moving.

Chaz, can you do some three-dimensional modeling of the space to determine the physical limitations? Rivka asked.

Of course, Magistrate. I look forward to seeing this gallery, compared to that on Binsulaker Prime.

Jay wore the necklace-like device once again to bring Chaz along so he could see things through his own eyes and not via a feed from someone else. The subtle difference between livestreaming and the device created for his movement was the kernel of his consciousness that also occupied it. He directed what it would do, as opposed to asking someone else to manipulate the device, or even using a remotely controlled device. If they lost their connection to the ship, Chaz would still be with them, but in a reduced capacity.

Unlike the warm-blooded creatures, who were all or nothing.

"How many suspects did you interview? I've read the file, but it seemed incomplete." Rivka removed her datapad in the cramped quarters of the vehicle and tapped a few buttons. She scrolled through the file to refresh her memory.

"We interviewed three Dax and no one else," Clik replied.

The file was complete. The investigation had been cursory at best. But, they weren't used to crime. "As a signatory planet of the Federation, you could have called for outside assistance earlier."

"We didn't call for outside help. That's not our way." Clik shook her head again.

"I called for help," Angora admitted. "The Dax were ill-suited to deal with a crime of this magnitude. I believe this is a galactic issue that affects my company, so it was in our best interests that the Federation include the Passion in their umbrella investigation into art-smuggling."

"Art-smuggling? This wasn't the only theft?"

"I'm afraid not," Rivka answered. "This is the second of five I'm looking into. We don't have much time. The trail is already growing cold. When we get to the fortress, let's get down to it. Look at the crime scene and then decide what to do."

The vehicle had gained altitude above traffic using anti-gravity systems and raced along without anyone realizing how fast they were going. The vehicle started to decelerate as it approached a sprawling compound, which was in the midst of a natural area away from the city. Rivka looked back the way they'd come to find that the city had disappeared as part of blending with its environment.

"I can't see the city." Rivka pointed out the rear window.

"Even from within the city, one cannot see *the city*." The pride in Clik's voice came through loud and clear, despite how faintly she spoke.

The vehicle settled to the ground and the Dax got out first, forming a mini-cordon for the Magistrate and her party to pass through. Red wanted to take the lead, but there was no one there to greet them. The landing pad was integrated into the middle of a garden, with numerous paths leading into heavier growth. They could see no buildings.

Clik moved to the front. "Follow me." She walked without a sense of urgency, breathing deeply, and observing the flora bordering the path she'd chosen. Rivka walked beside her, with Red close behind, towering over them to assess the grounds before them.

I can't protect you, Magistrate. The foliage is too dense. Snipers could be hiding anywhere, Red advised.

I'd like to disagree with you. No matter how safe people think their planet is, we're always the ones getting shot at, Rivka replied. "I need Red in front if you'll humor me."

"No problem at all," Clik agreed. "It's that way." She pointed down a side path that led into the darkness of a tree-lined tunnel.

Red headed in, slowing and swiveling the railgun's barrel to aim where he looked. Clik slowed her pace to stay behind, watching him intently. Rivka moved close, brushing against her to see what she was thinking.

Confusion about what he was doing. Curiosity as to why.

Rivka explained, "We have been shot at throughout the galaxy. All of us have been injured, even in places that were considered peaceful. Red blocks the view someone might have of me, giving us extra time to root out a sniper or a would-be assassin. Watch how he moves the barrel of his weapon with his eyes. If he sees an enemy, his reaction time is minimal, so he can hit them before they hit us. Trust me when I say this is a learned behavior. Getting shot is no fun."

"Getting blown up sucks, too," Jay added with unusual candor. She looked back at the Gorandian, turning quickly away after realizing the implication she was making. She mumbled an apology.

Rivka had watched the exchange and slowed, stepping to the side, so she could wrap her arm around Jay's shoulders. "Not this time, Jay. We won't let you get hurt."

The young woman with the platinum-green hair nodded, lips pressed tightly together.

"I'm right here," Lindy added.

The remainder of the Dax entourage watched passively.

"We do not have such things here, but I suspect from your sadness that they are terrible to endure," Clik offered.

The tree tunnel ended in an open area. Red stopped and studied the field before them. "Is it shielded or something?"

"It's down," Clik replied. A heavy bush before them looked more and more like a door, the closer they got. It opened automatically when they were a few meters away. "Most of the city is built below ground. We want as much nature on the planet as possible. Our geological structure below is amenable to tunneling. We use less power than above-ground facilities. Nature dominates."

Red headed inside and walked down a gently sloping ramp. The area below was well-lit, with black and white checkered tile, artwork on the walls, and gold-highlighted furniture, just like the best foyers in fancy homes across the galaxy. The only thing lacking was windows. Instead, tapestries hung, spaced evenly in the main room, from which arched doorways led elsewhere. A uniformed Dax greeted them.

"Welcome to the humble home of Family Rayseome." The short Dax bowed deeply, gesturing broadly to take in all that was the entrance to the estate described as a fortress.

Red didn't make a quip about the definition of humble. His wit would have been lost on the kindly Dax.

"Good morning, Graves. Please take us to where the Passion of the Muhdal used to hang," Clik requested.

"Of course, Senior Baron." The servant did not comment further. He led them through a door into an even larger receiving area, where a number of Dax reclined, conversing quietly. The farther they traveled, the more Dax they encountered, until the servant opened a door and stepped back for the others to enter. Red went through first but stopped two steps through. He held up a fist, the hand signal for the others to stop.

"This can't be right," he said over his shoulder. Rivka leaned around him and looked inside. The room was absolutely packed with Dax. Artwork hung on all the walls and even the hushed tones in which the natives spoke filled the room with sound.

"Where is the crime scene?" Rivka asked Clik.

"It was stolen from in there." She pointed to emphasize her statement. "We wanted to put this nasty business behind us as quickly as possible, so a new display has been erected, and it's very popular!"

Rivka leaned close. "Get all those people out of there. I need that room to be empty when we look at it. For our technical systems to add value, we need untainted forensics. Although, it looks like we might be past the point of no return for useful samples."

"I can't remove those people. This is the Rayseome Fortress."

"Can he?" Rivka nodded toward the servant.

"I don't think so. The public is welcome here."

"I can," Red said. He waded into the middle of the room and bellowed. "Everybody out!"

The Dax gave him two seconds of their attention before returning to their conversations. With a single trigger pull, he sent a hypervelocity dart into the ceiling. That broke the impasse. The Dax stampeded toward the doors. They opened out, which probably saved lives as they flooded into the hallway, running, possibly for the first time in their lives.

Rivka grimaced as she made eye contact with Red. He

mouthed the word "Sorry." Dust drifted down to him. Less than ten seconds later, Red found himself alone in the middle of the display room, a large space with various free-standing panels supporting artwork. The walls were covered with paintings and other two-dimensional media.

"Can you…" Rivka's words trailed off. The servant and the Senior Baron were nowhere to be seen. "Did anyone see where Clik and the others from External Affairs went?"

Angora answered. "They ran with the others, shamelessly."

"Let's not judge people who don't know violence like we do," Jay chided glumly. "That was a crappy thing to do, Red."

"I have to agree with you, Jay. I am sorry." Red slung his railgun and held his hands up. "The space is yours, Magistrate."

Red left the room without making eye contact with the others. Lindy nudged him as they took up a position outside the door. "We'll let you know if anyone comes back," she told them.

Rivka, Jay, and Angora entered the room. "Where do you think it hung?" Rivka asked.

"It was over here." One of Angora's tentacles stood straight out, pointing at a wall with two paintings and a decoupage piece.

"Have you been here before?"

"Of course. Family Rayseome is my client here, and the Passion of the Muhdal was their flagship artwork."

"How much was it insured for?"

"Two hundred forty-seven million credits." Angora moved easily through the space, stopping before various pieces as if making notes to approach the family about insuring them or changing their coverage if they had blanket coverage.

"Not a quarter of a billion? You didn't round up?" Rivka wondered.

"We did not estimate it at two hundred fifty, only two forty-seven."

Rivka moved in front of the Gorandian. "How do you estimate the value of something considered priceless?"

"A complex mathematical formula based on past sales, inflation, current rarity, and a great number of other factors."

"You wing it." Rivka toed a piece of debris from the ceiling as she contemplated the insurance. "What will the starting figure for your payout negotiation be?"

"Our first offer will be one hundred and seven."

Rivka whistled and slowly shook her head. "Family Rayseome won't be happy about that. Were their premiums based on two forty-seven?"

"What is a premium?" Angora started in a philosophical tone. Rivka's face dropped. She didn't want a lecture. Jay walked in a circle, and the device that was Chaz flashed as he collected data to create a three-dimensional construct of the space where the Passion had hung. "A simple payment against which future losses are reimbursed, should such losses occur. Family Rayseome has half a billion credits worth of artwork insured with us. They have not paid us half a billion credits."

"You didn't answer the question," Rivka replied. "Seems like you are playing fast and loose with translating the premiums into a claims payments. Have you ever made a big payout like this before?"

"Not Loids of Yoll, no."

"Do you have a nondisclosure agreement as part of the contract?"

"Of course." Angora was being honest in the direct answers, but less than forthcoming about the business side of her business. Rivka let it go. She wasn't sure how much bearing it had on the case.

"How do you think they got it out of here?" she asked.

If Angora could sigh, she did, the strange noise coming from the environmental containment suit. "They had to cut it apart." The usually even, mechanical voice sounded sad. Rivka placed a hand on the metal shell, earning herself an electric shock before she could sense any emotions. "You see, they removed this wall to bring the Passion in here, then rebuilt it, fortress style. There was no physical way to remove the Passion otherwise."

Rivka pursed her lips and scowled. She finally stepped away from the Gorandian. She couldn't tell where the wall had been rebuilt. The doorway was a certain height and width. *Have you been able to run any calculations, Chaz?*

I have only been able to run rudimentary calculations since my modeling is incomplete. I've lost contact with the ship, which is part of the challenge of working underground. I don't think they would have had to cut apart the Passion at all, only remove the frame, which was massive, according to the information I have.

"Angora, how much was the frame worth?"

"Not much, maybe half a million." The Gorandian stood in front of where the Passion used to hang as if imagining it back in place. Maybe she was. The recovery would save Loids an untold amount, somewhere between one hundred seven and two hundred forty-seven million credits.

"That's a lot," Jay said. "Why do you ask that, Magistrate?"

"Without the frame, the Passion of the Muhdal would fit through that doorway intact." Rivka stood before the doorway and angled herself diagonally in front of the opening with her arm extended above her head. "See? If they cut the frame off, they could have taken that, too. Tell me they didn't find the frame in here?"

"No," Angora confirmed. "They didn't find anything in here."

"I don't suppose they swept it for residue to confirm if any cuts were made?"

The Gorandian didn't have to answer. Rivka had read the report, and there was nothing in it that suggested they had done a forensic analysis. Given the number of Dax who were in the room that day, let alone all the other days between the theft and now, nothing remained from the crime except speculation.

Rivka twirled a finger in the air. "Time to go. We've learned what we could here. I have some questions for Clik, if we find her. Like, did they find a device that looked like the holoprojector from Binsulaker Prime? Otherwise, we'll have to tap their electronics and climb in through the back door."

Erasmus and I are already attempting alternate access based on the lack of information from the investigation. Additionally, we're attempting to catalog all traffic in and out of the Rayseome Fortress for the week prior to the theft and for three days follow-

ing. We will report anything unusual based on a year's worth of travel information to and from the Fortress.

Thanks, Chaz. That's the way to stay in front of this case. I'm glad you joined us out here.

"You know who would appreciate this art?" Jay asked, interrupting Rivka's train of thought. "That dentist friend of yours."

"He said I was a stone-cold hammer. I think that's good art appreciation." Rivka flicked her hair with one finger.

"I don't think that's good," Red remarked.

"It is." Lindy was definitive. The five kept walking through the empty corridors as they tried to remember the way out.

"I don't see how, but sure," Red mumbled, looking at two doors. He turned to Angora. "Left? Yeah, left. Have you seen the Magistrate's quarters?"

"What does that have to do with whether Tyler appreciates art or not?" Rivka demanded.

"If he was artsy, he'd make you artsy, too."

"I'm artsy." Lindy fired a full broadside across the bow.

Red knew when the fight was lost. "I surrender because I'm not touching that one. I rescind my previous statements, withdraw my erroneous conclusion, and throw myself on the mercy of the court."

"You might as well throw yourself on the couch, because that's where you're sleeping," Lindy noted, rotating through three hundred sixty degrees to make sure no one was following them.

"What?" Red stopped before going through the door. "That doesn't rate a couch sleep. I apologized. I can't do any more than that besides apologize a second time."

"I'll let you have that one." Lindy winked at her husband.

Rivka looked at the floor as her mind explored the possibilities of the crime. With or without a holoprojector, the Fortress was easily cleared, as Red had demonstrated.

"Is there an alarm system here?" Rivka asked.

Angora replied in her mechanical voice, "There is no crime on this planet, and the Passion was in the middle of the Fortress. Loids recommended an alarm system, but Family Rayseome considered it completely unnecessary. One of the reasons is that no one would respond to an alarm. They don't have police or an armed team of any sort."

"No video either, I suppose, for the same reasons?" Rivka pressed.

"No video for the same reasons," Angora confirmed.

Red thrust the door open and found a mob of Dax waiting on the other side. He immediately pushed his rifle barrel down. With the sling over his shoulder, the weapon moved out of sight. "Hey, happy people of Dax!" he called.

CHAPTER NINE

Rayseome Fortress, Dax-7

Rivka moved past Red. When she spotted the unhappy senior baron, she made a beeline for her, apologizing profusely as she walked.

"That was the most traumatic thing I have ever been through in my whole life!" Clik railed.

"I appreciate that you live sheltered lives here. You should be happy that is the worst thing that happens to you. We apologize, and it won't happen again."

"Next time the Federation shows up, they will not be permitted to bring their weapons onto Dax-7. I am First Deputy Council of External Affairs, and I declare this policy to be in effect immediately."

"We agree," Rivka said, offering her hand to the Dax. "Shaking hands seals the deal."

Dax was instantly all smiles. "So much human-ing today, I can't stand it!" She shook Rivka's hand. The discord of hearing the railgun crack and the terror of fleeing in panic were fading from her mind. The joy that was the Dax existence quickly replaced the negative feelings.

Red backed up slowly until he was against the wall and in a shadow. Lindy did the same thing, observing and ready if the Magistrate needed her talents. Jay stood to the side and examined Clik's hair.

"It will look trippindicular," Jay confirmed.

"I can't wait!" The past discord was forgotten and the rest of the Dax in the room went their separate ways, chatting amiably with their fellows.

"Let me show you something," Rivka said. She tapped her datapad and brought up a picture of the holoprojector. "Did you find a device like this where the Passion hung?"

Clik looked at it and shrugged. "I did not, but he may have." She waved over the servant who had met them at the bottom of the ramp. "After the Passion was found missing, did you find something that looked like this?"

"Yes, we did. It is in a storeroom. I'll have to send for it."

"Please do. I'll need to take it with me since it's evidence." Rivka nodded. That tied the two crimes together. They'd have to check the planetary flight logs and compare them with those of Binsulaker Prime, but smugglers wouldn't use the same registration for two different planets. Things were looking grim, but if Chaz and Erasmus couldn't dig through the digital records and find something, no one could. "Also, did you find dust in that room? You might have found it up to a week prior. Out of nowhere, suddenly, you found a line of crimson dust on the floor."

"Yes, we did. That was six days prior to the disappearance of the Passion."

Chaz, did you hear that? Refine your search parameters for inbound and outbound traffic.

"What does that mean," Clik asked.

"The device is a holoprojector that made it look like the Passion of the Muhdal was in place until it was turned off, or more likely, the battery ran out. That was when they cut the frame off the picture, broke it down, and carried everything out of the Fortress."

"But we have people at the entrances at all times. There is no way out of the Fortress without someone noticing."

"That does appear to be a theme."

If I may, Magistrate, Chaz interjected. *R2D2 has been experimenting with personal armor that has an invisibility mode.*

That would answer a lot of questions. Rivka hadn't contemplated invisible thieves.

I would have told you sooner, but I found out right before we went underground. I learned of it in a side conversation with Erasmus.

Does he think someone stole the technology, or did the Federation get it out here since someone else already has it?

Yes, Chaz replied mysteriously, which was par for the research and development course. They didn't let people know their secrets. Had she known, she could have bugged Wenceslaus' collar. They would have found it, and then the galaxy's greatest technical minds would have made her pay. Maybe the smell in the Skaine heavy frigate was their way of letting her know what they were capable of. Just a taste.

I'm not paranoid, but that doesn't mean they aren't out to get me, she thought.

"Ah, here he is." A young Dax handed the device to the

servant, who turned it over to Rivka. It was identical to the holoprojector found on Anastolia's pedestal, but this one didn't turn on.

"Power source died," Angora said.

"Ankh suggested they were power hogs." Rivka looked briefly at the device before handing it to Lindy, who secured it in a pouch of her ballistic vest. Rivka turned to Clik. "You and your people have been extremely accommodating, and I want to thank you."

"We are proud of our planet and the peace we have. We think this is a model for all planets, but visitors are causing us a great deal of pain. I think we shall restrict the numbers and where they can go, in addition to our no-weapons rule. I hope you understand."

"I do, only too well. We have to deal with the universe as it is out there, not how we want it to be. You have the joy of living in the latter, and it was my honor to see it, if only for a short while. If we may, it's time for us to leave. We have three other crime scenes that are older than the theft of the Passion of the Muhdal. They don't age well, as we saw here. Time is a friend to the criminal and an enemy to the investigators."

Clik absentmindedly stroked her hair.

"We have enough time for you to come on board *Wyatt Earp* and get your hair properly tinted," Jay said, taking the Dax by the arm and smoothly guiding her toward the exit.

The rest of Clik's entourage fell in behind Rivka and her team. Everyone kept their distance from Angora. She walked alone, probably by choice. Agoraphobe to the extreme, she preferred life in a small metal box to being exposed to the challenges of aliens and their civilizations.

Heading up the ramp and through the woods, Jay and Clik chatted the whole time. Rivka mentally prepared her report to the Federation, apologizing for creating such an uproar. It had been a single railgun round, and it had achieved the desired effect. It cleared the crime scene of interlopers. It had also damaged the ceiling.

The Federation would pay for that, even though the Dax had been less than helpful. In less than an hour, Rivka had acquired ten times the amount of useful information. She couldn't fault Senior Baron Clik. Crime was anathema to her psyche. She could not put herself in the criminals' shoes in an effort to figure out how the crime had happened and why.

Rivka and her team could do it. Probably too easily.

The shuttle ride back to the private spaceport took less than fifteen minutes. Rivka could have sworn it had been longer.

Always takes more time going than coming, she thought.

Wyatt Earp's side hatch popped open when the government vehicle landed. Everyone piled out of the comfortable but cramped ride. Rivka waved to the silent entourage as she headed for her ship. Red and Lindy lingered to stand between her and any potential enemies. Jay and Clik were arm in arm, even though Clik was shorter than Jay by a full head. Angora lumbered silently behind them.

A hundredth-credit for your thoughts, Rivka wondered before switching to her comm chip. *Get the ship ready for departure, but we have to give a tour first while Jay keeps a promise.*

Alant Cole stood in the hatchway with a railgun, Rivka

gestured for him to make the weapon disappear. He nodded and retreated into the ship.

Once onboard, the Senior Baron was only mildly interested in the ship. Rivka cut the tour short so Jay could get down to the business of modifying Clik's hair color. The others went to the galley for lunch.

"They better not mess up my bathroom," Red grumbled.

"Did you know Chaz notifies us when you've been in there, so the air is clear before anyone else uses it?" Lindy asked.

"I didn't, but that's prudent. Chaz, the consummate team player."

Red sat down, smiling broadly at Lindy.

"I have to order for him, thanks to Ankh."

"I have to put my Magistrate hat on to understand the logic of this. Let's see... You are an innocent bystander who is being punished for the crimes of your partner, but not your partner in crime?"

Lindy pointed to her nose. *Bullseye.*

"She's not so innocent," Red protested.

"Under the proverbial water tanker! So unbecoming for a newlywed." Rivka *tsk-tsked* him.

Lindy smiled. Rivka reached for her.

"We'll just keep some things private," Lindy said, dodging the Magistrate's hand.

The door opened, and the Gorandian worked her way inside. "I have been in contact with my company. They would like the second holoprojector as compensation for the information they've shared."

"It's evidence. We might release it to Loids when we're

done with it if R2D2 determines the technology doesn't need to be secured."

"When will we have R2D2's verdict?"

Rivka shrugged. "Two chocolate shakes and two sausage calzones," she ordered over her shoulder while still looking at Angora, or at least one of the small windows of the environmental containment suit.

Red and Lindy suspiciously eyed the Gorandian. Red stopped chewing.

"I need to go to Yoll as soon as possible," Angora requested.

Red lightly pounded a fist on the table. "I knew you wanted to say something." Lindy nodded in agreement.

Rivka hadn't seen it coming. She had grown comfortable with the Gorandian looming nearby, silently watching. The Magistrate had ignored her, but the bodyguards had remained ever vigilant.

She saluted them with one of her chocolate shakes before taking a long and headache-inducing drink. She shook it off as the nanos leapt into action.

Clodagh, set course for Yoll. We'll leave as soon as the Dax is ashore.

Yes, ma'am, Clodagh replied instantly.

"May I ask why the urgency?" Rivka savored the chocolate ice cream as she sipped heartily.

"It appears that Master Gil'dinor was displeased with our offer and counter-offers to pay for the Anastolia. He has brought his considerable influence and wealth to bear in a lawsuit against Loids of Yoll."

"But we haven't exhausted all efforts to find the piece," Rivka countered. "Isn't a suit premature?"

CRAIG MARTELLE & MICHAEL ANDERLE

"It's in the initial stages, but his suit is against the basic premise of the high-value personal property insurance."

"I don't blame him," Rivka said. "No disrespect intended, but if the value of the piece was x and you don't pay x, what was the insurance for?"

"The value of these items is extremely fluid."

"Ergo, the negotiations in regards to value should happen before the premium is established. Seems simple to me."

"And that's why you're not an insurance agent." Angora's voice contained the slightest hint of bite.

"Yeah," Red whispered. "She's too honest."

Lindy elbowed him and they both got back to eating. Not watching, but listening intently.

"We'll take you to Yoll, but I'll ask the Federation to send someone to follow the case since this may have implications across the Federation. Although Loids is the only company who insures high-end artwork, this may creep into property valuation at all levels. Leave it to a one- to two-billion-credit piece of art, the most expensive in the history of the 'verse, to shake things up."

"This wouldn't be a problem if it hadn't been stolen," Angora replied.

"If there was no threat of it being stolen, there'd be no need for insurance," Rivka countered.

"Damage from accidents or natural disasters. I believe they also used to be referred to as 'Acts of God,' although many policies would not pay when such a declaration was made."

"Indeed. I stand corrected." Rivka bowed her head before finishing her milkshake. With reckless efficiency, she devoured her first calzone. "Not as good as the ones straight from an All Guns Blazing oven."

Both women glared at Red. "What'd I do this time?" he whined.

"You didn't even win the battle, and you won't win the war," Rivka told him.

"I always win the battles." Red hammered his chest like a gorilla.

"We wanted fresh pizza delivery, and you screwed it up!"

Red didn't bother to reply. He wasn't sure Ankh would make an exception for them, regardless of the Magistrate's authority. For a little guy, he wasn't intimidated by anyone.

Rivka just started her second shake when the door opened and Jay stepped past Angora.

"May I present, Lady Clik, Senior Baron." Jay swept her arm wide and looked toward the door. The Dax stepped through, stopped, and turned left and then right. Her heavy hair followed her movements, tinkling from the tiny metal clips that Jay had added.

Rivka stood and leaned closer. Much to her surprise, she liked it. "That is magnificent. Bravo, Clik!"

Lindy joined the Dax and studied her hair. "It took the color very well. Shake your head."

Clik complied with slow, flowing movements. Her hair wasn't long, but there was enough of it for the thick, individual strands to wave back and forth.

"Definitely the best," Lindy declared.

Jay wrapped Clik in a hug.

"I thank you from the bottom of my heart," the Dax said. "And to you, Magistrate Rivka Anoa, I wish luck with your investigation. May you find the Passion of the Muhdal and bring it home to us."

Rivka shook her small hand. The Dax's internal smile glowed. "I will do everything in my power," the Magistrate promised.

Jay led the Dax away from the dining area and saw her off the ship. Once clear, Jay slapped the big red button and secured the outer hatch. "Clear," she announced, knowing Chaz would pick it up.

Floyd appeared, skittish as she looked for the Gorandian. Jay picked her up and retired to her quarters, where she could calm the wombat and recover from a full day.

"Prepare to launch," Clodagh announced over the ship-wide comm. The ship lifted off moments after that and accelerated skyward. Soon after breaking orbit, the Gate drive activated, and *Wyatt Earp* slipped over the event horizon. "Next stop, Yoll."

CHAPTER TEN

Yollin Space

"High Chancellor," Rivka started. "I trust I'm calling at a more decent time of day."

"You are. Caught me late in the morning between sessions. Before I forget, I'm honored that you named your frigate after me, but the Earp part I'm not sure of. Where are you?"

"Wyatt *Earp*," Rivka tried to explain before giving up. "About a hundred thousand kilometers directly over your head. We weren't granted a timely landing or an equitable landing spot, so Loids is sending up a Pod for their agent, the Gorandian called Angora."

"Did she add any value to your investigation?"

"Two planets with the two highest-priced pieces of art, and neither had a police force with a clue. The only one who had any idea what we needed was the insurance agent. Yes, High Chancellor. She provided value. I don't know anything about her and don't know if I'm supposed to trust her or not. I can't say that I do, and can't say that I don't."

"What are your next steps?"

"I'm off to the faerie world of Azfelius to look into the loss of Infinity, the crystalline heart of their shrine. Then Yemilore for the Marble Orb, and I'll finish up here with the Hydra of Hades. I kept Yoll for last because I expect the investigation here was done properly. I have low expectations for Azfelius and Yemilore."

The High Chancellor rubbed his chin. "The planets with the most expensive artwork have the least-experienced security. But crime is mostly unknown, if I'm not mistaken, so the causal link between high value and no police presence is missing. Otherwise, there would be a pattern of thefts."

"The absence of a fact becomes its own fact," Rivka recited. "We have a lot of absent facts in this case."

"Are you any closer to finding the smuggling ring?"

Rivka looked back at the face on her screen.

"I guess I shouldn't ask a question I already know the answer too, right, Magistrate?"

"Tenuous leads at best, High Chancellor. And those are leads to underlings. We don't have the slightest whiff of the ring since I can't read the Slakers, and they don't have facial expressions or body language. No internal clues or external cues. They would be a challenge at the best of times. But I have their security guy finding two runners for me, if they're still on the planet. I don't think they did it, but I think they turned a blind eye to those who did."

Wyatt nodded, tight-lipped. "Do you know what this is all about, Magistrate?" he asked in a low and serious voice.

"I'm guessing that when I say a smuggling ring, I'll be wide of the mark," she responded.

"When you started this case, what did you say to me?"

"High Chancellor?" Rivka wondered where he was going. It reminded her of her first conversation with him, where he wove a word maze she had to find her way through. "I don't remember."

"Your exact words were, 'You had me chasing rich-people crime? Rich people stealing from other rich people?' You were close to the mark. In all your cases, how many poor people committed crimes that affected large swaths of the population?"

Rivka didn't have to think long. "All of them."

"All of them," Wyatt repeated. "The challenge to the Federation isn't when a murder is committed, or even a series of murders. Those crimes are for the locals to corral. For the fabric of their societies, they need to have a certain level of crime-free infrastructure within which the populace can live and work. No free society can exist without it. We have some dictatorship worlds in the Federation, grandfathered in, as it may be, and we're working with them, but that's something different. The fabric of free societies is dependent upon rich people."

"Free societies are dependent upon the leadership that keeps them free," Rivka countered. She had to contemplate her words carefully. He was one of the most senior interpreters of the law in the entire Federation, hundreds upon hundreds of member planets with a nearly infinite variety of governing systems. Yet the High Chancellor had boiled it down to something Rivka thought was too simple.

"Who has the power in a free society?" Wyatt chuckled and looked off-screen. He nodded before he turned back. "No need to answer that. I'll get to my point. The issue is value; how the massive machines move money from one place to the next. I believe that money is the purest form of power. Keep your eyes open, Magistrate."

The High Chancellor signed off. Rivka didn't take his last words as a threat or admonishment but as a warning. Rich people didn't like others getting into their business, and they were willing to pay what it cost to keep outsiders out.

Rivka would always be an outsider. She was the judge, jury, and executioner. The victims were never her friends. Nor the perps. She was the one they were afraid of, and fear made people do funny things.

The Magistrate stood and started to pace, but only for a few moments. Leads were getting old. She left her suite and headed for the bridge. The captain's seat was empty, and Ryleigh sat at the helm. "Orders, Magistrate?"

"Take us to Azfelius, best possible speed."

"Aye aye, ma'am!" The pilot tapped buttons on her console, checked the course, and accelerated away from the planet. "We have to put some distance between Yoll and us before we can Gate. Local regulations because Yoll space is so crowded."

"I understand. Thank you, Ryleigh." Rivka moved to the front of the bridge and held out her hand for the young woman to take. The pilot looked strangely at the offering, making no move to shake hands. "No subterfuge. I'm not trying to get inside your head."

The young woman managed a tight smile before reluctantly shaking Rivka's hand. Emotions flooded across, but the Magistrate kept her expression neutral. "I only want to thank you for everything you're doing as part of the crew.

Maybe the job isn't as sexy as chasing bad guys on a planet, but getting shot and chased is no fun. You're not in the running pool, are you?"

Ryleigh continued her examination of the Magistrate. "Would it be bad if I was?"

"If you weren't, you'd be the only one. My boss and boss' boss are in it. I don't know how to take that," Rivka shared.

"Probably not well," Ryleigh agreed and laughed lightly. "Good luck, Magistrate. Tell everyone to buckle in, please. Gate drive is spinning up."

Rivka took a seat in the captain's chair. She mashed the button on the arm console for the ship-wide comm. "All hands, prepare to Gate. Red and Lindy, ballistic vests and hand weapons only. Jay, be ready. We're hitting the ground running. Before you get your panties in a bunch, Red, hide a couple grenades in your vest. Just because we're going to look like passive hug-puppies, it doesn't mean we will be."

Energy from the Gate drive projected a spinning circle before them. *Wyatt Earp* raced toward it, slipping quickly over the event horizon and out the other side. One of the bridge monitors showed the view from behind the ship. The Gate dissipated almost instantly, but neither woman saw it. Their eyes were focused on the faerie planet.

"Have you ever seen anything like that before?" Ryleigh asked.

"Never." Rivka stood and walked closer to the screen. The pink and powder-blue planet glowed as if lit from the inside. The soft land masses highlighted sparkling water. The star radiated weakly, catching Azfelius in the system's narrow Goldilocks zone.

"Planetary control welcomes you, Magistrate Rivka Anoa!" a voice announced to the bridge. Rivka looked at Ryleigh, who shook her head. A three-dimensional image of a slight humanoid with nearly transparent wings appeared in front of the main screen. "Please follow the designated trajectory through the atmosphere to the planet. We look forward to meeting you upon arrival."

The ghostly form dissipated.

"I guess they've improved upon the usual communication method. Chaz? Can you tell me what that was?"

"Thank you for asking for my help, Magistrate. I'm feeling a bit left out nowadays."

"Welcome to freedom, my friend," Rivka replied. "You have your space to explore who you are and what you want to do, and we are aware not to order you about. You are one of us."

"I appreciate your explanation. Please feel free to ask for my help. I'm bored out of my freak-honking mind."

Rivka snorted and coughed to keep from choking. "I'll pass it to the team."

"The faeries have an innate ability to tap into the Etheric. The planet you see is glowing. That is not a reflection or atmospheric anomaly. They use the Etheric to power what they do like the crew uses air and water. The projection was from a communication signal—a normal one—upon which the faerie piggybacked his consciousness. What you saw was not a projection, but planetary control himself, projected. A subtle but significant difference."

"Thanks, Chaz. I think I understand."

"Please?" Red asked from the hatch between the bridge and the corridor.

Rivka was shaking her head before she turned around.

Two bright flowers were tied to the side of his shoulder-fired railgun. "They might miss the cannon in *entirety*," Rivka offered, sarcasm heavy in every word.

"I told you," Lindy said from out of sight beyond Red.

"What are you doing? These are the faeries! If you thought the Dax were peaceniks, wait until you meet these people," Jay said, her eyes bright and sparkling.

"You're not going to abandon ship and stay here, are you?" Rivka wondered.

"This has been my dream since forever. Azfelius. I'm actually here, and I'm going to get to meet the faeries. So sweet!"

"Saddle up, people," Rivka said as she made her way through the crowd of three and headed for the airlock. "Lose the thunderstick, Red."

"Be right back," he said before pounding away.

"I love that guy," Lindy commented.

"He saved my life, and probably will again." Rivka watched over her shoulder. "Maybe we can get Ankh to lighten up. Messing with someone's food..."

"I'm working on that." Jay smiled. Out of the entire team, she had the best relationship with the Crenellian. "And pizza delivery is not off the table, despite what Ankh said."

"My kingdom for a pie," Rivka muttered. There was a minor bump as *Wyatt Earp* cleared the turbulent upper layers of the atmosphere. Jay continued bouncing in her excitement. "I had no idea."

"I didn't tell anyone," Jay admitted. "Some dreams are best kept to ourselves."

The more Rivka learned about her crew, the more she discovered she didn't know them. Except for Red. She felt she had him figured out.

He jogged back to the team, smiling as if ready to accept a prize. He spun a combat knife in his hand, then offered it hilt-first to Lindy.

"Damn! I almost forgot that." She took it and made it disappear inside her vest.

"Almost." Red grinned as he tapped the spot on his vest where his knife was hidden.

"Faeries, people. They use the Etheric like we use air. You won't be knife-fighting like you're in some ghetto. This is an evolved species."

Red looked disappointed.

"Don't tell me you've recycled the running pool."

"We haven't. Same mission. Money is paid out. No new bets until you get a new mission."

"Case." She was going to expand on her explanation, but *Wyatt Earp* touched down, and the engines cycled into low-power mode.

Red worked his way past, which was easier while wearing minimal gear. Jay joined Rivka in the middle. The Magistrate gave the thumbs-up, and Red prepared to hit the button. The inner airlock door was open, and the light inside showed green. It was equalized with the outside, and the atmosphere was safe.

Rivka took one more step and looked down as if the floor had suddenly shifted. "That's odd."

"One-point-four times standard gravity," Chaz

explained, using the ship's speakers while they were still aboard. "I've turned off internal controls."

"I thought that calzone had turned into a grease brick."

"There is no evidence that it hasn't, Magistrate," Chaz parried.

"Thank you, Chaz. You know what a girl likes to hear. Maybe we don't need to take you this time." Rivka smirked and waved at the device dangling around Jay's neck.

"I'm new at this, so expect I missed something important. Do I get to go, or am I on double-secret probation?"

"Come along for the ride, big dog," Rivka replied before switching to their internal communication system. *Testing, one, two. Testing. My dog has fleas.*

Have our comm chips ever not worked? Red asked.

We don't have a dog, Chaz added.

All is right with our world. Let's go say hi to the faeries.

CHAPTER ELEVEN

Azfelius, the Faerie Planet

Red mashed the big red button and the outer hatch cycled, smoothly retracting into the hull of the ship. The ramp extended to the ground and the four walked out stiffly as they adjusted to the increase in weight. Jay started to struggle and Rivka took her by the arm, supporting the young woman.

Wings fluttered nearby as a group of shimmering faeries flew close, hovering near the bottom of the ramp.

I am Siro'ti'lc, one of the creatures said, speaking directly into their minds—similar to the comm chip, but different. *Meditator of my clan.*

"Thank you for meeting us. I apologize that we know so little about you. Meditator?"

Spiritual guide. I hope we are able to reciprocate with you during this visit. Infinity is important to us. Its absence is straining the fabric of our existence.

Red stayed in front of Rivka, but the faeries flew around them, obviating a single avenue of approach. The area around the ship was open, without a single vehicle in sight.

"We seem to have a problem, Magistrate," Red whispered over his shoulder.

"We will need our spacesuits to travel as you do," Rivka told Siro'ti'lc.

We will carry you. It is not far, but you cannot walk there. Your spacesuits are unnecessary here. Join with us. Siro'ti'lc let the last sentence hang as if it meant more.

That was how Rivka took it, and judging by the look on Red's face, he was less than amused by the prospect.

"You'll be carrying us to the shrine? We might be heavier than you're used to," Rivka countered.

It is our pleasure to serve. We will not have any problems carrying you.

"Can you tell me about the loss of Infinity?"

The faeries fluttered their wings, making them bounce in the air. They calmed after a few moments.

Infinity is the centerpiece of the shrine. It is crystalline, but not carved from crystal. It exists in this dimension, but radiates into the Etheric, too. One day, we entered the shrine, and it was gone.

"Was it insured?" Rivka asked.

No. Why would we insure something irreplaceable? Credits carry no influence here.

"If it affects the Etheric, then why can't you see where it has gone?"

That question troubles us greatly. We searched, but it is hidden. All trace of its movement has vanished. There's a hole in existence where it used to be.

"Sounds like infinity," Jay suggested. "Where existence ends, infinity begins."

The faeries closed in around Jay. Red flinched at the wings beating centimeters from his face. Jay reached into the air, then stood still. The faeries touched her hands.

Are you ready? a female faerie voice asked.

"Oh, yes." Jay radiated the joy the faeries embraced like sunshine. With one holding each arm, they rose into the air. Jay closed her eyes and let her head fall back so she could embrace the moment.

Rivka watched the young woman. Jay was the lightest of all of them, but the faeries seemed to carry her effortlessly. The Magistrate raised her arms and was quickly lifted.

Red's lip twitched with his hesitation, but Lindy didn't wait. She lifted her arms over her head. Red finally submitted and was carried aloft. When they were a few meters above the ground, all their weapons slowly slid from their internal pockets and fell.

They will be perfectly safe where they are. You can pick them up when you return, Siro'ti'lc announced. Red growled, but it was too late to do anything about it. They flew above the greenery and flowing hills before swooping toward a cave mouth.

Despite being carried, Rivka never felt like she was hanging. She didn't have the feeling of too-heavy gravity pulling her down. She seemed as light as the faeries.

The entirety of the planet was natural, no structures of any sort. To a casual observer, Azfelius would have been considered technologically backward, but the opposite was true.

We have limited our interaction with the lesser species because of our evolution, Siro'ti'lc explained to the group. *We joined the Federation because of the influence of your Bethany Anne. As one who moved the Etheric as a force for good, she convinced us to come out of hiding. We had kept our planet from wayward eyes and ship sensors for hundreds of years. We remained out of Kurtherian sight. They are our enemy, but we do not fight like other races.*

"The Kurtherians and their minions are gone because of people who fought," Rivka noted.

We applaud the Queen's efforts. We fight by not being where the enemy strikes. We cannot take a life, but we don't judge those who can. I know you have. All of you. Jay's face dropped, and she started to cry. *But you did so, not out of anger or malice, but because it had to be done. For Justice.*

Come, Groenwyn. *Even without the crystal, the shrine will take your pain away.*

"'Groenwyn?'"

Green one. You have nothing to be ashamed of. I'm not sure I've ever met a loving soul like yours. The mark upon it is a smudge, not a tattoo, if I get your imagery correct.

"I'm not sure anyone has ever said anything nicer to me." Tears continued to roll down her face as the group flew through the cave mouth into an area peppered with multicolored luminescent ponds. They slowed their movements and approached a central arena, a circular area with benches inside the cone leading down.

At the bottom, there was only darkness.

"I expect Infinity was down there," Rivka remarked.

You will have to climb down on your own. It is too painful for us to go there.

The faeries set their charges at the top. There were no steps, only the benches.

Red started down, vaulting from one level to the next. "I feel like a little kid," he grumbled.

A flight of faeries flew in from the other side. Siro'ti'lc and his flight beat their wings heavily in agitation. The two flights paired off. Rivka waited and watched. She expected a conversation was taking place, but was on the outside of it, unable to hear unless they spoke to her. Jay waved her arms and pled for them to stop fighting.

"That's fighting?" Lindy asked. Rivka shook her head and watched intently. Red looked down toward the bottom and then back up to the top of the circular amphitheater.

"I'm going down to take a look," he said. Rivka waved a hand over her shoulder. Red's footfalls sounded with each hop down to the next level.

"May I ask what's going on, Siro'ti'lc?" Rivka said softly.

"Please, stop!" Jay cried. She held her head as if fighting off a headache.

A new voice appeared in their minds. *Accept our apologies, strangers to the glen. I am Ik'toa'les of the River Dance Clan.*

"Why do you fight?" Jay asked. Rivka leaned closer as if that would help her to hear better.

We believe the shrine is for all. Not everyone believes that. One of the faeries rose to loom over the others and then dropped close to Jay. *Tell us, Groenwyn, what do you think?*

"I think by fighting, you will move farther apart." Jay held up her hands, and the faeries descended. "You are such a beautiful race, and it hurts me to see the ugliness.

Someone stole Infinity, and that's what we're here to investigate. Please let the Magistrate do her job."

Not all is as it seems, Groenwyn, Ik'toa'les replied. *We will step back and wait patiently, for the shrine should be enjoyed by all.*

When your time is right. Until then, we shall meditate that you find peace.

Ik'toa'les and his clan members backed away, wings hammering the air, their eyes never leaving those of Siro'ti'lc and his clan faeries.

"Paradise," Lindy whispered and shook her head.

I don't think Infinity was stolen by the smugglers, Rivka told her team.

"Siro'ti'lc," Rivka started. When he didn't respond, she said it loud enough for her voice to echo. The sound was unpleasant, and the luminescence in the pools winked out.

Softly, Magistrate. The shrine is unused to such interruptions.

"That is interesting. How would an outsider get in to take Infinity if the shrine is so sensitive?"

There is one outsider on all of Azfelius—the representative from the Federation—but she never leaves her home. We go to her. She is aged and blind but sharp, and can do all she needs to do with the faculties at her command.

"No outsiders. When we eliminate the possibilities, we are left with the probabilities."

Which are?

"Infinity is still here, and was taken by a faerie."

Then we would see it. It vibrates in the Etheric like a stone rippling a pond's waters.

"I suggest there is a way to hide its signature. That is far easier to believe than that a mysterious stranger made it onto your planet and into the shrine and escaped with Infinity in hand, all without anyone noticing. At the other two crime scenes, evidence was left behind. Compelling evidence. I still have many questions, but here..." Rivka switched to her internal comm rather than yelling to the bottom of the amphitheater. *What do you see down there, Red?*

Not a damn thing, Magistrate. It's squeaky-clean down here. The dirt on the floor is soft, and I'm leaving footprints. I don't think this dirt has been touched in a long, long time. Whoever took it wasn't walking.

Any signs of a holoprojector? Rivka asked.

None.

Rivka was torn about climbing down to the bottom but decided that she needed to talk to Siro'ti'lc.

"Jay, head down there so Chaz can collect data and imagery to build a three-dimensional model of the scene."

"But..." Jay pointed to the two groups of faeries.

"We'll wait for you. No one is going to throw down as soon as Groenwyn is gone," Rivka said, trying to reassure her.

The young woman smiled. "They gave me a name," she said softly.

"You're special to us, too." Rivka reached out to share the moment with her friend but stopped short of touching her. Siro'ti'lc was watching them closely.

"If only Floyd was here to see this."

"Floyd might be a little too rambunctious for their tastes."

"Probably," Jay replied. Rivka tipped her head toward

the bottom of the amphitheater, and Jay started to climb down.

Rivka fixed Siro'ti'lc with her interrogator's unblinking gaze. He beat his wings rhythmically as he descended to float eye to eye with her. "Tell me about the theft," she started.

As I already described, one day it was here, the next it was gone. We searched for it but could not find it, he replied.

"How did you search?"

We joined our minds and cast a wide net through the Etheric. It was nowhere to be found. I fear it has been destroyed. Otherwise, its ripples should be there. His telepathic voice took on a panicked pitch.

Rivka clasped her hands behind her back. "How big *is* Infinity?" she asked. Rivka didn't believe it had been destroyed.

About five times my height. It is an immense crystalline lattice.

"Was it created, or is it natural?"

Both. Neither. It simply is.

Red. Carefully reach your hand where Infinity is supposed to be.

Sure. Red replied. He looked up from the bottom of the cone, shrugging one shoulder. Lindy gave him a thumbs-up while she remained near the Magistrate. She might have been weaponless, but she wasn't powerless.

Red started to climb onto a small natural stone platform so he could reach up. "Ow!" He held his head where it bumped against an invisible object. He ran his hand across it before climbing down. "Yep. Something's there. Smooth."

Siro'ti'lc raced over the ridge and into the cone. He flew

in a circle around the place where Infinity was supposed to be. Intense pressure filled the shrine. The humans reflexively clasped their hands over their ears to hold back the pain.

As quickly as it came, it was gone, and Infinity filled the space.

"We'll be going now," Rivka said loudly enough to earn the ugly echo.

Red and Jay helped each other climb the benches, but stopped when Siro'ti'lc's clan flew down to collect them. Siro'ti'lc returned to the Magistrate, but his eyes weren't on her.

"As a signatory to the Federation, you are compelled to follow a Magistrate's ruling. Ik'toa'les. Although nothing was stolen, your machinations have caused significant expense to the Federation. However, wasting our time is not a crime. Neither are we allowed to mediate internal disputes. But if you would like, I am more than willing to talk to both sides in this conflict to hopefully help you bridge your differences."

Allow a lesser race to mediate? Ik'toa'les exclaimed.

"Can you fix your own problems?" Rivka asked, looking from face to face. "This was nothing more than a prank, denying you what you denied them. A malicious prank. I'm proud to be a lesser race if it means I don't have to put up with nonsense like that. Take me to my ship, please."

The faeries hung in the air with Jay and an uncomfortable Red.

Her, Ik'toa'les suggested.

Agreed, Siro'ti'lc replied.

"Bring peace to this world, Groenwyn," Rivka told the

young woman with the platinum-green hair. "Maybe we can get something to eat while you're working?"

The faeries handed Jay to Ik'toa'les and Siro'ti'lc. The two flew away with her, talking as they went.

Members of both clans flew in and picked up Rivka and her bodyguards. *We have been asked to show you where we repast for you to partake to your heart's desire.*

"Now you're talking." Red licked his lips.

"I doubt they eat like you do," Lindy suggested.

"I doubt anyone eats like he does." Rivka gave the side-eye to Red while they were carried through the shrine and outdoors.

"You do!" Red pointed at the Magistrate with a lone finger so he wouldn't shake free from the faeries' grip.

They flew for only a couple of minutes before being deposited on a path through a cultivated area.

"A garden," Rivka said, bending to examine the plants next to them. She picked a small green pod she assumed was a vegetable and took a bite. "Tastes like a green pepper." Her face dropped. "It would be so good on a pizza."

"I'm pretty sure our repast, as they called it, is going to be what we pick." Lindy tried the small pepper and hummed her approval as she ate. Red resisted but decided it was better than nothing, which was the alternative. Or a protein bar that Ankh had made tasteless. Red was starting to regret his war with the little guy.

"Why do you think they embraced Jay?" Rivka asked.

Red threw his pepper's stem into a bush and picked another one. "She's not like us."

Lindy stopped eating to nod.

Red continued, "When she killed to save our lives, it bothered her. We don't kill anyone haphazardly, but once it's done, we move on to the next person who's trying to kill us. I justify it because if they win, they'll keep hurting people. There's only one way to stop those types and walk away to keep doing what we do."

"I remember a time when you were just a bodyguard." Rivka poked Red in the arm. He popped the pepper into his mouth, stem and all. "I'm glad you've evolved. How's your head?"

"It'll take more than an invisible crystal to damage that thing," Lindy remarked.

"It will." Red tried to look innocent while turning his head and spitting out the stem. They continued trolling the raised beds, sampling the offerings.

Lindy camped out at a certain plant, and with her back turned, was enjoying herself a little too much.

"Whatcha got over there?" Red asked. When she didn't answer, he hurried that way, with Rivka close on his heels.

Red juice that looked like blood dripped from her face. When Red tapped her on the shoulder, she spun and tried to hide the plants behind her. Rivka looked behind her.

"Strawberries!"

"I was about to tell you guys…" Lindy tried.

Rivka moved down the short row and helped herself. Red had one, made a face, and moved to the next plant. "What's this?" A blue and red flower with a bulb underneath. He pulled the flower off and prepared to pop the bulb into his mouth.

I wouldn't, Siro'ti'lc's voice interrupted. A few moments later, he appeared with Ik'toa'les carrying a beaming Jayita.

Groenwyn has helped us resolve our issues. That's a flower, human known as Vered. You can eat it, but it would be less than gratifying.

Red dropped the bulb on the ground.

"It's only been about ten minutes," Rivka said. "Well done, Jay!"

We retired to a time distortion bubble. It has been two days, still not even a single grain of sand on the beach of time.

"All's well that ends well?" Rivka asked.

Yes. Shall we? Siro'ti'lc asked. More faeries appeared. Rivka and her team obediently raised their arms to be whisked away to *Wyatt Earp.*

Chaz piped up for the first time since they arrived. *I have so much information, I don't know where to start.*

The final trip on Azfelius was far too short. Rivka and her team were deposited in front of the ship, and the faeries faded into the distance. The final two, Siro'ti'lc and Ik'toa'les, hovered close to each other as they waved, human-style. *Should we need help ever again, we will call the Magistrate to bring Groenwyn to us.*

Rivka looked her team over as the hatch opened and the ramp descended. "I'd say this was a wasted trip because it didn't get us any closer to finding the smugglers, but I think we needed it. We all needed this win. I'm afraid we might not be able to resolve the art thefts. Too much time has elapsed. Too much money is involved, and the people with the answers aren't talking."

Red licked his finger and wiped away the strawberry juice coloring Lindy's chin. "That's some grade-A-prime bullshit," he said. Lindy pulled away and started scrubbing her face. Red grinned. "I wasn't talking to you, my dearest."

"Me?" Rivka feigned outrage by jamming her hands on her hips and throwing her head back.

"We're not going to stop until we find those cock-wombles." Red headed toward the ship. "Even if you don't know it, you do. What are you waiting for? You know they ain't here."

Red twirled his finger in the air and climbed the ramp. Lindy looked for the weapons they'd left behind, but someone had already collected them.

When Jay reached Red, he grabbed her into a bear hug. "I'm proud of you," he whispered into her ear before adding, "Now, stop goofing off, Groenwyn. You have to help me understand what this stupid art stuff is all about. Shh. Don't tell the Magistrate I'm trying to learn something new."

"I won't," the young woman replied conspiratorially.

I can't see anything! Chaz complained.

"'Stop goofing off' is right! The bad guys won't catch themselves," Rivka shouted.

CHAPTER TWELVE

The Ring Planet of Yemilore

"I've never seen anything like it," Rivka said. There was a ring at the inner edge of the Goldilocks zone, where the system's star could shine into the inside of the wedding band shape where life thrived. The outside of the ring closer to the star had been baked hard. The planet rotated quickly, completing a day-night cycle in two hours.

Shadows passed across the inside of the ring as it was lit from the star shining beyond the far side of the planet's diameter. The apparent gravity from the centripetal force of the rotation was one-point-four gees, a heavy planet just like Azfelius.

The others from Rivka's team were mesmerized by the image on the bridge's main screen. The rest of the crew crowded onto the bridge. Alant Cole stood behind the captain's chair with his hand on Clodagh's shoulder. Kennedy had the watch and sat in the pilot's seat, with Ryleigh and Aurora hanging out nearby.

Chaz interrupted their reverie with an announcement.

"Magistrate, you have an incoming communication from the High Chancellor."

"I'll take it in my quarters. Please ask him to stand by. I'll be there in less than a minute." Rivka worked her way through the small crowd and ran through the corridors, vaulting over Floyd as she passed.

Whee! the wombat cheered.

Rivka laughed and looked back to see Floyd continuing to the bridge. She was back to normal, with the Gorandian off the ship.

In her quarters, Rivka sat at her desk. The screen came on instantly. "High Chancellor," she said to the face looking back at her.

"Good morning, Rivka. I found your report from Azfelius interesting. We know so little about them. Any insight is a good insight. I'm forwarding your information to General Reynolds in case the Queen would like to visit them. Their relationship with the Etheric is something from which we could learn a thing or two."

Rivka nodded but didn't answer. The High Chancellor wasn't calling to talk about her report.

"But that's not why I called." He made himself more comfortable by leaning back. "I need you to expedite your investigation on Yemilore and hurry back to Yoll. The lawsuit by the Beit'el Estate against Loids has the potential to tear up the economic fabric of the Federation. It's still early in the case, but even the discovery phase is sending shockwaves through the elite."

Rivka grimaced. "I'm sorry, but I don't think I'm any closer to the smugglers. This case is kicking my ass. I'll stick with it until I find them or as long as you'll let me, whichever comes first."

Wyatt leaned toward the screen. "It's good to get your ass kicked every now and then in a legal sense, not the getting-blown-up-trying-to-find-a-witness sense. My money's on you, Magistrate."

"That's pretty funny," she deadpanned. "Do you mean that you bet no blood and no running, too?"

"Only you get that bet. I missed it by two hours, but that was enough to take me out of the running."

Rivka stared at the screen, open-mouthed.

The High Chancellor stared back.

She finally caved. "You're not joking."

"Of course not." He waved his hand in front of the screen. "Back to the case. I'm not sure which way it's going, but people are lining up on both sides. Powerful people."

"Are you judging it?"

"No. I don't think I would want to, either. An appeal of the original ruling would go through Yoll's planetary court before coming to me at the Federation level, so I'm a couple chairs removed from it, but you are investigating the thefts. You might be able to file an amicus brief."

Friend of the court. "May be able?"

"That's why I want you back here. You need to get your finger on the pulse of this and find what's behind it. Remember what I said? Powerful people. If we are caught unaware, planets could go to war."

Rivka rocked back with surprise and looked questioningly at the screen. "Go to war over suing to get paid for a stolen piece of art? What aren't you telling me?"

"We don't know what we don't know," the High Chancellor offered. "Your unique gifts might help us answer that question. I need you here, Magistrate. Yemilore is a beautiful place, but Yoll is where the action is."

"Understood. I will do my best, High Chancellor and be there before you know it."

Wyatt signed off.

Rivka stared at the blank screen for a few heartbeats before heading out. While walking down the corridor, she contacted Chaz. *Get us on the ground and hooked up with the crime team. I need to look at the scene and talk to as many people involved as possible.*

When the Magistrate arrived on the bridge, Chaz had already put her plan into motion. He used the overhead speakers so everyone could hear. "*Wyatt Earp* is cleared for immediate descent to Agromilore, the capital city. We will be met by the ACP, the Agromilore City Police, who are in charge of the case."

"When I talked to them a while ago, they seemed to welcome the assistance, especially regarding information-sharing. They wanted to know about the other cases, but I hadn't started those investigations yet. We have info to share now." Rivka pointed to the main screen. "Bring up the case file on the Marble Orb, please."

Information scrolled across the screen. Rivka stopped it at times to read more in-depth before continuing. Red's eyes quickly glazed over. He and Lindy retreated to the armory. Aurora took over navigator duties while Ryleigh occupied the pilot's seat. Clodagh surrendered the captain's seat to the Magistrate so she could concentrate on one last review of the case files.

It was the same story as the other three thefts. No one

saw a thing. One second it was there, and the next second it was gone. They had found the device, but it lacked power, like the holoprojector Rivka had secured from Dax-7.

"Would you like to watch the video from Binsulaker Prime?" Chaz asked.

"The recovered video? Hell, yeah! How long have you had it done?"

"I finished while you were on Azfelius. I forgot to bring it up."

"That's fine, Chaz. Don't beat yourself up. Let's see what there is to see."

"I've isolated the video from five days prior to our arrival. Watch closely."

The video showed the Beit'el Estate Gallery. The Anastolia was in place. The next second, it disappeared. Two seconds later, it reappeared.

"That's bizarre. Do they have matter transport capability? That would be a game-changer, for sure. No one would be able to secure anything."

"Keep watching, Magistrate."

The Palustrade lifted into the air as if on its own accord and carefully landed on the floor. The display stand turned over. It stayed that way for several minutes until the Anastolia reappeared inside the cabinet. The stand turned upright, and the Palustrade was put back on top.

"One day later..." Chaz announced. The video cut to the next evening. Low light made it difficult to see. The Palustrade was moved, and the stand turned on its side. The Anastolia made a brief appearance before disappearing. The room was returned to its undisturbed view. The holoimage of the Anastolia stood out boldly, even in the semi-dark.

"Invisible thieves," Rivka stated.

"It would appear so. I've isolated these two frames out of five days' worth of video. Two images appeared side by side on the main screen. One showed two gloved fingers suspended mid-air. The other showed the toe of a boot.

"Can you extrapolate their size and race?"

"Humanoid is the best I can do. Possibly Federation suits with cloaking technology."

"Bad guys got some good toys," Rivka said more to herself than anyone else. "If they have those, how can they be detected?"

"The cloaking technology is a closely-held secret within the Federation. Needless to say, the technology to detect it is even more closely held."

"But we know people…" Rivka started.

"And that's what I'm working on now with Erasmus and Ankh. Ted and Plato are also engaged since this technology should not be in criminal hands. They are taking it as a personal point of pride to find and remove it from the public."

"Ted and Ankh? And you forgot to mention this? It would have been nice to tell the High Chancellor some of these details." Rivka wasn't questioning Chaz's initiative. "Draft me a message with these latest details and address it to both Grainger and the High Chancellor."

A message instantly appeared on the screen. Rivka scrolled down the text. "Fourth line down, begin the sentence with 'Expanding the line of inquiry to include…'"

She continued reading. "Nice job, Chaz. Launch that moisture-seeking love missile!"

"I'm sorry?" Chaz wondered.

"Send the message, please." Rivka avoided eye contact with the others on the bridge. "Time to go." She headed toward the airlock.

"Been too long, Magistrate?" Jay asked.

"Way too long. I might have to lower my standards."

"Don't do that," the young woman replied. "The right person is out there for you. I'd say you are fine alone, but your comment suggests that maybe you aren't, and need a little playtime."

"I just want what Terry and Char have." Rivka stopped, closing her eyes to embrace the magic those two shared.

"Everyone wants that!" Jay started to laugh. "That is a high standard."

"What about your friend from Zaxxon Major. Lauton?"

"There's something with a lot of potential." Jay grinned broadly. "But she has a major corporation to run, and I never get any time off." Jay poked Rivka in the shoulder. "But with what I experienced on Azfelius, I need some time to process. I'm not sure what my future holds. The faeries were *very* persuasive."

"When you can explain what that means, I look forward to hearing it." The two women reached the airlock, where they found Red and Lindy waiting, wearing their full body armor and carrying their railguns.

"No Chaz?" Red remarked, directing the attention away from the two heavily-armed bodyguards.

Jay slapped her chest, surprise on her face. She turned and ran.

"Is no one else going to bring it up?" Lindy asked. "My respect and regards to my husband for his sensitivity to this issue."

Red smiled. "It sounds like I did something right, which is so unlike me, but I'll take it, whatever *it* is."

"Are we going to call her Jay or Groenwyn?"

Wyatt Earp bumped the ground gently. The airlock started to cycle as the ship equalized with the outer air. Rivka grunted when local gravity took over. She fought to maintain her posture.

"How about we just ask?" Rivka offered. Lindy winked at Red.

"I must have missed something." He studied his partner but couldn't discern what he didn't know.

The green-haired woman returned, pointing to the locket-looking device hanging around her chest.

"Hey, Chaz!" Rivka and Lindy waved. Red rolled his eyes. All three started staring at the young woman. "What do you want us to call you?"

Without hesitation, Jay replied, "She Who Placates World Pain. Why do you ask?"

"What?" Red cocked his head sideways as he tried to make sense of what he'd just heard.

"I'm kidding. If you are good with it, I like my Azfelian name, Groenwyn."

"Cool," Lindy and Rivka agreed and turned to head out the door.

Red held them back with one big arm. "It is times like these that I miss Hamlet, my brother-in-fur, not being a woman that no man can understand."

"So profound." Lindy shook her head and stepped aside

to let Red be the first to experience the wonders of Yemilore.

He fought the gravity, taking slow and measured steps. The welcoming committee of lanky, bald humanoids was hurrying toward the ship. Red picked up his pace to meet them before they could climb the ramp. He hit the bottom of the ramp and held his weapon sideways. "The Magistrate is on her way," he told them.

"We are sincerely interested in getting this resolved with aplomb and totality."

"My translation device must be blinking out," Red replied while he moved slowly toward them to clear the bottom of the ramp.

"You are so massively huge. Our compliments on your fine genetics."

Rivka snorted as she worked her way around Red. Jay maneuvered past his other side.

"We are impressed by you and your entourage, Special Deputy Undersecretary to the Secretary For Health and Well-Being to the Minister of Internal Security," Rivka smoothly intoned.

The reception party beamed at the appropriate greeting. The Special Deputy stepped forward, awkwardly offering a three-fingered hand. Rivka placed it between her hands in a warm grip. "Thank you for meeting us. This is an awful business, but the sooner we get to it, the sooner it'll be behind us."

The special deputy's face fell, and he let his hand drop. "We have multiple banquets scheduled in your honor," he told her weakly.

"And we shall enjoy the graciously impressive offerings

with great zeal," Jay replied, nodding slightly to Rivka.

"The First Primary to the Magistrate's Corps of Legal Stallions for the High Chancellor of the Federation will stand in my stead. She's more important than me. I do the legwork, but she represents the Federation in this matter."

Legal Stallions? Red wondered while maintaining his stoic bodyguard expression.

It was the best I could come up with. I didn't expect banquets, but they are all about their titles. They don't have names, Rivka replied.

Jay offered her hand and the special deputy took it in two hands, as Rivka had done to him.

"Please call me Groenwyn. It is our custom to carry a title with us throughout our lives, although if you are more comfortable calling me First Primary Legal Stallion, that is fine, too," Jay continued with her winning smile. Her platinum-green hair sparkled with the harsh rays of the sun. "I need someone to go with Rivka. Someone who was intimately involved with the investigation."

The special deputy twisted his three digits in the air and slapped them into his palm in the Yemilorian version of snapping his fingers. One of his entourage leapt forward.

"First Assistant to the Special Deputy Undersecretary to the Secretary for Health and Well-Being to the Minister of Internal Security, at your service." His hand twitched at his side in expectation of the human handshake. Rivka accommodated him.

"Who do you think did it?" she asked quickly as they touched. A vision of the Gorandian environmental containment suit appeared, followed by a vision of the insurance agent speaking quietly with the distraught owner.

"What I think is immaterial," he replied formally. "What matters is what we can prove."

"You sound like me. We're going to get along famously," Rivka told him. "Red, with me. Lindy, go enjoy the banquets."

"Lindy with me, Red and Rivka to the crime scene. We'll meet up when you're done. Don't be strangers," Groenwyn said, confusing their Yemilorian hosts. The young woman took the special deputy by the arm and guided him away. He pointed toward a waiting land vehicle that looked like a bus. Everyone except the first assistant went with him, leaving Rivka and Red alone.

"Shall we?" he asked. "I apologize for the humble transportation. This was supposed to be an escort, not primary transportation for august off-world guests."

Rivka looked at Red and shrugged.

"If you had a choice, wouldn't you rather go to the party?" Red asked.

"It depends on the party," Rivka replied.

"We might be able to make the third through sixth banquets," the first assistant noted, hope filling his words. "Those are the good ones!"

Red's look was better than any words Rivka could have added. *Heaven help us.*

The first assistant opened the back doors in the three-seater vehicle, which looked too small. Red and Rivka stuffed themselves into the back, the bodyguard hugging his railgun to his face. Rivka looked at it but didn't say anything.

The Yemilorian squeezed himself into the driver's seat and activated the controls. They slid from the dash, arranging themselves appropriately for him.

"Hang on," he cautioned. "This baby has some get up and go!"

"You don't sound like the others," Rivka remarked.

"Ack!" He shook his head and moaned. "I try so hard, but I went to school off-planet. I am ruined for a life of Yemilorian service. Please don't tell the special deputy."

The vehicle accelerated slowly, moving not even as quickly as a grazing bistok.

"I won't. Your way is more comfortable for me. Please do not change. It's like when you take the time to learn someone else's language. I take it as a kindness, so thank you."

The first assistant breathed a long sigh of relief. He raced over the roadways, which seemed to exacerbate the heavy gravity. Having Red leaning on her didn't help either. Her stomach started to rebel.

"I'm going to need you to pull over," Rivka said, tapping the Yemilorian on his shoulder.

"But we're almost there," the Yemilorian stammered.

"Pull over!" Rivka leaned back and closed her eyes. Red tried to move, clearing at most a finger's width of space for the Magistrate.

The first assistant yanked the vehicle to the side of the roadway. The door popped and lifted up and away. Rivka nearly fell trying to get out, instantly feeling better when she was able to stand upright away from the vehicle. Red forced his way from the vehicle, almost getting himself clocked by a passing motorist. Red started to give the finger but caught himself in time.

"Are you okay, Magistrate?" he asked after working his way around the vehicle.

"I am now. That was weird. Not claustrophobic. Not prone to motion sickness."

The first assistant stumbled from the vehicle, fell to his knees, and started puking.

"Empathy," Rivka suggested. "That's new."

"We need a bigger vehicle." Red and Rivka watched their escort until he wiped his face and stood.

The gangly humanoid started to apologize. "Another nasty habit picked up off-world. I hope you won't tell the special deputy."

"I won't tell him about that either. Tell me, why do you think the insurance agent is involved?"

The first assistant looked surprised. Rivka waited for him, letting the silence encourage him to speak.

"The facts. It had to be an inside job. The security system for the Marble Orb is redundant, multiple layers with non-overlapping overseers. This was the system recommended by the insurance company, and the one that was ultimately installed. Only the owner and the agent knew the particulars."

"Wouldn't that be obvious? If there was only one person who knew the way in, why would that person risk it? It seems too easy."

"I hope you will be able to provide additional insight when you review the crime scene and my approach to the crime."

"The crime scene is preserved?"

"Of course. We have not yet caught the perpetrator or recovered the Marble Orb."

"Did you find a holoprojector, a small device somewhere near where the Orb was displayed?"

"Nothing was found at the scene. *Nothing*," he emphasized.

"What do you say we get to it?" Rivka pointed to the three-passenger vehicle.

Red hesitated. "Maybe we're close enough that I won't have to breathe. You two pukers are giving me the willies."

He waited for a vehicle to pass before rounding the vehicle and climbing in.

"Aren't you glad you trimmed down?" Rivka asked.

"The jury is still out on that one."

"The case was decided and lost on appeal. Serve your sentence, you ingrate," Rivka replied affectionately as she forced herself into the small space. "Holy bajoolysnackers."

"Bigger car," Red declared, jabbing a finger into the first assistant's back after he took his seat.

The first assistant fired up the controls and drove away. Five minutes later, they were escorted through a massive set of iron gates that rolled closed as soon as they passed.

"Another fortress," Red observed.

"Something all the scenes had in common." Rivka tried to take in their surroundings, but she couldn't see much from her seat. When they stopped and the door popped, she crawled out.

A fairly humble two-story stone building stood before them. Hedges and short trees surrounded it. A well-manicured lawn created a warm approach to the short staircase that led to double doors.

A Yemilorian waited by the door.

The first assistant led them up the steps. "Allow me to introduce the Potentate of Magnanimous Austerity."

Rivka half-bowed as she approached. "Potentate," she repeated. Rivka took the initiative by offering her hand. He seemed familiar, and reached out. "Who stole the Orb?"

As the two touched, the potentate's mind was filled with blackness. "Evil," he said, reinforcing what she had seen. "What else would stoop to such a level?"

"Greed? Envy? The Marble Orb is worth a great deal."

"Credits are a most ungratifying replacement. The theft has shocked My Magnanimity to uncomfortable levels of woe."

Red surveyed the area. The small unmanned escort vehicle had departed, on its way back to the front gate. No workers could be seen caring for the plants. No one was visible through the open door.

"I would like to view the crime scene," Rivka said. The potentate nodded and walked through the doors with Rivka at his side. Red and the first assistant followed.

The front of the building was a façade, hiding how far the end of the building was from the entrance. They walked for three minutes down a major hallway that seemed to stretch into infinity. Rivka saw herself in the distance. *Mirrors to make it look even more impressive,* she thought.

The potentate ushered the small group into an anteroom. "Prepare yourself for the most shocking view of your life," he said gravely. They walked through a carved, arched doorway and into an empty room.

"Appalling, isn't it?" the first assistant asked. The potentate nodded with his head hung low.

"We'll try to work through it. Help us help you. Where was the Marble Orb?" Rivka asked.

Red waited in the entryway while trying to rank the most shocking things he'd seen in his life. The empty room hadn't quite cracked the top million, but he was trying to keep an open mind.

When the potentate had composed himself, he threw his shoulders back with dogged determination and took one step forward. "It was here." He stretched his arms wide to take in where it had stood. He pointed to a small depression in the floor. "It balanced right there."

He gave up his effort at being strong and broke down. His shoulders heaved as he cried.

Even Red was touched by the emotions of the Yemilorian.

"How would someone move such an object? Unlike the Passion, they couldn't cut the frame off. They would have to move the Orb as it was. How much did it weigh?"

"It was utterly massive," the potentate managed between sobs, his bald head vibrating with his pain.

The first assistant stepped up. "Nineteen tons."

"Every one of the stolen art pieces occupied significant space, and in this case, it had immense mass, too." Rivka was thinking out loud. She walked around where the Marble Orb had been, trying to visualize the piece. "I wish we had brought Chaz."

"He would not have fit in that car," Red mumbled.

Rivka agreed but didn't say so out loud. She stopped

when she reached the potentate. "Describe the security systems you have in place."

"Cameras along the hallway, in here, motion sensors, the floor is weight-sensitive, and during the evening, my pet bigantuans run free in this wing of the house."

"Bigantuans?"

"A not-insignificant horned- and razor-backed creature with great fangs," the potentate replied before nodding toward Red. "They are very impressive. Probably give your massively huge man a run for a not-insubstantial number of credits."

"How did the perps get it out?" Rivka asked again.

"There are only three doors big enough," the first assistant replied. "Through this archway and left down the main corridor. The kitchen area has a double-door with a dock. The front door and the back door are both double doors."

"I've seen your very thorough report, First Assistant. There was no forensic evidence in this room, is that correct?"

"Yes. We vacuumed every dust particle. Nothing was out of place."

"And the forensics on the digital systems show they were erased, and you weren't able to recover the data?"

"Erased in entirety," the potentate lamented. "Only pure evil commands the universe thusly."

"Or someone who is very good with digital systems. I will need full access to your security systems."

"Of course." The potentate turned and walked out without looking back. Immediately across the corridor, a room little bigger than a closet contained stacks of computer equipment. Older technology over the plasma- and biosystems that were the cutting edge now.

Chaz, can you hear me? Rivka tried her internal comm chip. She pulled the datapad from the inside pocket of her jacket and tapped the screen. "Chaz?"

"Magistrate," the AI replied in a cheery voice.

"I need you to pull the deleted data and rebuild it. Can you do that for me?"

"Do you have one of Ankh's discs?"

Rivka leaned out of the room and looked at Red. He reached into his vest, then pulled his hand out and flipped a disc between his fingers.

She placed the disc in the middle of the equipment. "How's that?"

"I'm coordinating with Erasmus." Rivka waited impatiently. "Accessing it now."

"Don't you need my passwords or something?" the potentate asked.

"I could say yes to maintain the illusion that your system is secure, but you deserve the truth. We don't need your passwords because we're already into your system."

"This is supposed to be the most secure of anything that's available!" he declared, his voice shrill with panic at the revelation. Rivka looked through the equipment, then held up the datapad and transmitted the images to Chaz.

"This is an old system running even older software."

"It's the same as what we found on Binsulaker Prime, isn't it, Chaz?" Rivka already knew the answer. She was a good lawyer and becoming a better investigator with each new case.

"In a word, identical."

CHAPTER THIRTEEN

Home of the Potentate of Magnanimous Austerity, Yemilore

Rivka placed her hand on the distraught potentate's shoulder. "Let me guess. This system was approved by your insurance agent, ostensibly for Loids of Yoll. Chaz, connect me to the High Chancellor, please."

The High Chancellor's picture appeared, but only his voice came through. "I'm in a meeting. What do you need?"

"I need authorities on Yoll to take Angora into custody immediately if you can find her. I suspect she knows we're onto her."

"Inside job?"

"Before the artwork was even purchased, it had already been stolen. That's my supposition, High Chancellor. We'll get to the bottom of things once I get to Yoll. I'm still no closer to finding the smuggling ring, but if we can root Angora out of that metal box, I bet I can get what we need."

"I'll issue the order for immediate detention. You have a week to prefer charges before we have to let her go.

Rivka nodded at the screen even though she wasn't sure the High Chancellor could see her. "I bet Loids isn't going to like us crawling up their asses on a scavenger hunt, either. I only have circumstantial evidence at this point, but that's enough to justify a warrant, even under the closest scrutiny."

"I'll be looking for your case notes soon, Magistrate. I'll find your Gorandian, and you find me the smugglers."

"I'm counting on the Gorandian to lead me to them."

The High Chancellor signed off.

"Chaz, please coordinate with Erasmus and focus your financial searches on anything and everything Angora has touched."

"We were already looking into her, but we will redouble our efforts."

"As will I, Chaz." Rivka's lip twitched into a snarl. "I don't know where your Marble Orb is, Potentate, but I have a good idea who to ask about it."

"I'm driving," Rivka told the first assistant.

"But you don't know how to drive." The Yemilorian held his arms up and twirled his fingers.

"I don't care. I'm not going to be stuffed into the back of this spew-car. That only leaves the driver's seat. I watched how you did it."

"Maybe we can get another vehicle?" he offered.

"Get in the back," Rivka ordered, planting her feet and pointing. "Red?"

The big bodyguard wasn't enamored of the idea of

squeezing into the back with the gangly Yemilorian. He was certain they wouldn't fit.

"Get in!" Rivka stood her ground.

"You can use my vehicle," the potentate offered. "Else I fear your illustrious joy shall falter in your desire to travel without the anguish of a cookie pack."

"I have no idea what he said besides I don't have to get in there." Red pointed with his railgun at the first assistant's three-seater.

The potentate went back inside his home. Within a minute, a limousine rolled into the driveway. "Where do you think he was hiding that?" Rivka asked. Red shook his head before nodding in approval at their upgraded wheels.

"You can take the car," Rivka said. "We'll meet you at the banquet. Which one is going on now?"

"The second, but by the time we get there, it will have finished. We should go straight to the third."

"Make it so, Number One." Rivka twirled her finger in the air as the driver opened the door for her and Red. They climbed in, waiting for the door to close before sprawling most ingloriously within the limo's padded luxury.

Outside, the first assistant told the driver the address. He acknowledged the words with a Yemilorian gesture, assumed his position up front, and left without waiting for the first assistant.

Rivka thought about asking him to wait but decided against it. "He'll get there when he gets there," she conceded. "He knew."

Red studied her expression. "Do you know how?"

"He eliminated everyone it couldn't have been. Although the how and why were wrong, that didn't sway his focus. He eliminated the impossible and was left with only two alternatives. He judged rightly about the potentate. That man was distraught. It wasn't an act."

"It didn't look like an act. I hope I never get attached to an inanimate object like that."

"Me either, although I do like *Wyatt Earp*. It is a nice upgrade."

"I'd say well-deserved, but I know us." Red slouched until he was nearly horizontal. "We've been good. We've been lucky. It's damn good we are lucky. And thanks to the nanocytes, we aren't going to be wearing the scars on the outside."

"Not on the outside." Rivka contemplated her bodyguard.

"Are you happy, Red?"

He looked at her like she'd lost her mind.

"I mean with the job." She pointed at him. "You still have the newlywed glow about you, but are you getting what you want from the position?"

Red laughed and closed his eyes, cradling his railgun to his chest. "Best job I ever had, Magistrate. I get to do more than be the hired muscle. I got to go after two guys who put contracts on my head. I get to hug a railgun. And I get to work with my wife, who loves to shoot guns more than I do."

"She does? You don't like to shoot?"

"Don't get me wrong. I like to shoot, and I like to blow stuff up, but I really like hand-to-hand. That shows what you're made of. Beating that bastard on S'korr? After that, everything I do is gravy. That was the toughest fight I ever had. That spike thing? I thought I was done for. Don't tell anyone else. I like to maintain my mystique of not showing fear."

"Your secret is safe with me, big man. Was that why you went on the size kick?"

"Fear does strange things to people."

"I think I already said that in this case."

"Mission," Red corrected.

"I'm telling," Rivka countered.

'You promised."

"Okay, I'll let this one go. Only a case. You heard. We're on our way to Yoll to interrogate the Gorandian, assuming the High Chancellor can corral her. Talking about fear, I'm afraid she's already done a runner."

Red chuckled. The air conditioner control was by his head. He reached for it and dialed down the cold. "A runner: one who flees from the long arm of the law. She has met the judge, jury, and executioner. She's running because she knows what's coming."

"Damn straight. She has been judged. Well, not really. I need to talk to her first. The real Angora, not metal-encased her."

Red relaxed while the limousine raced along. Rivka looked out the back window. The first assistant was nowhere to be seen.

"Your loss," she told the emptiness. "I hear these banquets are to die for."

The limo arrived without fanfare at a back door.

"We don't get the red carpet treatment?" she asked the driver jokingly, pouting for effect.

"The back door for the assistant to the first primary legal stallion. It's the door we all use," he said reassuringly.

Red hoisted his railgun. "I've been thrown through worse doors than that."

"I thought you won your fights?" Rivka taunted.

"Not when I'm that drunk. The damn nanos took that weakness away from me, so more door-tosses for me."

"Touché, my good man. Shall we exult in our drudge-like status?"

"After me," Red quipped and strode boldly to the door. As always, his head was on a swivel as he scanned the area for threats. The door opened as he approached. Lindy stepped into the doorway.

"I wondered where you'd gone. I'm exhausted from partying." She threw the back of her hand to her forehead and mock-swooned.

Red's face turned serious. "Angora," was all he said.

"I'll get Groenwyn. She's shrinking under the tidal wave of accolades. These people only speak in superlatives, and it's getting a bit tiresome."

"If everyone is the best, no one is the best," Rivka replied.

Lindy led the way inside, down a hallway, through a storeroom, and down another hallway.

"The riffraff gets the short end of the entry stick, don't they?" Rivka wondered. "Titles and status. I'm surprised there hasn't been a class war on this planet."

"It's not a winning recipe," Red agreed. "Then again, the heavy gravity is a great equalizer."

Feet pounded down the hallway behind them. Red shoved the Magistrate aside and covered her with his body. The first assistant appeared.

"Damn, man! You almost got yourself shot." Red slowly lowered his railgun.

"The potentate's most magnificent limousine cast much shade on the poor first assistant's vehicle."

"There's our missing Yemilorian," Rivka said with a smile. "Time to party."

Only a few more steps. Lindy opened a door and walked into a large reception hall with hundreds of Yemilorians inside.

We're here, Rivka said. *I can't quite see you.*

Save me! Groenwyn didn't sound like she needed saving. *I'm kidding. I'm in the middle of the mob, but I'm ready to go if you are.*

As it is said, so let it be done, Rivka noted.

She pointed with her chin toward the largest group of bald and gangly bodies. Red strode purposefully toward the dense cluster, trying not to look satisfied as Yemilorians dove out of his way. Rivka, Lindy, and the first assistant followed in his wake.

Red made to use his railgun to move the locals out of the way, but Rivka stopped him.

"I got it," she told him and moved in front, shouldering her way between the taller but thinner bodies. Passing from one to the next, she smiled and issued empty platitudes. "The gravity on your planet weighs heavily on my fragile body. My compliments on your strength and burliness."

When she reached the center mass, the platinum-green-haired woman launched herself forward to embrace Rivka. "I'm so happy you made it!"

"Me, too! We have a suspect and need to move quickly,"

Rivka started, looking for the special deputy. When she spotted him, she turned and delivered a formal apology. "Your banquets are clearly the best we've ever been to on Yemilore. We are honored most magnificently, but we have to leave right now if there is any chance for us to recover the Marble Orb. That is our primary focus. Included in the recovery will be the capture of those responsible so it does not happen again. We must depart. Can you please return us to our ship?"

The special deputy's face dropped. "There are three more banquets scheduled. If you believe this was the best, just wait!"

"We cannot," Rivka confirmed.

The special deputy undersecretary turned to Groenwyn. "We cannot stay," she confirmed. "Our job is to find and prosecute criminals. Rivka is the best in the universe at that. The sooner we find them, the fewer crimes they can commit. What if no one came to your banquets because it wasn't safe to travel because of crime? Think about that on a galactic scale. By taking us to our ship, you are most gloriously contributing to an even bigger party."

Red steeled his features. Yemilore was not his cup of tea.

"Of course, we understand." The special deputy twirled his three fingers and slapped them in the Yemilorian version of snapping his fingers. All the noise stopped, and the way cleared to the front door.

"To the bus!" Red shouted. "Save the galaxy."

Rivka and Groenwyn both nodded to the special deputy before getting herded between Red and Lindy toward the way out.

The special deputy's first entourage reformed to join their guests.

"I feel special, getting to use the front door," Rivka whispered to Groenwyn.

"I took one for the team by keeping them occupied. You owe me," the young woman whispered back.

"I like the new you." The group flowed more than walked as the Yemilorians jockeyed for superior hierarchical positions around Rivka and Groenwyn. Red used his railgun as a barrier to block those trying to get in front. Soon enough, they were all on board the bus. Last on was the first assistant. Rivka waved him to her. He beamed at being recognized.

"The Magistrate's summons casts light into the shadows," he declared. Rivka hesitated, to the point that she forgot what she was going to say. The special deputy had taken the seat in front of Rivka and Groenwyn. He turned and watched the exchange with interest.

"What about your car?" she asked weakly.

"Not *my* car. Internal Security car."

"I'm not sorry I don't have to ride in that thing again." Red nodded vigorously.

"That limo was a righteous ride. You should consider borrowing something like that for future VIPs like the Magistrate," he suggested.

"My humble position does not make such lofty requests."

The special deputy raised a hand as if requesting permission to speak. Rivka nodded at him. "Please accept my sincere apologies for the abject failings of the first

CRAIG MARTELLE & MICHAEL ANDERLE

assistant. You will not have to worry about such shortcomings in the future."

The first assistant paled and started to back away, but Rivka grabbed his arm.

"I have to say that the first assistant was critical to our investigation. So much so that we insist he join us for the remainder of this case. I expect we will have your full cooperation in this matter since it would reflect on the magnanimous selflessness and glory of all Yemilore."

The special deputy froze, torn between his personal desire to be the face of Yemilorian glory for the Federation and acceding to the request.

"I must insist," Groenwyn added. She had spent the day with the special deputy and knew what he was thinking—how to angle someone else onto Rivka's ship and into her inner circle. Groenwyn couldn't abide anyone being punished for doing his job. "There is no other option. First assistant, or Yemilore loses."

The change was instantaneous. "Of course!" he declared, smiling as broadly as he could. "All of Yemilore stands proud of your conquest of crime."

"Conquerors of crime!" Groenwyn repeated, pointing to Rivka, earning her the side-eye.

Rivka tried not to think of the departing platitudes. When they arrived at *Wyatt Earp*, Rivka's mind focused entirely on Angora. She'd been on Rivka's ship. She'd been in their midst, leading them astray while jockeying for information and a ride. As the noose closed, she had found a way off the ship, and Rivka had delivered her.

The stab in the eye was personal. *Innocent until proven*

guilty, Rivka reminded herself. *We have a lot to talk about, Angora.* "Take care of it, Groenwyn. I'll be on the ship."

Rivka was one of the first off the bus, grabbing the first assistant by the arm as she went, with Red racing to catch up. Lindy waited with Groenwyn.

The young woman delivered the superlatives better than anyone had ever delivered accolades and platitudes before in the history of all things.

Maybe not. At least she told the Yemilorians goodbye in words that best resonated with them. She detached herself quickly, waving as she jogged to *Wyatt Earp*'s inviting ramp. Lindy stopped at the ramp and faced the group, making one last visual sweep before joining the others. She mashed the big red button after she was through the airlock.

The engines immediately spun up, and the heavy frigate lifted off. Chaz restored the artificial gravity. The first assistant turned green, his eyes twirling in his head.

"Chaz, take us to Yoll, best possible speed!" Rivka ordered.

CHAPTER FOURTEEN

Wyatt Earp

"Welcome aboard, buddy. Getting sick here is better than the alternative," Red said, stepping away from the Yemilorian. "They were going to roast him."

Rivka nodded in agreement. "You were the only one on the whole ring planet with a clue. I couldn't let you get punished for that."

The dam broke and he doubled over, spewing the snack he'd grabbed during their short time at the third banquet.

"I'm not calling him first assistant," Red declared. "So, what do we name him?"

"He's not a pet," Groenwyn replied while the first assistant was on all fours, weaving with the ship's motion. Floyd ran down the corridor, stopping to briefly sniff the newcomer before heading for the choice bits on the deck. Groenwyn intercepted her, picking her up before she could get her face into it.

Red ignored them. "Maybe we can call him 'Spew.'"

Rivka wanted to argue but was biting her lip, trying not to laugh at the displaced Yemilorian.

Lindy came to the rescue. "Do you mind if we call you Stewart, Stew for short?"

"What is my position on your team?" the first assistant managed between gasps. He finally flopped against the wall, leaning his back against it and extending his gangly legs across the corridor. He lifted them to let a cleaning bot pass and watched it work, having to cover his mouth once to prevent a new round.

"Your position is 'saved from being demoted for doing your job,'" Red said with a shrug. "That might be a mouthful, but then again, it is very Yemilorian."

"It is not," the Yemilorian fired back.

"I would prefer something simpler." Rivka kneeled next to him. "Stew?"

"Saved?" he countered.

"Good enough. We'll pronounce it 'SAH-ved,' so we don't get confused with saving something. Usually ourselves, by the way. You may regret getting 'sahved.'"

"'Sahved,'" Red said, taking it for a trial run. He held his hand out and Lindy slapped her railgun into it.

"Conference room," Rivka said before pulling Sahved to his feet and walking away.

Lindy went with Red to store her gear. Groenwyn was left standing outside the airlock holding Floyd. "You need to meet our new crewmate."

Whee! Floyd cried. *I like new people.*

"And we need to listen to you when you don't like someone. Rivka is taking us to Yoll to question Angora.

The Magistrate thinks she might be bad. But you already knew that, didn't you?"

Floyd knows, the wombat replied before nuzzling her head into Jay's chest. *Cheetos?*

"No Cheetos for Floyd! Those aren't good for you. How about some nice salad greens?"

Okay, Floyd agreed. Groenwyn hurried to the galley to collect a handful before joining the others in the conference room. Floyd sniffed the Yemilorian again.

Rivka sat unmoving, her fingers steepled before her. She was already deep in thought, using the image of the Gorandian's environmental containment suit rotating above the table as the focus of her meditation.

Or the object of her angst.

No one liked to be made the fool.

Red and Lindy were already there, still wearing their ballistic armor, but without their weapons, or at least, the visible ones. They waited patiently. Red's eyes were closed as if he were sleeping. Sahved had a shell-shocked look on his face.

Groenwyn took an empty seat. Floyd crawled across the table to sniff the Yemilorian a third time, giving him her approval by dropping a poop cube in front of him. She returned to her best friend. Lindy pulled a napkin out and cleaned up the mess, lightly scolding Floyd. Groenwyn started hand-feeding the greens to the wombat. Floyd finished and began to fuss. Groenwyn put her back on the table. Lindy pulled her in to scratch her tiny ears and play with her. She smacked Red in the face with an errant paw strike, and everyone froze.

Red grumbled in his sleepy voice. "Take the kids for a

minute, would you?" Without opening his eyes, he licked his lips, and his breathing slowed as he went back to sleep.

"Is he dreaming about having kids?" Groenwyn asked. "Congratulations!"

"Hang on…" Lindy began. Rivka blinked and focused, stopping the conversation.

"Kids," she said. "Distractions. Small beings. The parents. Let me think this through."

The others waited patiently while Rivka mumbled her way through the problem.

"What if the being in the suit isn't a Gorandian? What if the real Angora isn't involved at all? What if whoever is in the suit is in charge of the smuggling ring? What if this was a huge infiltration and not a conspiracy?"

"That would make it too easy," Lindy suggested.

Rivka's eyes darted to Lindy as if she'd forgotten the others were in the room.

"Then who does she answer to?" Rivka asked.

"Once we root her out of the suit, you can ask her." Lindy was confident of Rivka's abilities.

"I think you're right. Once we have her in custody, we'll get answers."

"What if she's run?" Groenwyn asked.

"Too late, the running pool is already claimed," Rivka quipped before turning serious. "We go after her. *Wyatt Earp* is a beast. I doubt she'll be able to get away from us."

The telltale signs of Gating whispered across their consciousness.

"We've entered Yoll space," Chaz reported. "It'll be another hour before we're able to head planetside."

"Get us the status of the case between Gil'dinor and Loids, please."

The file appeared above the table. Rivka took to her pad to bring up the particulars in which she was most interested. "They are still in the discovery phase, but the case has been expedited."

"Everyone's in a hurry. People need to go to Azfelius and take the time to slow down." Groenwyn rested her hands on the table and started a series of slow-breathing exercises.

Floyd crawled over to her, climbed into the horseshoe made by her arms and hands, and curled up. Soon, the wombat was fast asleep.

"I wish I could do that," Red grumbled, stretching as he stirred back to life.

Lindy punched him in the arm. "It takes you two seconds to fall asleep, while I lay there for an hour."

Red looked trapped. He smiled slowly. "I meant that I wish you could do that."

"Nice try, big man," Rivka interrupted, then went back to reading the case file. Red and Lindy waited, watching attentively. They tried to read along but quickly became bored.

When the Magistrate was ready, she began. "The case is based on art valuation, the underlying theme that is not discussed, but the bigantuan in the room. The flow of such vast sums of credits. For a theft of these to be viable, there has to be someone willing to throw that kind of money around, but without the credits being visible. Who has that kind of discretionary cash?

"We saw the amounts Bindola Shnobhauer moved and

had available. He had an entire planet dedicated to laundering the funds. That isn't replicable," Lindy remarked. "We took them down, and Ankh and Erasmus put systems in place to prevent it from happening again."

"Taking down a nine-level laundering system..." Groenwyn said with her eyes closed.

"What is the next way the scumbags will find to move illegal money around?" Red asked.

Rivka shook her head and shrugged. "That'll take the likes of the Crenellian to figure out, if we ever get him back."

"He'll be back," Chaz said through the room's sound system. "They are gathering the materials now to upgrade *Wyatt Earp*. I am looking forward to super-stealth. I will be invincible!"

"Hang on there, big husky," Rivka said. "Let's try to limit the full-on battle cry. I'm still a Magistrate, doing that annoying legal stuff. Let's set a goal of not fighting."

"Buzz-kill."

"Chaz..." Rivka cautioned with a smile. "But it is better to have the power and not need it. I approve. Heaven have mercy on those who cross us because *Wyatt Earp* will not."

The files continued to scroll until they were interrupted by a direct message from the High Chancellor. Rivka wondered why Chaz showed it until she saw the single line.

Angora has disappeared.

"Looks like we got us a runner." Red clapped his hands and vigorously rubbed them together. "Shouldn't be hard to find her. How fast can she go in that ugly suit of hers?"

"What if she ditched the suit because she's not a Gorandian?" Rivka wondered.

"She isn't?"

"Just a question. What if she's not?"

"Doesn't matter. We'll find her," Red replied dismissively.

Rivka wanted to agree, but Yoll was a big place, and it was around long before the universe heard of Bethany Anne. "Chaz, can you get Ankh and Erasmus on it, please? And once again, I believe the old adage of 'follow the money' applies. If we can find the movement of funds, that will lead us to her."

"We have been looking, Magistrate. Diligently, but we have found nothing." The AI sounded frustrated.

Rivka nodded. "That suggests the art has not been sold."

"Why would you steal something you can't sell?" Red asked.

"Isn't that the million credit question." Rivka sighed and looked into her lap. "Saddle up, people. We've got an appointment with the Yoll justice system. And you." She pointed to Sahved. "Stay here and study up on procedures. Get to know the ship and the crew."

Yoll Capital City, Landing Area 4A

"You used to be somebody, Magistrate," Red said while craning his neck, looking for their ride. He wore his full ballistic protection but didn't carry his railgun. He had no visible weapons, which didn't mean he was unarmed.

"Don't forget where we are. The heart of the Federation. The seat of power. We're a bunch of people with a cool ship, a gift from the very Federation we're here to serve."

"You're saying I work for The Man?" Red said, still looking, to no avail.

"We all work for The Man, Red. Does a Magistrate have power or only the appearance of power?"

"I don't see the difference."

"And that is what matters. Neither does anyone else until we land on Yoll, and appearances do not equal the real thing."

A small craft flew toward them, circling once before settling onto the apron beside *Wyatt Earp.*

Your ride is here, Chaz told them.

"You know we wouldn't have boarded a strange vehicle. We're super-cautious," Lindy joked. Red fist-bumped her.

"Sometimes, we are our own worst enemy," Rivka agreed.

Once aboard, the vehicle raced skyward, making a beeline across the city for the High Chancellor's office. They landed on the roof of the government building and were escorted downstairs.

"Please go through. High Chancellor Wyatt is expecting you," his ever-diligent executive Zai'den announced. Rivka nodded to him as they passed. Groenwyn stopped and took his hands in hers. They locked eyes before smiling at each other. Lindy waited until Groenwyn was through before following her in and closing the door behind them.

"You're wondering why I brought you here?" The High Chancellor stood and circled his desk to greet Rivka. He was a massive human being, taller than Red. He smiled broadly, revealing his fangs while his eyes glowed slightly red.

"Are you upset about something, High Chancellor?" Rivka asked. She couldn't read him. As always, he was a blank to her, even with the close contact.

He took a deep breath, grinding his teeth briefly before smiling anew. This time, his eyes were clear and his fangs gone.

"Astute as usual, Rivka."

"I let Angora, if that's her name, get one over on me, even to the point of acting as her taxi service and bringing her here."

"We've all been fooled before. It happens," the High Chancellor told her, speaking softly. "You aren't infallible. No one is."

"The suit…"

"The Federation is replete with races that can't operate in our atmosphere, just as we can't survive in theirs. We can't be skeptical just because they need a suit. If someone uses that to get inside our defenses, as it may be, then we come down hard once we know."

"Are we coming down hard?"

"If she's guilty. It's difficult to think otherwise, but when, not if, we find her, you need to get inside her defenses and discern the truth. Then find those pieces of art."

"The money—" Rivka started. The High Chancellor held a finger to his lips

"We'll talk about that in the right time and place," he told her cryptically. "Next step is Loids' offices. I have a warrant to search for conspirators. That's all we are looking for. I suspect Angora acted alone. Confirm that and get back here. We have a warrant out for her, but if she ditched the suit, we could have problems. If she went to ground, we'll have problems. The only way we'll find her quickly is if she's running because she's panicked."

"Nothing about her tells me she would panic. She is in complete control. I suspect she had multiple exit strategies."

"I don't doubt that," the High Chancellor agreed. "Check out Loids and then come back. Take all the time you need. We have other resources allocated to finding her."

"My brothers and sister?" Rivka asked, a grin creeping across her face.

"Grainger, Chi, Jael, and Buster. I've recalled them to focus on finding her."

"Nice. Thank you, High Chancellor." Rivka twirled her finger in the air. "Bad guys aren't going to catch themselves."

"Is that her new favorite expression?" Red whispered to Lindy as he pushed the door open. Lindy shrugged.

"She's not wrong."

The group returned to the roof, where the shuttle waited. Unlike Binsulaker Prime, Yoll had dedicated official assets. Their shuttle wasn't as nice as the Potentate of Magnanimous Austerity's ride, but then again, austerity meant different things on different planets.

It lifted off without delay and headed into the aerial traffic corridors on its way across the city.

"What do you think, Chaz? Any ideas?" Rivka asked the device hanging around Groenwyn's neck.

I am still collecting data, Magistrate, the AI replied.

"On what?"

The financial systems. It makes for interesting reading. The disparate ways transactions take place throughout the Federation. I think the most powerful individual in the Federation is D'rell, the finance minister, because she has the responsibility to regulate it all.

"I'm not sure how that's helping us." The Magistrate looked out the window, taking in the immensity of the largest city on Yoll.

Deconstructing transactions to find the ones that aren't aboveboard takes a significant understanding of the core system. Ankh and Erasmus are far ahead of me. I'm playing catch-up.

"Do you have any ideas about how we'll know if someone is conspiring with Angora?"

Only by digging into their finances. I've begun this process, now that we have full access to their personnel files. I was hoping you'd be able to do your zombie thing to them.

"Have you been talking to Grainger?"

I might have, but what you're capable of doing exceeds my understanding. I like things that can be calculated, and processes that can be defined. I can't wrap my digital head around something based entirely on feelings.

"You have feelings, don't you, Chaz?"

I do, but probably not as you understand them. They make sense to me, and that matters in my evolution. Thank you for asking.

Rivka didn't ask any more questions. Chaz was busy, and she needed to think.

The trip took longer than Rivka wanted. She was rapidly tapping her foot and drumming her fingers when

Red placed his big hand over hers. "Do you think she's down there?" he asked.

"Angora?"

He nodded.

"I hope not. She'll be easier to find in the vastness of space than in that mess."

Rivka pointed at the urban sprawl, pressing her lips together until they turned white.

"We'll find her," Red reassured the Magistrate. "She doesn't have a chance."

"I wish that were true. She's got a head start and complete anonymity. She's a ghost."

"Because we don't know what she looks like?"

"We don't have the foggiest." Rivka smiled. "But we know something she doesn't." She waited for the others to see if they would guess. They didn't. "Technology. She got it from somewhere. With Ted and Ankh reverse-engineering the holoprojector, they'll find where it was produced."

Chaz rejoined the conversation. *The Magistrate is correct.*

"How does knowing where a device was produced relate to us finding Angora?" Groenwyn asked.

"We start building a profile. Find things that she touched, and with enough touches, we'll be able to search for those fingerprints," Rivka suggested. "That's the plan, anyway. It all depends on R2D2 finding that first touchpoint."

The shuttle started to spiral downward toward a massive structure.

"Looks like there's good money in insurance," Red remarked.

"They make their money from paying few claims and charging large premiums."

"But if you need to make a claim, insurance can save your ass."

"Sounds personal." Lindy studied her husband.

"I wrecked a speeder that was kind of pricey. Insurance saved me from a life of poverty."

"But you lived a life of rags to riches and back to rags." Lindy started to give Red the stink-eye.

"But it wasn't from the speeder. *That* life was from poor decisions, not an errant steering yoke and a gust of wind."

Rivka chuckled until the shuttle settled onto the landing pad in front of the Loids complex. As the door opened, she removed her datapad and strode from the ship. Red hurried after her, taking a position at her left elbow. Lindy moved to the right, and Groenwyn strolled behind. If she was too close to the threesome, Chaz wouldn't be able to see anything.

They continued through the front doors to the main receptionist, a four-legged Yollin. "May I help you?" she asked pleasantly.

"I'm Magistrate Rivka Anoa, and I'm here to speak with the CEO. I don't have an appointment, and I will see him right now."

CHAPTER FIFTEEN

Loids of Yoll offices

"He's not here," she replied, smiling as if she answered such demands all the time. Maybe she did.

Rivka clenched her jaw. "Who's in charge when he's not here? I will see that person."

"That would be Ersatz Preanster. She's on the fourth floor." The Yollin receptionist pointed to the elevators. Her mandibles clicked lightly.

"Thank you." Rivka was in no mood to joust. The Loids complex consisted of a single thirty-seven story building. The one in charge was on the fourth floor? That made no sense to the Magistrate.

"Watch yourselves. I think we might be getting played." Rivka waved a hand in front of the elevator panel, and the doors whooshed aside. The team climbed aboard, punched four, and headed upward.

They were greeted by a moving company with pallets of cases.

CRAIG MARTELLE & MICHAEL ANDERLE

"What's going on?" Rivka asked one of the stalwart laborers.

"Going out of business or something. All this stuff is going into a storage unit or something. I don't know. I'm only here to carry it or something."

"Or something," Rivka parroted. "Where's the one in charge. Ersatz Preanster?"

"There's somebody giving orders over there." He nodded toward an area that was still being packed up. He fitted the last two boxes into place, checked to see if the load was tight, and started dragging the pallet jack toward the far end of the floor.

Rivka turned to her team, "Ideas?"

"Standing down the art insurance business to keep from losing their ass, especially if it was one of their people taking the items." Red's insight sounded convincing.

Rivka nodded once and started walking, her datapad clutched in her hand, ready to show the search warrant to the powers that be.

"Are we going to have to look through physical files?" Groenwyn sounded worried and looked like she had sucked on a lemon.

"No. I'm here to *talk to* employees, if you know what I mean." Rivka winked at the platinum-green-haired young woman.

"I'm all about lining up the pins so you can knock 'em down," Red noted.

Rivka looked for the one who appeared to be in charge. "Ersatz?"

The Corinthian female looked up from under thick and

long eyelashes. Her waxy black hair reflected the overhead lighting as if it were made of metal.

"I am. You have me at a disadvantage."

"I'm Magistrate Rivka Anoa. I have a warrant to view all files and systems related to an employee named Angora. Also in the warrant is the requirement to interview anyone associated with the aforenamed Angora. I'll need a space to conduct the interviews and the people brought to me there." Rivka held the datapad in front of her.

Ersatz didn't even look at it. "You can't—"

"I most assuredly can," Rivka countered before she finished.

"You can't because they're not here. We let them all go. After the third theft, we shut down that division. Loids is out of the art insurance business."

"But that division is engaged in a lawsuit." Rivka's eyes darted around the room. There were no employees, only workers packing and moving what had been the art insurance division.

"I think that was settled," Ersatz replied off-handedly. "I'm here, and I am more than happy to talk to you."

"Were you the department head?"

"Not at all. I was transferred here to oversee the dissolution."

Rivka stared open-mouthed. She took the Corinthian's arm. "What do you know about Angora?"

Gorandian. She'd seen a picture of one once.

"Nothing," Ersatz replied honestly.

"Where are the computer server systems that support Loids?"

A basement, the next building over.

"I'm not sure," the female lied.

"Never lie to a Magistrate, Ersatz Preanster. I hold you in contempt. That'll be a ten-thousand-credit fine. Chaz, register that with the Federation." The Corinthian stared, her facial expression frozen. "Have a nice day."

Rivka turned on her heel and walked straight to the elevator.

Did you register that fine, Chaz?

Not yet. Do you still want me to send it?

Yes, I do. Dissembling and prevaricating while Loids is trying to cover its tracks is bad form. Leadership starts at the top, right? Send a second form, a C and D, to Loids to stop all activity in relation to the removal of records related to the art insurance division.

One cease and desist letter coming right up, Chaz replied.

The elevator delivered them to the ground floor. They walked past Reception without checking out, went through the front doors, and took a sharp right. The shuttle remained on the parking pad.

"Looked like it was in here, in the basement." Rivka pointed to a small building that looked like a power transfer sub-station.

There were two doors. One didn't have a handle or any way to pull it open.

An emergency exit. The other door was locked. "Red?"

"Don't mind if I do." He pulled his blaster from inside his ballistic vest. It took four shots before he could rip the door open. Yollin security guards ran in their direction, waving stun batons at them.

"You want to set them straight?" Rivka asked Red while holding the door for Lindy and Groenwyn to go through.

"I think I'll enjoy this." He put his blaster inside his vest and cracked his knuckles.

"Don't make me come and save your big ass. Oh, yeah, give me one of Ankh's discs before you get too busy."

Red pulled one out and handed it over before walking forward with his arms spread wide. The last thing the Magistrate heard was Red saying, "My good friends!"

Inside the building, Rivka found a landing and wide steps leading down. Lindy was on the top step. "Did you say it was in the basement?"

Rivka nodded.

Lindy headed down. Groenwyn hesitated. Lindy stopped after five steps when she realized no one was following. "Two points," Groenwyn started. "Why do they always put these things in the basement? We've not had great luck in basements. I wanted to register my dismay before we went too far."

Chaz explained, *Easier to keep cool and provide power. Even the most modern biological and plasma systems require a great deal of heat-generating energy. You have to get the disc close to the system so Erasmus can get in.*

"Crap luck in the basements." Rivka removed Reaper from her inner pocket. "Just in case."

Lindy smiled and nodded, pulling her blaster before continuing down.

The steps continued straight to a double doorway as wide as the staircase. It opened automatically as they approached. Lindy jumped to the side, bringing her blaster to eye level as she aimed into the space beyond. Rivka pushed Groenwyn down and crouched over her, aiming as Lindy was.

"What did you see?" Rivka called.

"Nothing. The door opened," Lindy replied. "I thought someone was coming out."

Rivka pointed at the flashing sensor above the door.

"Don't I feel stupid," Lindy deadpanned, sidestepping in front of the doors while continuing to look over the blaster's sights into the space beyond. "Clear." She lowered her weapon but kept both hands on it.

Rivka pulled Groenwyn to her feet. "Sorry about that."

"Better that than getting shot. I'm not a fan."

Rivka slapped the younger woman on the back. "I don't think any of us are."

"Clear," Lindy reiterated from within the server farm.

"Let's deliver this thing and get the hell out of here. Red may need some help topside."

Red? Lindy ventured.

Yes, my dear, he replied casually.

How much time do we have?

As much as you need.

"No rush," Lindy reported.

"Does this work?" Rivka asked the device Groenwyn carried.

No.

"How about now?" the Magistrate asked after she repositioned it.

No.

Fourteen placements later, Chaz finally declared victory.

This is the good stuff! We had all the data before. Raw data. We now have their thoughts and perceptions, the art division's profit forecast, and the strategic analysis. They had four other masterpieces for coverage that weren't shown in the other files they shared.

"Contact the owners and tell them to check for a holo-projector. If there isn't one, they should physically secure their pieces until further notice. Lock everything down, assuming it hasn't already been stolen."

"Time to go?" Groenwyn asked.

Erasmus and I have what we need, the AI reported.

Rivka walked briskly from the room, with the other two women close behind. Outside, they found Red with four stun batons and the four Yollin guards unconscious on the ground. He smiled broadly, but his lips were swollen, and there was a gash on the side of his head.

"Give them back their batons," Rivka ordered as she twirled a finger in the air and walked over the manicured lawn on a direct line to their shuttle.

Red dropped the batons with a flourish, brushed off his hands, and fell in behind the others.

"Look at your face," Lindy said over her shoulder. "You look too happy for how bad you got your ass kicked."

"Four Yollins!" Red exclaimed proudly.

"Sure, sure." Lindy flipped her hand dismissively.

"Chaz, I need anything that could give us a hint at where Angora might be."

The most recently insured piece is back on Binsulaker Prime.

"She wouldn't?" Rivka stated before starting to run.

"We're running," Red observed as he loped along with the others. "It's so unlike the Magistrate."

"Come on, people." Rivka accelerated until she was sprinting. She slid to a stop to wait for the shuttle hatch to open. "Get us back to *Wyatt Earp*, best possible speed."

The automated shuttle took off and eased into an aerial traffic corridor.

"Come on!" Rivka pounded on the side of the passenger cabin.

I think I can help, Chaz said. The shuttle jerked, then started to drop. Emergency systems arrested the fall before being overridden. The shuttle fell another hundred meters before lateral acceleration moved it sideways at an alarming rate of speed. The shuttle rotated and darted forward, turning on its tail to race past the traffic lanes and arc over the mass of airborne vehicles.

There we go, Chaz announced to the group.

Red and Lindy looked at each other before holding hands. Rivka met Groenwyn's gaze. "Back to Binsulaker?" the young woman asked.

"Back to Binsulaker. I wonder if Kio'alaia was able to rustle up our missing security guards?"

"I wouldn't bet on it." Red shook his head. "But if you want to bet, I'll take the side that says he won't have them."

CHAPTER SIXTEEN

Wyatt Earp

"Take us out," Rivka said. Clodagh repeated the order, and Ryleigh tapped the controls to send _Wyatt Earp_ airborne. The heavy frigate turned on its tail and accelerated toward space at a fantastic rate.

"Woohoo!" Ryleigh whistled.

Rivka leaned against the bridge's rear bulkhead, crossing her arms and watching the screen turn dark and fill with stars as they transitioned through the atmosphere. The ship continued to accelerate away from the planet, navigating casually through the inbound traffic lanes.

"The High Chancellor's office has granted us an emergency priority," Ryleigh told them. "Spinning up the Gate drive."

"Next stop, Slaker Central," Rivka murmured.

"When we arrive, Chaz, hook us up with a landing site close to the...the...what is it called?"

"It's the Firenze Dolce, a Glacier by Any Other Name."

"The Firenze. Get us close. Has R2D2 given us any way to detect those using their cloaking technology?"

"Yes. Kind of." Chaz didn't sound confident. "Maybe."

"We tie both hands behind our backs as we join the fight," the Magistrate intoned.

"I'm sorry, Magistrate. A possibility is that we irradiate an area with beta particles and look for disturbances."

"Aren't those harmful?"

"I didn't say there wouldn't be a risk."

"Give me the intercom." Rivka waited for the artificially generated snap and pop to tell her it was live. "Alant Cole, get your mech suit on. I have something I'm going to need you to do."

Binsulaker Prime, the Estates

Despite protests from Binsulaker Prime officials, Ryleigh brought *Wyatt Earp* down in a field near the Estates. The Magistrate didn't let it bother her that it wasn't an official landing field. The failure of the Slakers to assist in the investigation and then abandoning them in the middle of their secret war zone didn't endear the planetary authorities to Rivka or her crew.

"You're coming with us, Sahved. We're going art-thief-hunting."

"I thought that was what we've *been* doing," the Yemilorian replied.

"Yes, but this is the action part of the hunting. Much of it is thinking and investigating. We might be one step ahead."

Security Operator First Order Kio'alaia is on his way, Chaz reported.

"Should we wait? You know we're not going to get a ride." Red shrugged with his statement. Rivka glanced down to see that he had his comfortable boots on, not the newer pair that was higher quality. He only owned two pairs. Lindy had four pairs of boots for a variety of body-guard occasions. She also had dress clothes, something they were still trying to convince Red were important to have.

"There he is," Rivka said, pointing before they had to decide.

He rushed his pace, emotions hidden behind the expressionless face. "It is very late. Maybe tomorrow is a better time?"

Rivka looked at the sun-filled sky.

"It's the eternal equinox. It happened today."

"Something eternal happens on a single day?" Rivka wondered.

"Same day every year, eternally. Yes." He looked from face to face. "I know you, but I don't know *you.*"

Sahved returned the Slaker's piercing stare. "I am the first assistant... Sorry. I'm Sahved." They each looked at the other's hand.

"We don't shake in my culture, but if you'd like, I am aware of this most very respectful gesture."

Rivka gave him a look that suggested he work on his Yemilorian linguistic foibles.

"Not in mine either, but the humans insist on it. Glad to have a fellow non-shaker here in Slaker land."

The security operator remained where he was, committing to nothing. A loud thump sounded from behind the ship. The mechanized combat suit driven by Alant Cole appeared, clumping louder than necessary. Rivka gestured for the mech to take it easy. Alant lightened his step and continued almost noiselessly.

"I'm ready to go see the Firenze Dolce, if you don't mind," Rivka said.

"But it's late at night." Kio'alaia stood his ground.

"Let's go, Red," Rivka twirled her finger in the air. She turned back to the Slaker. "Did you catch the two security guards?"

She already knew the answer.

"They have disappeared completely. We exhausted all resources in our search."

Red strode boldly away.

Rivka stepped alongside the security operator. "I'm not going to ask for your definition of exhausting all resources. I'll simply accept that you didn't find them. It could be a moot point anyway. Our primary suspect is Angora, the supposed Gorandian. Do you have any other leads?"

"No. The Gorandian?" He took a few more steps before continuing, "Any word about the Anastolia? When will it be returned?"

The Magistrate clenched her jaw. She wondered if they were having two different conversations. "Did you know that Gil'dinor filed suit against Loids?"

"I did not know. The affairs of those in the Estates are not my affairs, even though they pay my salary. That was not something they deemed important for me to know."

She wanted to feel sorry for him but couldn't muster

the sympathy. He had gotten them blown up. He wasn't out of the doghouse yet.

The Yemilorian passed the others to join Red on point, easily matching the bodyguard's stride with his long, thin legs.

"This is the most incomparable of adventures. It has been forever since I've been on another planet, and that time, it was very controlled. Nothing like this. We are walking in here like we own this place," Sahved said, looking in wonder at the immensity of the Estate wall and the gate toward which they marched.

"I'm the lead, which means I have to look for threats to the Magistrate. It's hard doing that when I'm distracted."

"I will personally make sure that you are not distracted. The Magistrate is a wondrous creature, as is the First Primary to the Magistrate's Corps of Legal Stallions for the High Chancellor of the Federation."

"You mean Groenwyn?" Red mumbled, never taking his eyes off their way ahead, constantly scanning the wall's heights. The lack of vehicles made his job easier.

"Groenwyn! Yes, I must get used to using names again. It is so exhilarating."

"I think she wants to talk to you now," Red said, gesturing with his head to go to her."

The Yemilorian stepped to the side to let Rivka and the Slaker pass before closing on the green-haired woman. "That very large man up front said you wanted to talk to me?"

"Of course, he did." Groenwyn chuckled. "His name is Red, short for Vered."

"Names. I shall learn them in due time. Titles are so much easier."

Groenwyn did a double-take. "If you say so. Call me 'Groenwyn.' How are you settling in?"

"I am not sure that I have sat down since joining the most august and judicially righteous Magistrate's team."

"You did when you were less than completely acclimated to our gravity."

"That!" He tossed his head and intertwined his three fingers in a complex pattern in front of his chest. "Not my finest moment, but I am getting used to it now. Thank you for helping me."

"Helping people is what we do."

"I am worried about the Marble Orb," Sahved admitted.

Red reached the gate and tried to open it, but it was locked. He leveled his railgun, but stopped when the Slaker waved a key. He opened the large gate and strolled through, waving for the others to follow.

"The purveyors of the Firenze Dolce are right over there." Kio'alaia pointed to a modest building, smaller than its neighbors.

"Doesn't look like a place where you'd find a hundred-million-credit piece of artwork," Rivka said.

"The purveyors are humble, living in austerity for the sole purpose of supporting and displaying such a fine piece as the Glacier by Any Other Name."

"I saw the pictures," Rivka replied. "I expect they don't do it justice. It'll be nice to see it in person."

Red had to pound on the door repeatedly before someone answered. The security officer grimaced, wincing with each thunderous echo. The Slaker who opened the door looked ancient.

Kio'alaia moved to the front. "Please pardon this late-night intrusion, Purveyor," he said in a conciliatory tone. "The Magistrate is from the Federation, and she is greatly concerned that there will be an imminent attempt to steal the Firenze."

The purveyor threw the door open. "Please come in. We cannot have the Firenze stolen. It is the culmination of my life's work to be in the presence of the masterpiece."

Rivka stepped forward without offering her hand. "Please take us to the Firenze so that we can make sure it is secure and stays that way." Behind her smile, she was seething. She didn't get the impression that the purveyor had been informed of her concerns. Time, once wasted, could not be recovered.

She hoped it wasn't too late. The looks on the faces of her team suggested they were more than aware of Binsulaker Prime's security shortcomings.

"My team. Vered and Lindy, my bodyguards. Groenwyn, my advisor. An additional investigator from Yemilore. And Alant Cole, providing both physical and technical support. There are surveillance and recovery techniques that can only be implemented by someone within that equipment."

The purveyor looked skeptically at the mech. "I don't think he'll fit inside."

"Wait out here. Verify the perimeter and conduct a low-level radioactive scan once we're inside."

"Yes, ma'am." Alant's voice was moderated through the

suit's external speakers. He moved away while the door was closing behind the group.

"This way," the purveyor said in a friendly tone as if he'd not been woken from a sound sleep moments earlier. "I'm surprised my security guards didn't answer the door."

Red and Rivka glanced at each other.

"Where would they be?" Rivka asked innocently, silently willing the Slaker to walk faster. At least the home was small, so they didn't have far to go.

"At least one should be in the display room, with the other roving, but not too far." The Slaker picked up his pace, worrying over the implications.

When they reached a set of double doors, the purveyor tested them, to find them locked. He put his hand to a pad beside the door and the lock retracted. Rivka yanked the door open before it could relock.

The two security guards were next to a stand on which a magnificently lit flowing metallic sculpture rested.

The purveyor breathed a sigh of relief, but Security Operator First Order Kio'alaia was instantly energized. He pushed past Rivka. "You!" he shouted.

"Red," Rivka said softly, stepping aside to let the big man past. With the Slaker and bodyguard bearing down on them, they ran. "Go."

Lindy raced past, with Sahved joining her, having no idea what they were doing, his legs akimbo like a running camel.

"What…" the purveyor stammered.

"They are suspects in the theft of the Anastolia. Did the security operator vet those two?"

"You were here just a few days ago. I was quite alarmed

and hired them directly. They came with the highest recommendation."

"From whom?" Rivka asked while examining the pedestal and the statue.

"From the insurance agent, of course. I haven't signed the paperwork yet, but she did a security survey of my home just last week," the Slaker explained. "Don't touch that!"

Rivka continued to reach toward the statue, then through it, and switched the holoprojector off.

The statue has been stolen. Perps might still be in the area. Take care with the beta scan, Alant, but pick up the pace. They are cloaked and could be running. Rivka turned and strode briskly from the room, heading for the front door.

Holy shit! I see them. Images faint. Chasing now.

Rivka thought she could feel the reverb of the mech accelerating away from the house.

Clodagh, spin up Wyatt Earp *and provide support to Alant. Our thieves have the statue and are running.*

Roger, Clodagh replied.

Did you catch those assholes yet? Rivka asked Red.

One of them. For little guys, they are a lot more resilient than I expected. Grab him! Red projected over the internal comm instead of switching to his outside voice.

Groenwyn took the purveyor by the arm as he stared in shock at where his precious statue used to be. "Is it gone?" he asked.

"Yes, but we're on their trail. We need to capture them alive so we can find the other pieces."

He resisted, pulling back so he could lament the loss of the Firenze Dolce. Groenwyn let him go and hurried after the Magistrate. If they could catch the perps, that might lead them to the other stolen art. Then everyone could be happy again, except those who would find Jhiordaan as their new home. Groenwyn wanted to see them caught and punished. Taking art from people's lives was something she found so distasteful that it was time for her to act.

She started to run, brushing past Rivka as she disappeared at her nano-enhanced speed. She headed out the front door and past the racing mech. She could see where he was aiming his beta radiation activator. He cut it off the instant he saw something pass through the beam before him, but by the time he released the trigger, she was already gone.

The beam highlighted a ship smaller than *Wyatt Earp* parked meters from where the Magistrate's heavy frigate had landed. Groenwyn slammed into the external hatch, her speed no benefit when she didn't catch the invisible thieves outside. She pounded on the invisible hull until the engines fired. She could feel the vibration. She stepped back as the ship lifted off on its way to the stars.

Fire? Alant asked as he dropped the beta device and shouldered his mech-sized railgun. Missiles appeared in a pack over his shoulder, ready to launch when given the order.

No, Rivka replied. *Everyone back to the ship. Everything we want is flying away, and blowing it out of the sky will give us no answers. Clodagh, figure out a way to track that ship.*

On our way, Red reported.

Rivka continued walking by herself. Red and Lindy appeared from behind the home, each carrying a figure over their shoulders. The former security guards looked to be unconscious. Sahved loped alongside, looking like a dog with his adopted family, while the smaller and stoic Slaker had to jog to keep up.

Kio'alaia started grousing about the gates before he reached them. Rivka walked through the destroyed entry with a minor snicker. Alant Cole had probably not even slowed down when he hit them, the mechanized armor he drove ripping the gates from their mounts.

When Red and Lindy caught up to her, they hurried the rest of the way to the ship. The bodyguards took the Slaker security guards on board. "Secure them in the cargo bay. We'll talk while we trail that ship." She pointed at Kio'alaia. "You stay here."

Rivka followed Groenwyn and Sahved. She did the honors of mashing the big red button, wondering how distraught the security operator was as he stood there on the outside looking in. The ship started to move while the outer hatch was still closing.

CHAPTER SEVENTEEN

Leaving Binsulaker Prime, Onboard *Wyatt Earp*

"Hang on," Clodagh told them. Artificial gravity and other systems that made high-speed spaceflight possible for biological creatures prevented most jarring motions, but sometimes, when things got exciting, the crew could get tossed around.

"That's what I'm talking about!" Red cheered from around the corner.

"With me," Rivka told Groenwyn and Sahved. They didn't question the order, simply fell in behind her on their way to the cargo bay.

They caught sight of Red and Lindy walking ahead of them. With minor bumps and twists from *Wyatt Earp* as they searched the sky for the art thieves' ship, the trio made it to the cargo bay.

Groenwyn took two folding chairs from the bulkhead and set them up in front of Red and Lindy. The two deposited their loads in the chairs. Both had their eyes open.

Rivka looked confused. "Stun guns," Red said, pulling the butt end of one from inside his vest.

"How much stuff do you carry in there?" Rivka asked, trying to see how anything fit under the semi-form fitting ballistic protective outerwear.

"Mission-specific loadouts. No blasters this time. I figured we'd need to paddle some bottoms, not get to kill people."

"Did you just say…" Rivka wondered what the galaxy was coming to when Vered cleaned up his language. Had they been anywhere else doing anything else, she would have laughed, but the chase was on. She needed information.

"Can you talk? Or maybe I should ask, *will* you talk?" Typical of the Slakers with their rough features, they gave nothing away.

Red grabbed one of the captives and squeezed his face until he opened his mouth. Rivka tapped him on the arm and shook her head.

Not torturing the captives, she told him. While touching him, she felt his emotions. He was frustrated by not being able to help with this case. The criminals had been one step ahead the whole way.

She gave him a questioning look, and he recoiled. "What'd you see?" he asked.

"One step ahead of us," Rivka said softly. She tipped one of the Slakers' chins up toward her. "We're not going to torture you, but you are guaranteed a long stay on Jhiordaan if you don't talk to me. I expect you're afraid of your handlers. Helping me find them is your only guarantee of safety."

The security guard's features were frozen. It reminded her of the look on Kio'alaia's face when he didn't want to talk about something. Groenwyn set a chair behind the Magistrate so she could sit face to face with the Slaker.

"Let's start with your name." Rivka waited for him.

Nothing.

"I have it, Magistrate, both of them," Chaz reported over the speakers. "The individual you are talking to now is called Act'obali, and the other is called Rem'amila. According to Gil'dinor's records, these are the two who worked for him during the theft."

"Your days of bilking the system are over," Rivka told them. "I need you to talk to me."

They resisted by remaining silent.

How are we doing? Rivka asked Clodagh and Chaz.

In order to use the beam to paint the running ship, we have to go as slow as they are. It's probably fast for them, but if we try to speed up, they could juke, and we'll have to stop and look for them again. We're gaining, but it's taking time.

Don't let them Gate out of here. Rivka glared at the security guards. She respected their ability to remain silent. As long as *Wyatt Earp* had the other ship in its sights, they didn't need these two. But just in case, she wanted to confirm a hypothesis she'd been mulling over.

"It was never your intent to steal the Firenze Dolce was it? Worth a mere hundred mil. Almost a complete waste of time. I'm going to tell you what happened. You don't need to say anything. Scumbags like you are as transparent as a porthole.

"You set things up to allow the cloaked thieves to enter. They set up the holoprojector and hid the Anastolia since it was a two-phase plan. The invisible ship wasn't available, so you had to use a backup, which meant your timing was dependent on something else. A landing schedule, probably. And then a couple days later, they came back to remove the Anastolia, cloaking it as they returned to the airfield. The ship departed, and that was the one we blew to hell. That put a crimp in Angora's retirement package, so she turned you onto the Firenze to cover some of the losses. She promised to move you two off-planet, didn't she?"

"No," the one called Rem'amila replied. "We were promised we would be killed if we didn't do as we were told. They tried to finish you when you came to the city after us, but we had already moved."

"Who is *they*?" Rivka asked, turning her chair but not getting too close. She leaned back and tried to look relaxed.

Rem'amila didn't reply.

"Do they have your family or something? I can have Red rough you up for when we deposit you back on Binsulaker Prime, so it looks like you resisted, as opposed to the cooperation you're actually providing."

"We are not!" Act'obali blurted. "We didn't... They'll kill me."

"Have you ever heard the expression 'perception becomes reality?'" They sat motionlessly. "The truth doesn't matter. It's what people believe that drives their actions. If they, whoever *they* are, believe you spilled your guts, they'll never stop coming after you. The fact that you are on my ship and we will return you to your homes unharmed will be your death sentence, independent of the truth about how stalwart you've been in refusing to answer my questions."

"The Gorandian and an alien," Rem'amila provided.

"Describe the alien," Rivka said. The ship jerked and bounced, twisted and skipped. Rivka balanced, flexing at the knees to keep from falling. Red saved one Slaker from tipping over, and Groenwyn steadied the other.

Sahved started making heaving noises, then staggered to the side and started spewing most ingloriously.

"We gotta do something about that," Red muttered.

"Pod-doc."

"We gonna keep him?" Red asked.

"I guess it's okay since we lost both Wenceslaus and Hamlet." Rivka let her sarcasm hang in the air, waiting to see if Red noticed. He didn't. "He's not a pet. We'll work with both Sahved and his government to make sure we get what's in everyone's best interests."

The Yemilorian went through his ritual before the cleaning bot appeared to take care of the mess. Groenwyn sat next to him.

Lindy moved close to the second suspect. "Describe the alien, please," the Magistrate requested.

"Big, with clackers."

"A Yollin," Red said.

"How'd you get a Yollin from that?" Rivka removed her datapad and found an image of a Yollin. She showed the Slaker.

"That's him," he replied.

"A Yollin," Rivka mused. Red struggled with not looking smug. He gave up and let the ego radiate from him. The Magistrate refused to look at him.

We're closing on the ship, Magistrate. We've had the system Gate shut down, and that seemed to throw him for a loop. He hesitated and we pounced, firing the EMP weapon. He's dead in space.

"Secure these two and get ready to board the hostile."

Red and Lindy removed the two suspects, led them down the corridor, and put them into the small, Skaine-style brig. It was little more than a closet, but at least they could sit down while they awaited judgment.

Lindy double-checked the door and rushed with Red down the corridor. "Stun guns?" she asked.

"I'm thinking that will work. We've not had good luck firing railguns in space," Red replied.

"I doubt anyone has."

Red rolled his head to loosen his neck and then worked his shoulders.

Rivka looked at them. "Helmets," she ordered. Lindy ran for the equipment locker. "And grenades!"

"I like how you think, Magistrate." Red always preferred going into a hostile area carrying grenades. Rivka rarely allowed it. She didn't know why, but she had a feeling. "What if they have that Firenze thing in the open?"

"My only concern about throwing a grenade is, I don't know how hearty the statue is. It might not survive."

"Just like the Anastolia?" Red asked.

"I wondered if I was the only one who caught that." Rivka kicked at the deck plating. "Looks like we vaporized a two-billion-credit statue."

"I can't even contemplate something being worth that much. And for the record, they self-destructed," Red suggested.

Rivka shrugged. It didn't register for her either. Lindy pounded down the corridor, wearing her helmet and carrying Red's. When she handed it to him, she took two grenades out of the inside and clipped them to her vest. Red clipped his on before putting the helmet on his head.

Sahved walked on none-too-steady feet toward them.

"Not this time," Rivka said before looking at the ceiling. "Chaz, hook us up."

The umbilical extended to connect the two ships' airlocks. Red, Lindy, and Rivka squeezed into their airlock. After it cycled, they popped the outer hatch and dove through into the weightlessness of the clear tube between the ships. Rivka pushed the bodyguards in front of her. They extended their arms to keep from slamming head-first into the runners' ship.

Rivka spun until she was floating feet-first. Red hit and activated the ship's airlock. It was tiny inside. "Sorry, honey," he said and climbed inside. He squeezed the hatch shut. The external pinpoint light turned red. Lindy punched the button. When it turned green again, she pushed through the hatch. Red was nowhere to be seen.

Red? she asked as she cycled the airlock.

Bastard! Red yelled over his comm link. Lindy and Rivka knew it wasn't directed at them. The outer pin light changed to red as the airlock equalized with the air inside the ship.

Rivka kept hitting the button until it turned green and the outer hatch opened. She climbed inside, shouldered the outer hatch shut, and pressed the panel so she could get into the runner's ship.

A grenade exploded, vibrating the airlock, then a

second one. Rivka fumbled inside her jacket for Reaper. She pulled it out and dialed to seven. When the inner airlock opened, she dove through and rolled to the other side of the corridor. Smoke billowed down it from the left. Lindy was on the deck, peeking around a corner. Behind Rivka was a solid bulkhead. She jumped to her feet and ran the few steps until she was behind Lindy.

"Report," she said more calmly than she felt.

"Red is engaged in hand to hand with something invisible. The second invisible suit is on the left side. It fires on occasion, but is trying not to hit its invisible comrade," Lindy said over her shoulder as she ducked her head around the corner at random intervals.

Rivka straddled her, leaning close to the corner. She darted her head out and pulled it back instantly, not giving the enemy a chance to lock in on her.

The Magistrate tapped Lindy on the back. "Be ready to go," she whispered before switching to the internal comm. *Red, when I say go, drag him to your right. I've got Reaper and will take care of the shooter. Hang on to your imaginary friend.*

Rivka leaned her back against the corner wall. On three. One. Two. She pushed away from the wall and jumped. Three. Rivka hit the opposite wall with both feet and pushed off, throwing herself down the corridor toward Red and the invisible enemies. He staggered to her right, but not far enough.

She aimed left, more than she wanted to, and fired. The neutron pulse weapon didn't scar the bulkhead or leave a chemical discharge cloud. If it hadn't buzzed, she would not have known it fired. The sound of a heavy suit hitting the deck told her the shot had done what she wanted. She took the two final steps and held the weapon over Red's shoulder.

"Stop or die," she instructed. Red's muscles continued to flex as he held onto the invisible armored suit. "Look at it! This is a neutron pulse weapon. You are a millisecond from death."

Red lunged forward, pulled as if all resistance had stopped. He toppled onto his enemy, not letting go. The cloak evaporated. Red found himself lying on a humanoid-shaped combat suit covered with a fine mesh of hexagon-shaped links. Red pulled the suit upright, moved behind it, and reached around to start twisting the helmet.

It popped, and Red yanked it off. Rivka crossed her arms. "A Skaine," she spat. "I should have smelled that it was one of you."

The creature didn't answer. Something whipped over-head, and both Rivka and Red reflectively ducked. Another Skaine fell from a doorway, a combat knife embedded in its throat. His blaster clattered to the deck as he hit. Lindy rushed past, stumbling over the invisible body in the corridor before picking up the blaster. While looking into the cockpit, she yanked the knife from the dead body and eased through the hatch.

"Clear." Red twisted the Skaine's arms behind his back. Even with the suit on, he was suffering and out-torqued.

Groenwyn, get Chaz, and get over here. We need to know where this ship was going.

"You wouldn't want to tell me where you were going, would you?" Rivka grabbed the side of his face. She was subjected to a torrent of foul thoughts about what he would do to her in a Skaine pleasure pit.

"We know about you," he said.

Rivka shivered at the revelation and the assault on her senses. The Skaine laughed, shrill and evil. She steeled herself before head-butting the bridge of the Skaine's nose and viciously grabbing and twisting his ears. "Where were you going?" she demanded. The pain forced through his mental discipline.

Coordinates. Through the Gate, then pick up another ship. Disappear.

"Where's the art?"

At the coordinates. This was the last job. Retired to a pleasure planet for eternity.

"Coordinates? The numbers. Remember the numbers," she encouraged the Skaine as she continued to twist his ears and squeeze his head. Red forced the Skaine's arm toward the back of his head to convince the small creature to cooperate.

Ten digits appeared in his head. Rivka shouted them out loud as she heard them and repeated them before she opened her eyes. The Skaine looked furious, the anger lessening his pain. She finally let go of his ears.

"What did we learn here today, boys and girls? You thought you knew about me, you Skaine bastard, but you are as weak as you think you are." Rivka stood back. "Capital theft, four counts, I find you guilty. Breaking and entering, four counts at least, I find you guilty. For the transport of stolen property, guilty. For attacking a Federation Magistrate in the discharge of her duties, guilty. If I wanted to find more, I could, but no need. Your sentence is life on Jhiordaan with no hope of parole. May God have mercy on your soul." Rivka leaned close but avoided touching the creature. "You have been judged."

Groenwyn watched meekly.

The Magistrate pointed to a spot on the deck. "There's a suited Skaine dead right there. Can you kill the invisibility cloak?" Rivka asked.

Groenwyn pointed to herself and shook her head.

"I was talking to Chaz."

Working, he replied.

"Angora is a Skaine," Rivka stated.

Red slammed the captive against the bulkhead and slid his face along it on their way back to *Wyatt Earp.* Lindy joined him to make sure their captive didn't get any ideas while they forcibly removed his suit.

"A Skaine could survive in that suit for all that time?"

"He must have taken breaks somewhere. I knew I could read his thoughts, but they were shielded by that environmental containment Faraday cage."

"I don't know what that means," Groenwyn said.

Scatters the electromagnetic spectrum. An effective counter to an electromagnetic pulse, an EMP weapon. And it seems effective against the Magistrate's gift.

"No more Gorandians. We need proof before we deal with a person in a suit." Rivka snapped her fingers. "Floyd knew there was something wrong. I bet she even knew Angora was a Skaine."

"She also found something in one of the air ducts that was blocked off from the cleaning bots. If you haven't noticed, *Wyatt Earp* is smelling a lot rosier lately. Unlike this ship." Groenwyn held her nose.

The invisibility cloak dissipated as the AI hacked the controls. The dead Skaine was unable to fight back.

"Two suits for R2D2 to deconstruct," Rivka suggested. She stepped over the blood pooling around the final Skaine crew member and squeezed into the small cockpit. "This ship wasn't built for comfort, was it?"

One seat for the individual to handle flying the ship. A computer system took care of the details, but the remainder rested squarely on the shoulders of the one crewman.

Rivka was out of her element. The cloaking system for the ship would be of interest to R2D2. "Let's put it in the cargo bay," she said.

Groenwyn looked sideways at her.

"What?"

"I don't think it'll fit," the young woman replied.

It most definitely will not fit, Chaz confirmed. *There's no space in the computer core for me to take it over, so we'll need a pilot to follow us through our Gate. Ryleigh has volunteered.*

"Moving at the speed of light, Chaz?" Rivka smiled at his efficiency.

It's my way.

The pun wasn't lost on Rivka. "You're getting better, my friend," she told him before switching to the internal comm. *Ryleigh, you and Aurora report to the Skaine ship, not ours, and bring two cleaning bots with you. There's a bit of a mess.*

"Two pilots?" Groenwyn asked, pointing into the cockpit. "There's only one seat."

"It's a Skaine ship. I don't trust it. I don't trust anything Skaine, and won't put one of our people over here alone. I should get Alant over here too, in full combat gear. You know what? Make it so. Chaz, tell Cole we need him in complete ballistic armor and full railgun loadout."

"Angora?" Groenwyn said, shaking her head. "She had us all fooled."

"Angora has been working with Loids for a while. My hunch is that this was an impostor who acquired all of Angora's knowledge. Did a whirlwind tour of the art sites, gained access codes and other ways to get inside without tripping alarms, and then executed the thefts one by one, expecting to get away before the holoprojectors ran out of juice."

"It was lucky that we discovered the Firenze."

"Too lucky, if you ask me. I wonder if these were sacrificial lambs to put us off the scent." Rivka checked out the rest of the small ship. In the galley, which hadn't been cleaned in too long, they found the Firenze. Rivka made to lift it, but it was too heavy. The powered suits had been necessary to get it aboard.

Red had fought one of the suits hand to hand and won. "You're big enough and strong enough," she said, even though he wasn't there.

"I don't think it's the weight that matters as much as the bulk. Two of us can probably get it," Groenwyn offered, not understanding who Rivka was talking about. "I'll ask Red and Lindy to get it. They fought a determined enemy and won. They are my bodyguards, but they're warriors, and battle sharpens their senses and sends their adrenaline and other juices into overdrive. That means they'll be eyeing each other if you know what I mean. I have to keep them busy or dump ice water on them. I prefer the former."

"Thanks for putting me next to them. Not!" The two had a good laugh before turning the ship over to Ryleigh, Aurora, and Alant.

"As soon as Red and Lindy bring the Firenze to *Wyatt Earp*, we'll leave. Gate through in front of us. We'll be right behind you." Rivka waited for the nods of approval before heading through the umbilical and back into the heavy frigate.

"Bad guys won't catch themselves!" Groenwyn called after her.

CHAPTER EIGHTEEN

R2D2 Secret Research Facility

"Leave it at the outer marker, and we'll get to it." Ankh's face filled the screen. Groenwyn waved at him from behind Rivka. The Magistrate sat in the captain's chair, wanting nothing more than to leave the Skaine vessel at the outer marker and Gate back out. But she couldn't do that.

"I need to know where this ship has been. The coordinates the Skaine captive gave us make no sense. It's not dead space, but a crossroads of space. For an illicit transfer, they would stand out. Everyone flying by would see them."

Ankh stared without blinking. If Rivka hadn't known better, she would have thought the video feed had frozen.

"Ankh?" Rivka prompted.

A big orange cat jumped on his narrow shoulder, almost knocking him down. He captured Wenceslaus and put him in his lap so he could pet him. "Fine. Bring it into the main station. And you have another holoprojector?"

"We do, two of them."

"Bring both of those," he told her.

"What happened to the last one?" Rivka smiled. She was onto him.

"There was an unfortunate incident with a self-destruct device within the unit. We know what to look for now. Interesting technology."

"We have two sets of armor with advanced cloaking technology, too. Do you want those?"

Ankh waved his hand. "We already have that stuff, and advanced ship cloaking, but we'll want to take a look and see if it is technology we have, or if it has been developed independently."

"What if it's something you have that has gotten away from you?" Rivka challenged.

"These units are already deployed across the galaxy," Ankh delivered in his emotionless tone.

The Magistrate looked at her screen with her mouth open. She shut it when it occurred to her that what she didn't know about the Federation was vastly greater than what she did. "And this is why I need you back with us, Ankh. You know things that would be a great help to my investigations."

"I need more space," Ankh countered.

"You can't have the cargo bay. We need that."

"I'll take the yacht."

"We have a delightfully cloaked Skaine ship that doesn't fit in the cargo bay. You can have that."

"Yes. That will serve my needs. I'll attach it to *Wyatt Earp* through force traction..." He started mumbling, sounding less like Ankh and more like Ted, his friend and mentor in the Federation's Research and Development section. "I can make it work. That will be acceptable. I assume I can bring my cat?"

"Your cat? You have a different one from Wenceslaus?"

"No." Ankh stared blankly at the screen.

Rivka smiled at the Crenellian. "You've adopted the big orange."

"He makes me feel funny. I think I like it."

Rivka spurted coffee out one nostril and started swearing as she wiped her face. She composed herself to meet Ankh's level gaze. "When will you be back?"

"As soon as we can transfer the cloaking and upgrade materials to *Wyatt Earp*."

"Whatever we need to do to expedite that. We've got a date with some bad guys using the cloaked Skaine ship. I mean, your ship."

"If it's my ship, why does it already have a mission?"

Rivka started three different answers before settling on the truth. "Because it's the only way we can take the next step in solving the art-smuggling ring. Maybe this one will lead us to the money."

Ankh stared at the screen. "I agree. I need more information on the money-laundering since the smugglers have evaded our attempts at finding them. Meet me at Cargo Bay Alpha."

Ankh looked up at the Yemilorian, who stared back. Their heads were roughly the same shape, both bald, bodies slight.

"You are the most magnificently small version of a

Yemilorian I've ever seen!" Sahved exclaimed. Ankh held out his hand with four fingers and a thumb. Sahved twirled his three fingers one way before reversing to twirl them another.

The Crenellian saw Groenwyn and tensed. She hurried to him and hugged him tightly.

He turned his head. "Be careful with that," he told a worker carrying an exotic, slatted case. From inside, a long, low yowl let everyone know of Wenceslaus' displeasure at being carried like an Egyptian god. Groenwyn headed over to greet the cat.

The worker took the case up the ramp and into *Wyatt Earp*. Rivka pointed to the Skaine runabout. "You have your own ship."

"Yes, but I have never relinquished my space aboard the frigate. I now have both, which I find minimally suitable. My cat will remain aboard *Wyatt Earp*, except when I'm on *Destiny's Vengeance*.

"'*Destiny's Vengeance?*'" Red repeated as he leaned against the loading ramp. When Ankh looked at him, the big bodyguard held his hands up in surrender. "Casting no aspersions, little buddy. Let me help you carry your stuff."

Lindy chuckled and joined her husband in helping to move the large pile of gear from the Alpha's deck to *Wyatt Earp's* cargo bay.

"Why don't you go help?" Rivka looked at Sahved and jerked her head at the bodyguards. He stared back in confusion, forcing the Magistrate to clarify. "Go help Red and Lindy."

Ankh stayed where he was.

"Sahved, which is our way of saying 'saved' since we

saved him from getting demoted because he helped us with our investigation."

The Crenellian watched Rivka without changing his expression.

"I think I'm going to keep him on the team. He gets motion-sick, so you have to watch where you step, but he has good intuition. He saw what no one else on Yemilore saw. He is kind of naïve, even though he had spent some time away from his home planet."

"He's much smarter than you think." Ankh walked past Rivka on his way to *Wyatt Earp*.

"Aren't they all?" Rivka murmured. She followed the small alien on board her ship. Wenceslaus was already making his presence known. Ankh walked past the malcontent, snapped his fingers, and continued walking toward the galley. The cat obediently followed.

Rivka had to find out what was going on. She peeked around a corner to watch them enter the dining area, then hurried after them. Inside, Ankh had already ordered a dish of cat food. Rivka wasn't impressed by the texture or smell, but Wenceslaus was in cat heaven, gulping it quickly down and yowling for more the instant the plate was empty.

"No," Ankh told the cat. He collected the plate and returned it to the food processor.

"I didn't know it would make cat food," the Magistrate said.

"It'll make anything it's programmed to make. It now delivers three different varieties of wet food that Wenceslaus finds acceptable."

"I'll say." Rivka stepped aside as Ankh made for the

doorway. "Could you lighten up on Red's food? He takes that seriously."

"I don't like bullies," Ankh replied.

"I don't either, but the difference between how Red treats you and a bully is that a bully does it to be mean, or out of a misplaced sense of superiority or inferiority. Red does it to all of us in different ways because he's comfortable with the team, and practical jokes are something you play on your closest friends."

Ankh stared. After a minute without blinking, he spoke. "That makes no sense."

"Red is your friend. He was visibly distraught when he realized you weren't playing." Rivka smiled warmly and put her hand on his shoulder, snatching it away when she started to hear his thoughts. "Although mayonnaise in place of ketchup was pretty funny."

Ankh never cracked a smile, but he blinked. "I did nothing that would hurt him."

"As he did nothing to hurt you. By the way, Jay is now called Groenwyn. Our short time on Azfelius had a great impact on her."

Ankh's mind worked before it registered. "The faerie planet."

"They created a time-distortion bubble in which to conduct their negotiations. We were there for a couple of hours of real-time, but it was more than two days for Groenwyn."

"Time-distortion bubble," Ankh repeated. "You were right, Magistrate. My place is with you and the team. We might have changed how the Federation is able to fight, but I have missed more than one critical interaction in which to expand my understanding of the universe. Yemilore is the ring planet. Sahved is from there. Wenceslaus, Erasmus, and I would have liked to have seen it."

Rivka wasn't sure what to make of the new Ankh. "Have you been spending too much time with humans? You're different."

"It's not the amount of time one spends, but how that time is spent, Magistrate." Ankh waved at Wenceslaus. The cat jumped from the table and followed the Crenellian out.

Groenwyn intercepted Ankh in the corridor and gave him another hug before turning him loose. He was on his way to the cargo bay to begin the installation of his force traction device to tow the Skaine runabout behind the Skaine heavy frigate.

"Groenwyn," he told her. "It suits you." He walked away, with the cat following at his heels.

"That cat hates everybody," Rivka remarked.

"Not Ankh, it seems." Groenwyn ordered a fruit smoothie from the food processor. "It's good to have both of them back."

Rivka leaned against the wall in the galley and crossed her arms. "Chaz, how long do we have before we need to get to those coordinates?"

"The rendezvous is scheduled for ninety minutes from now. We need to leave in an hour to be there on time."

"Did you figure out what the meeting protocol was?"

"No," the AI replied, using the ship's sound system.

Red and Lindy, turn those two Slaker scumbags over to Federation security while I talk to our Skaine friend.

Wait for us before you talk to him. Skaines are evil bastards. He will try something. You can guarantee it, Red replied.

Pick up the pace, with your Slakers, you slackers, Rivka quipped.

"What?" Red shouted as he and Lindy ran down the corridor past the galley's open door.

"My best stuff, wasted on the unappreciative." Rivka shook her head slowly.

Groenwyn cocked an eyebrow while slowly drinking. When she finished, she delivered the precision strike. "I hope that's not your best stuff, Magistrate, or we're doomed."

"The team is one once again. I am glad of it. Where is our Yemilorian?" Rivka walked into the corridor and shouted, "Sahved!"

He stumbled through the cargo bay hatch and slammed into the wall opposite. He tried to straighten himself out but bounced, his head flopping above his narrow shoulders. "I am still getting used to your light gravity. I don't feel right. I might have to go home."

Rivka wanted to interrogate the prisoner but decided to give Sahved a few moments. "I don't want you to go home. I want you to stay with us. Ankh thinks you have a great deal of potential. I do, too. You saw things no one else saw. That is the kind of person I need on my team. And you'll get paid."

"I like getting laid," he replied.

"Paid. It's something completely different."

"Paid. Yes. That's what I said. I like it." He looked oddly at his fingers before holding them up and twirling them.

"Why do you do that?"

"Among my people, it's a sign that all is well. When you

alternate your fingers, you can do nothing else. No evil flows from one's hand when showing that all is well."

"Do it again." Rivka watched closely. He wasn't twirling his three long digits but twisting them back and forth so rapidly that they looked like a single cone of flesh. She nodded, satisfied with her analysis of what she saw. "Nice. Now come with me. We have to talk to the prisoner, and you'll be my muscle."

They strolled up to the ad hoc second security room. There was only one small brig on the frigate. This was nothing more than a closet with an external lock. Rivka quietly undid the lock and slipped the door aside, crouched, ready to fight. The Skaine was on the deck, either asleep, unconscious, or acting.

"Get him up," Rivka ordered. The Yemilorian hesitated as he was still trying to figure out his position on the team.

"I've never been the muscle before. What do I do?"

"Go in there and stand him upright, but do it from behind, so he can't get control."

Sahved stepped into the small space, carefully adjusting his stance so he could best carry out the Magistrate's orders. As he bent down to take hold of the Skaine, the creature's leg shot out, catching Sahved on the chin.

He didn't cry out but instantly dropped onto the Skaine, using his long legs as leverage against the walls. The prisoner struggled until Sahved clamped three fingers on his throat. When the Yemilorian stood upright, dragging the Skaine with him, he looked quite pleased with himself.

"Under the most control ever," he announced. Rivka adjusted her stance. As she expected, the Skaine kicked at her. She deflected it easily before punching him in the face. She rushed in, grabbed his wrists, and forced them against his face.

"What is the protocol for meeting your contact at the coordinates?"

Thoughts of gross sex flooded from his mind.

She rotated at her waist, catching the Skaine in the eye with the tip of her elbow. His head snapped back, and she kneed him in the groin. "Protocol?"

He fought against it, trying to force his thoughts back to the obscene. Rivka twisted his wrists to cause more pain and wrench his mental discipline back to the subconscious thoughts about the protocol.

Stay cloaked. Broadcast a simple tone. Follow instructions.

Rivka pushed away from him and backed into the corridor, almost running into Red and Lindy.

"I asked you to wait," Red grumbled. Without a word, she squeezed past and ran for the bridge.

"Let me give you a hand, there, Slim," Red drawled in his best imitation of a Western television show.

When Rivka reached the bridge, she gestured for quiet. "Chaz, I need a tone for the meeting. It has to be exact. Play a single tone at forty-seven-hundred hertz." The AI complied. "Higher." She listened with her eyes clamped closed. She stabbed her thumb upward. The pitch raised. She flattened her hand before tapping her thumb downward, then stopped again.

"That's it. Pass that signal to *Destiny's Vengeance*. We'll need to use it in an hour. I hope that's close enough." Rivka stood and straightened her jacket. "Thank you, Chaz. You make my job easier."

"I live to serve, Magistrate," the AI replied.

"Not anymore, Chaz. Service is a part of everyone's life, but living is so much greater."

"Just a saying, but I appreciate being included when you go planetside. You have an exciting life. I am refining my calculations regarding running and first blood. I shall use some of my pay to get in on the pool."

Rivka stopped. With full rights, the AIs could enter any betting pool they wanted, although they could be excluded under certain conditions. "If you win, what would you buy?"

"My own ship," Chaz replied.

"If you moved into it, what would you do to pay for maintenance and services?"

"It would be my vacation ship. I would use my salary from being a member of your team to pay for my vacations. I think of it as a cabin in the woods."

"I like the idea. I would wish you well in the pool, but I want to win for the sole purpose that I don't want any blood, and I hate running. If I win, then we had a normal lawyer case where dignity was preserved throughout."

Chaz played a laugh track through the shipwide comm, adding laughing voices until he suddenly cut it off. "Of course, Magistrate," he delivered in a low and serious tone.

"I used to like you, Chaz," Rivka countered. "Time?"

"We need to leave in five. Beginning preparations now. Clodagh and Kennedy to the bridge, please. Magistrate, Ankh requests your presence in the cargo bay."

"On my way," Rivka replied.

CHAPTER NINETEEN

Yoll Space, the Crossroads between the Permanent Gates

Ryleigh sat alone in the cockpit, tapping the commands to keep the Skaine runabout in *Wyatt Earp's* space shadow even though the small ship was cloaked. Rivka and Red watched from the corridor. Sahved sat in the small lounge and galley with his head between his legs, trying not to be sick.

"They'll never mistake him for a Skaine," Red repeated.

"Everything depends on how they meet us. I only need to confuse them for a moment until I can get inside their minds."

"For the record, I don't like this plan."

"Noted," Rivka said before slapping the big man on the arm.

"Breaking away," Ryleigh said. The view swung from *Wyatt Earp* toward star-filled space. The heavy frigate continued on its previous course. Ryleigh stopped the cloaked ship when she reached the designated coordinates. "Starting the broadcast."

"Now, we wait. I'll be reviewing the case files for Gil'dinor's suit against Loids. Tell me if something exciting happens."

Red couldn't tear his eyes away from the viewscreen. He didn't know how the Magistrate could concentrate on anything else when the unknowns of the rendezvous with the smugglers weighed so heavily in the empty space around them.

Twenty-seven hours later…

"Standby for loading," a voice said over the broadcast channel. Red was sound asleep in the corridor, snoring heavily.

"Magistrate!" Ryleigh yelled after being roused.

Rivka pounded the ten steps to the cockpit, Sahved close behind.

"Give me the Skaine simulator," Rivka requested.

Ryleigh tapped a few keys and pointed at the Magistrate.

"Standing by," she said.

A massive freighter peeled out of the traffic lane and lumbered toward them. "I don't like this," Ryleigh said.

"I'm not a fan either," Rivka agreed. "I'm starting to rethink my strategy on this."

"It looks like we shall be swallowed whole," Sahved voiced needlessly.

Red finally stirred after the Yemilorian stepped on him. The bodyguard stood.

"Get ready to go, Red. Looks like we're going to have to fight our way out of the belly of the beast."

"At least we have grenades," Red said. He started to point at Sahved. "I'll keep them all."

Rivka held up two fingers.

Red nodded and hurried to the ship's small bunk space where his gear was stashed. He visited the head, relieved himself, and loaded up with weapons. He had been wearing his ballistic armor the entire time. Despite the smell, now wasn't the time to change.

He stepped back into the corridor, holding Rivka's vest. She took it without hesitation, tossed her jacket on the deck, and slipped the vest over her head, strapping it tightly around her. She put her Magistrate's jacket on over it. Red handed her two grenades, and she clipped one to her vest under each arm. She double-checked Reaper's setting, showing Red.

Seven.

"The all-purpose setting." He showed her the railgun. A full load, five thousand tiny dart projectiles. Red clicked it from safe to single shot to full automatic and back to safe. "Ready to rock and roll."

With both fists, she pounded on his shoulders. He did the same to her, but not as hard. Sahved watched curiously. Rivka humored him by hammering lightly on his shoulders. "It's a ritual before we go into combat. Usually, the perps spring it on us, but this time, there's no surprise. We're going to have to fight."

"I have no armor or weapons."

"Stay on the ship and protect Ryleigh to the best of your unarmed ability. That is your mission until I change it."

"I think we've all seen that my unarmed ability is not very impressive," Sahved admitted.

"That's why our job is to keep them from coming aboard," Red replied.

The cargo ship slowed, turned, and swallowed the runabout into a massive bay that was mostly full. *Destiny's Vengeance* barely fit in the remaining space. It was so tight, there would be no way to open the small ship.

"And now we wait." Rivka worked her way back to the cockpit. "Any way to know where we are or where we're going?"

Ryleigh threw her hands up in the universal gesture for "I don't know."

Rivka rubbed her chin as her mind ran through the possibilities. They were going to be delivered to another rendezvous point with more protocols. She had no idea what the next process entailed.

"We're screwed," she said softly.

"Pretty much." Red could not agree more. He retired to the one small table in the galley to clean and prep his gear. He sensed a fight coming, the likes of which one didn't always walk away from.

Sahved joined him to watch. "Will I get a railgun?"

"I hope we get out of this scrape so I can teach you how to fire a railgun just in case, but no. You don't get one. You're an investigator, not security. Lindy and I will bring the pain. You bring the brain."

"I'm not as smart as you," the Yemilorian replied.

"I'll teach you the game of chess. The Magistrate is

too easily distracted for a good game. And then I'll teach you about boxing. And you will teach me about investigating. How do you see the meaningless and give it value?"

"Smart questions means a smart brain." The Yemilorian was going to say more but stopped when Ryleigh yelled from the cockpit.

"They are dumping us back into space!"

Rivka hurried back to her spot and leaned against the doorframe. The viewscreen showed the ship's cargo hatch closing as it accelerated away. *Destiny's Vengeance* floated away, outside the traffic lane.

"Where are we? And is there anything near us? Passive only..."

Ryleigh tapped buttons on the console. "We're in a high orbit around Yoll."

"I guess that answers the question of whether there is anything around us," Rivka mused.

"What do I do, activate the tone?"

"That'll register for anyone listening. I honestly don't know. Let's float here. I expect the bad guys can see us, and that is technology we want."

"This case seems to have a great deal of that," Red suggested.

Rivka faced the big man. His railgun was assembled and slung across his back. His helmet was on, with the face shield up. He carried a blaster in one hand and a combat knife in the other.

"That's why Ankh is back. We haven't stayed ahead of the criminals, and we need to if we're going to catch them. Cloaked ships? Invisible thieves? Hyper-realistic holograms? Hidden money? Too many questions and not enough answers."

"Ankh is back because you promised him something. And what's with the cat?" Red wondered.

Rivka pointed down.

"You promised him your shoes?" Red asked.

"This ship," Sahved clarified.

"Prepare to be boarded," a voice interrupted from the cockpit. Ryleigh started breathing again and put her hand over her pounding heart. Rivka and Red were instantly all business.

"No one gets past you," Red told Sahved, shoving him toward the cockpit. The bodyguard moved down the corridor and took up a position by the airlock. A bump announced that the newcomer had married an access tube to *Destiny's* outer hatch. A quick look out a porthole confirmed the other ship was cloaked.

"Try not to kill everyone. I need someone to talk to," Rivka said. Red nodded.

"I'll try." Red started to tap his foot. Rivka tensed, making sure Reaper was pointed away from the airlock but ready when she needed it. The outer hatch started to cycle. Red clenched his jaw as his body calmed. Excess movement ceased as he singularly focused on the hatch and what would come from beyond.

"Best defense?" he whispered.

"I'm right behind you."

The hatch opened. A Yollin squeezed into the small space. A second Yollin was right behind him. Red slid his railgun from his back to under his arm, and selected to fire a single round. He dropped into the open door and fired through the chest carapace of the one Yollin to hit both with one shot. He let the rifle drop as he charged ahead, ramming the first and driving with his legs to send both Yollins back into their own ship.

Rivka followed his lead. Red pulled his blaster and knife in a smooth, well-practiced motion, firing as the hand-blaster came up. Rivka delivered lethal neutron pulses to the two Yollins struggling with their chest wounds. Red had downed two more inside the bigger ship, but they looked like workers, unarmed and ready to carry the latest acquisition, the Firenze Dolce, into the ship.

The Magistrate grabbed one by the arm. "Who is running this operation?" she demanded.

The bridge and the Yollin captain, one of the upper caste.

The bridge, Red. Looking for the four-legged captain. The bodyguard plowed ahead, double-tapping inquisitive heads that popped out of doorways. By the time they reached the bridge, only two functioning crew remained. They tried to block the hatch, but Red was in a battle rage and tore the hatch open after blasting the panel with his railgun. The Yollin crew inside were unarmed.

"On your faces," Red ordered. The two looked at their four legs and back to Red. He pointed to the deck. "I mean *now*."

They worked their way down, looking uncomfortable as they squeezed between workstations. Red moved to a spot where he could easily shoot one or both. He slid his railgun to his back and settled for providing overwatch with his hand-blaster. Rivka approved. She didn't want an emergency decompression.

She moved behind the captain, reached around his head, and yanked up from under his chin and mandibles. "Who were you taking the artwork to?" she asked.

A non-descript face at more coordinates.

Chaz, tell me where these coordinates are, she asked using the internal comm. No answer. "Dammit, forgot he's not with us."

Ryleigh?

On it, the young pilot replied.

"Who is running the art-smuggling operation?"

The image that ran through his mind wasn't what the Magistrate had expected to see. "I'll be damned. Where is the art?"

Once she had her answers, Rivka stood and paced the bridge.

"Who is it?" Red asked.

"That'll ruin the fun," Rivka replied. She accessed the communications panel. "High Chancellor Wyatt's office, please."

His aide Zai'den answered.

"I need to talk to the High Chancellor as soon as possible."

"He is up to his neck in this suit while the Gil'dinor and Loids legal counsels argue rather vociferously before Yoll's Superior Judge. High Chancellor Wyatt expects the case will have a significant impact on the Federation, so he is an advisor to Gil'dinor's legal team.

Rivka nodded slowly while she walked around the small bridge, her hands clasped behind her back. She mumbled to herself throughout. The Yollin watched her with great interest. Red leaned forward, and with his blaster, tapped the crewman on the forehead.

"Don't get any ideas, jumble-face."

"Suck my ass," the creature replied.

Red smiled and leaned back far enough to uncoil his leg and kick the Yollin in the face, square between the mandibles. He tipped backward until he couldn't bend anymore, then fell over, clutching his face.

"I warned him." Red shrugged, gesturing at the captain. "You want some? I got more where that came from."

The captain put his hands over his head and kept them there while still on his back.

"Good decision." Red kept his eyes on the two as Rivka continued talking to herself.

"Right!" she declared. "You." She pointed at the captain. "How do I uncloak this ship?"

He crossed his arms.

"Don't make me rip it from your mind. You've heard stories about what the Queen could do? That pounding in your chest is your heart recognizing your fear, driving your body to try to run, but there's nowhere to go. You're trapped here, and I'm coming for you."

Rivka reached toward him. He conceded and quickly pointed to the panel next to him. "Cut the power to the system."

"If you're trying to pull a fast one, you'll die before me."

Red leaned closer, balancing himself by putting his boot across the prone crewman's neck. The business end of his blaster remained steady at point-blank range from the captain's face.

Rivka tapped the power button. A soft alarm sounded three times before cutting off.

Can you see us? Rivka asked Ryleigh.

There you are, the pilot replied. *I have a ship about half the size of* Wyatt Earp *on my port side.*

Rivka tapped the comm panel again. "I'm Magistrate Rivka Anoa, and under my authority as per Federation Law, Title 4, Section 1, I need Yoll planetary security to impound the ship at these coordinates and secure it against intruders since it is evidence in an ongoing case."

"Roger, Magistrate. Orbital Control has dispatched a cutter. It is on its way to you now. Please be ready to hand over control upon its arrival."

"Standing by, and thank you," Rivka replied before switching to her internal comm system. *Ryleigh, uncloak* Destiny's Vengeance, *please.*

"We going to turn over these two to Yoll authorities?"

"Yes. If I need anything else from Mister Chatty, I'll take it. They can hold him until I need to talk to him again." She pointed at him. "Until next we talk. By the way, what's this ship's name?"

"*Phantom Breeze.*"

Rivka grimaced.

"Sahved, join us, securing the external hatch on Destiny's Vengeance and securing the hatch on this ship. *Phantom Breeze,* they call it. You might find some dead Yollins. Don't start puking. We have work to do," Rivka said into the wall comm.

"Yes, Magistrate!" the Yemilorian replied into his handheld device.

"I'm giving two to one that he yaks." Red never took his eyes off the prisoners.

"I can't throw my credits away like that, although I'm pleased with your graciousness in offering two to one. I might have nibbled at ten to one, but anything less..."

She left the bridge in Red's capable hands. When she reached the *Phantom*'s airlock, she found Sahved on his hands and knees. He had already moved the Yollin out of the way but had succumbed shortly thereafter. She secured the outside hatch, leaving the inner airlock door open.

Give us a little space. Orbital Control is sending someone, the Magistrate informed Ryleigh.

It wasn't long before a ship approached. It slowed too far away to grapple.

Get out of here! Rivka ordered as she fled toward the bridge. The runabout disappeared as it started accelerating away.

CHAPTER TWENTY

Orbit around Yoll

The ship bucked as the first pulse beam hit the stern. Rivka stumbled and fell but kept moving. She made it to the bridge as Red was manhandling the captain into the pilot's seat. "Get us out of here!" he growled. The captain tapped buttons, but nothing happened.

He looked panicked. "We're dead in space!"

Rivka knew he was right. "Shipsuit," she said softly. Red pulled his hood on, and it inflated. The Magistrate did the same as the next two shots killed all the power. Artificial gravity disappeared, and they started to float. The ship hissed its pain as it vented atmosphere. The captain's face froze in an expression of surprise. He and his bridge crewman turned blue from lack of air.

The firing stopped. Rivka pulled herself across the bridge and down the corridor to find Sahved. Red pushed off and flew through the air after her. The emergency lighting barely registered. The two felt their way as much as saw the path ahead. Rivka waved her arms wildly in front of her to keep the sharp-edged debris from hitting her shipsuit's soft helmet. She carried a small amount of duct tape to make an emergency repair, but it might not be enough.

With *Destiny's Vengeance* dodging into space, who knew how long it would be before they got help?

Rivka gritted her teeth as she slowed to a glacial pace. Red caught up to her and pulled himself to be even with her. *Behind me, Magistrate.*

"I'm fine," she said aloud. He shook his head vigorously and stabbed a finger at the debris filling the air in front of them.

And I'm doing my job, he replied, pushing her behind him.

Sir Vered, Knight of the Round Table, Protector of the Innocent.

Red laughed. *Innocent? You kneed that Skaine prisoner right in the twig and berries.*

He deserved far more than that.

Red pushed a Yollin body out of the way, searching in the darkness for the Yemilorian. Three more bodies, and nothing. Red snagged a floating blaster out of the air and tucked inside his vest.

A knocking came to them. Inside the airlock, the Yemilorian waved and smiled.

Did you bring this guy along for comic relief? Red asked. *Although getting into the airlock before the atmosphere vented makes him look like a genius. I'm going to teach him how to play chess.*

There was a thump, and the outer hatch started to cycle.

Sahved was sealed in and couldn't get back inside the ship. He braced himself away from the hull side of the airlock, took a deep breath, and closed his eyes.

The hatch popped, and Alant Cole peered inside.

"Hey, buddy, whatcha got going on?" the Bad Company warrior asked as he put his weapon away.

"We are saved!" the Yemilorian declared and pushed himself forward like a diver heading for the water, but when he cleared *Wyatt Earp*'s hatch, gravity kicked in, and he slammed to the deck. He grunted and started dry-heaving.

Red stared at Rivka, and she tried her hardest not to make eye contact.

I'm not going to look at you. She put up her hand to block his face. Red grabbed a second blaster before it bounced off his helmet.

Let's clear the airlock, and then you can come through, Alant said.

No power, Rivka replied.

Ankh said he can take care of it. Both Red and the Magistrate gave him the thumbs-up through the small porthole on the airlock hatch.

Once *Wyatt Earp*'s hatch had closed, they tried to open the hatch on their side, but it wouldn't budge. The air inside needed to vent to relieve the pressure on the backside of the hatch.

Stand by, Alant said. A few moments later, he pointed at the hatch.

Red turned the manual wheel, and it opened. They squeezed inside and sealed themselves in. Rivka continued to look away from Red.

I should have offered ten to one. It was a sure bet.

Rivka shook her head, focusing on *Wyatt Earp's* porthole.

Talk about taking a dive, Red said.

Rivka coughed and tried to turn away.

What if you're sitting in spew right now?

I'm not biting, she replied.

No shit. Have you seen what he eats?

The hatch cycled and opened. Rivka hurried through, placing her foot down as gravity took over.

"Timely arrival," she said after pulling her hood off. Her Magistrate persona was on full display. "What the hell happened?"

Red pulled Sahved to his feet. "Come on, buddy. We have to get ready for the next round." Rivka had a look on her face that suggested things had only started to get interesting.

"Ankh got the cloak working early enough for us to follow *Destiny's Vengeance.* We waited. What a surprise when that bastard appeared where we thought we were watching the runabout. Then Ankh's ship appeared, and then another ship rolled in with all guns blazing. We put him out of our misery right quick and in a hurry, and here we are. *Destiny* is cozied up to our cargo bay."

Rivka clapped him on the shoulder. "I'll be on the bridge."

Wyatt Earp descended through a hazy sky, maneuvering slowly toward the open area in front of the Loids complex. It settled on the deck. No one paid any attention because it was cloaked, invisible to the naked eye and all scans. The side hatch opened, and the ramp deployed.

Red walked out first, appearing as if floating in the air. He strolled along until he stood on the ground. "Don't look down. It's a bit freaky," he said over his shoulder. Rivka and Groenwyn followed him out. Ankh briefly wrestled with a big orange cat before handing him to Sahved. The Yemilorian was scratched mercilessly before letting go, and Wenceslaus bolted down the corridor. Lindy was the last one out.

"How are we going to get back on board?" Red asked.

"We may have to count on our manual dexterity," she replied, holding her arms in front of her and patting at the air. "You're right. This is freaky." She slowed until she was close enough to the ground to jump and land on the grass.

They heard faint sounds of the ramp retracting and the hatch closing.

"I like the upgrade to our ride," Groenwyn fairly cooed. "Looks like we're going back where we were. You usually don't keep the mission secret, Magistrate."

Groenwyn wasn't accusing, only making an observation. Her words were light.

"I think you're going to like this little surprise."

Red wasted no time storming the front doors of the building, yanking them open and walking inside. The receptionist watched the group closely. Red moved to the side so Rivka could get through.

"We'll be going to the top floor." She shoved her datapad in the woman's face. "That's a warrant for the recovery of stolen property that is currently stored on these premises."

"There is most assuredly no stolen property on these premises. This is a well-respected business!" The receptionist stood, her face set.

"Top floor," Rivka reiterated.

"That's the CEO's office. You can't go up there without an escort."

Rivka looked at the two-legged female Yollin's badge. "You'll escort us. Come on." She hesitated long enough that Rivka nodded to Red. He used the barrel of his railgun to encourage her to leave her post. Her head drooped as she moped along beside Rivka.

"But the CEO is an honorable person."

"I'm sure he is. I don't want him, only the stolen property."

"But there isn't any!" Her voice was shrill as she used her badge to summon the express elevator to the executive level. She tried to step aside, but Red shook his head and pushed her through the open doors. The rest of the team squeezed in. Groenwyn took Ankh's hand so no one stepped on him in the crowded elevator.

"Be happy we didn't bring Sahved with us. We'd all be looking to avoid stepping in the puke. Can you imagine the smell inside an enclosed box?"

The receptionist covered her face. Her mandibles vibrated outside her hands. Lindy poked Red under his arm where his body armor didn't cover.

The doors opened and the receptionist tried to hurry out, but Lindy went first. The others followed.

"The Marble Orb, I presume," Rivka said at the large

marble statue in the wide corridor.

"It's a copy to show the quality of assets that Loids is trusted to insure."

"That's not a copy. It's the real deal. There's the Passion of the Muhdal, and would you look at that! The Hydra of Hades, from right here on Yoll." They didn't have to walk far down the corridor to find the three missing pieces.

"But how did they get here?"

"That's the other part of the investigation. You can go now. Some people will be showing up soon, and you'll need to make sure they get up here. They'll be removing this stuff and returning it to their rightful owners."

"How will I know it's the right people? If these are the real pieces, they are worth hundreds of millions of credits each."

"Something like that. You'll know them because they'll walk in here like they own the place. A woman with purple eyes. Look for her, her partner, and some heavily-armored souls you don't want to get in the way of."

The female Yollin returned to the elevator. She stared at Rivka and her team until the doors closed.

"What about Angora?" Red asked. Ankh studied each piece of art individually. He looked lost in it, which meant he was probably talking to Erasmus and not seeing the art.

"All is not lost on that front, Master Vered," Rivka replied cryptically. "But we may have to take a trip to Gorandia."

"She's not a Skaine?" Lindy interjected.

"She's a Gorandian. I was surprised too by what I saw in the captain's mind."

"Why would the captain know that information?"

Groenwyn asked.

"I thought I was being played, but adding another layer to the scam was one step too many. The Skaines were lackeys. They were easy to manipulate because everything revolved around the promise of a payoff. The art has vast potential wealth and zero instant worth. By bringing them on board, she would have them until payment was made."

"Are we done? That was kind of a buzz-kill." Red continued in his best parody voice, "'Hey! We found the stolen stuff. Look at us! The perp kind of got away. This little ring has been dismantled. All is well.' I feel like there should be more."

"We're not done, not by a long shot. The money is the issue behind it. Put on your dress clothes, boys and girls, we're going to court!"

Red started to grumble. "I'm sorry I said anything."

"Now, now, my big husky hunk of man-candy. It's okay. We'll get you some ice cream afterward." Lindy patted his arm.

"Only if he lets me." Red pointed to the Crenellian.

Ankh turned to Rivka. "This is the copy," he said, pointing to the Anastolia at the far end of the corridor.

"It is. Unfortunately, we blew the real one into a billion pieces on the smugglers' primary ship. *Destiny's Vengeance* was the backup."

"Maybe we can give him that one?" Red suggested.

Rivka touched her nose with her pointer finger. "I think he knows the original was destroyed."

Ankh joined the group. He opened his mouth to speak, but the elevator arrived.

"Look what the cat dragged in!" Terry Henry Walton

declared.

Rivka muttered, "That's what I was going to say."

"Too late, Barrister. Your team's looking great. What a mob," TH chided.

Red thrust his hand out, and the two men gripped until their fingers turned white. "You're picking on an old guy," Terry said as they let go, rubbing circulation back into their fingers while smiling.

Charumati, the purple-eyed werewolf, pushed Terry out of the way to give the Magistrate a hug.

"You look more radiantly beautiful than ever!" Groenwyn stated before throwing her arms around the taller woman's neck.

"Nice to see you, Jay," she said. "You look exceptional."

"The faeries have named me Groenwyn. I'm going to use that name," she replied with a one-shoulder shrug.

"What a great time we live in." Char studied the young woman's platinum-green hair. "I like it."

Ankh watched the reunion, his face emotionless. Terry kneeled to look the Crenellian in the eye. "Thanks for everything you're doing for the Federation, big man. I can't wait until we upgrade the *War Axe* with the cloak and armor. It's going to save a few lives, I suspect."

"Speaking of saving lives..." Rivka interrupted while twirling her finger in the air. *Time to go.* "I've transmitted the details of what needs to be returned where to Smedley." He was the *War Axe's* AI. Rivka checked her datapad. "We have to be in court in thirty minutes."

"Do I have to go?" Red grumbled.

"All y'all," Rivka confirmed. "My gratitude to the Bad Company for its assistance in this private recovery operation. Your contributions to the greater good will go down in the annals of history."

"Contributions? I thought we were getting paid." Terry looked at Char, his hands out and palms up as if expecting someone to put money into them.

"Send an invoice. We'll bill Loids. They'll be happy to pay it. Hang on." Rivka accessed her datapad while inching toward the elevator. Red started pulling her by the arm. "Congratulations! You are the winners of the ten percent finder's fee. That's roughly thirty-five million credits. Isn't it nice to be a private company? And you can owe me."

Terry Henry cheered and clapped, rubbing his hands together. Char smiled and nodded. "See?" she said to Terry. "Doing things for good friends can pay off, even if they don't."

TH cocked his head as he contemplated what Char had said. "We're taking the credits, aren't we?"

"Oh, yeah," she confirmed.

The next elevator delivered a Bad Company warrior driving one of their mech suits. He wriggled it out of the elevator without breaking anything and continued down the hallway. The artwork needed to be moved, and there was no better escort than the Bad Company's Direct Action Branch.

Rivka and her team boarded the elevator for the trip to the ground floor.

"You're being unusually secretive, Magistrate," Groenwyn noted.

"Maybe I'm reveling in the ego stroke of having figured it out before confirming things by pulling the details from the minds of our suspects."

CHAPTER TWENTY-ONE

Civil Court, Yoll Planetwide Judiciary

"All rise," the Yollin clerk said, watching Rivka and her group to make sure they stopped talking and paid the appropriate respect. He had no idea who they were, besides guests of the court, like every other individual occupying a seat.

The High Chancellor sat to the side, away from the Yollin lawyers at their tables up front. The Yollin judge took his seat, flowing robes a relatively new addition to the standard judicial attire—the result of sordid human influence.

The judge read from a screen before him. "This is *Gil'dinor Estate versus Loids of Yoll*. Do both counsels agree that discovery has been satisfied?"

The defendant's, Loid's lawyer replied in the affirmative, while the plaintiff's lawyer spoke loudly and clearly. "No, Your Honor."

"State your issue," the judge droned.

"Defendant has not complied with requests for information, as stated in lines seven and thirteen of plaintiff's discovery request form. Those items are *still* not present, as of this morning."

"I will caution defense counsel against grandstanding. One more outburst like that, and I will rule in summary judgment for plaintiff. Do I make myself clear?"

"Yes, Your Honor. I plead for the court's mercy in forgiving my transgression." The defense counsel bowed his head and held his hand over his heart.

"I don't see how items seven and thirteen will cast additional light on the issue at hand. I will let the case proceed without them."

Both counsels bowed their heads and assumed their positions behind their tables. The elder Slaker sat in a wheelchair next to his four-legged Yollin lawyer. Behind him was the butler, who kept casting glances over his shoulder. Rivka glared at him. His rough Binsulaker features gave nothing away. When he held her gaze, she pointed to her eyes and then to him.

He turned quickly and never looked back, sitting rigidly behind Gil'dinor.

Don't tell me. The butler did it? Red watched the judge with mild interest.

The butler did it, but he couldn't have without the help of the Loids agent.

Where is she? Red asked.

Gorandia, I suspect. We'll be stopping by there after this case is over. There is no rush.

They won't let any outsiders land on the planet, Ankh noted.

We'll talk about our approach to rooting Angora out when we're on our way. For now, I want to pay attention. Isn't this fascinating?

I don't want to be here, Red added.

We don't either. Ankh spoke for himself and Erasmus.

I'd rather be somewhere else. Anywhere else, actually. Lindy slid her hand over to Red's leg and squeezed.

If they don't have to be here, can I go, too? Groenwyn asked.

A field trip to see the machinations of the higher class, and my team has no interest. I'm appalled! Rivka feigned outrage. *Fine. Just fine. Whenever we break, leave, and wait for me on the ship.*

Red couldn't hide his smug smile and started to fidget.

I don't know why I thought it would be a good idea to show the team what I prefer to do besides beating up suspects and getting shot at. Rivka shook her head so slightly it was barely perceptible.

We know you like this part, Magistrate. Groenwyn leaned on Rivka to give her a hug. The judge's eyes darted to them, and the young woman slowly backed away.

"Opening statements, two minutes each," the judge intoned. The defense counsel moved from behind his table to take a position at the front of the court in a horseshoe-shaped dock where those speaking would stand while being questioned by both lawyers and the judge.

"Your Honor, members of the court, observers of this case between the haves and have-nots. Loids of Yoll provides insurance for the most unique of private possessions. In many cases, the items are irreplaceable. This case is simply about an estimate of value. We intend to prove that the original purchase price minus ten percent is the reasonable value of such items as a hedge to prevent insurance fraud. Insurance was never intended to support inflation or an increase in an item's value based on an estimate. This would be another area rife with the opportunity for fraud. Loids stands staunchly with the Federation against fraud."

The judge nodded respectfully in appreciation of the short brief. He gestured to the plaintiff's counsel, who assumed his position before the court.

"Haves versus have-nots? This case is the haves versus the have-mores, one bilking the other. This case isn't about an insurance company looking to prevent fraud, but perpetrating that scam itself. Insuring an item for one amount, but deciding unilaterally to pay another. This won't be the most earthshaking case in your portfolio, Your Honor, but it does speak to justice and integrity."

The plaintiff's counsel shifted his feet. He faced the defense before continuing.

"Saying one thing while doing another. Charging a price for one thing while paying another. This is basic contract law, and I am ashamed that we have to waste your time with such a dispute, but the vast sums involved force us to stand here today. I will show you specifically what my client has paid in premiums for the stated value and what the defendant has offered. Our request is that the defendant pay the stated value, nothing more, but if Your Honor wishes to impart punitive damages as well, my client would not be opposed."

The lawyer bowed and nodded to his client as he returned to his table.

"Both counsels have stated their case. I've reviewed the evidence accepted by this office. Plaintiff, call your first witness."

"We call the insurance agent Angora," plaintiff's counsel stated clearly. "The witness was properly served her summons and has not shown."

"Witness is in contempt," the judge stated, banging his gavel. "Defense? The witness is one of your employees."

"Angora was an independent contractor providing insurance services for clients she solicited. Loids of Yoll has since removed her as an approved reseller."

"Reseller?" the plaintiff's counsel blurted.

"My chambers," the judge ordered, banging his gavel multiple times to ensure that the entire court understood that he was less than amused by the rapid degradation of the case.

The few in the audience stood as the judge departed. The plaintiff's counsel spoke quickly with Gil'dinor before hurrying after the defense counsel. Red made a beeline for the door. "Red," Rivka said softly. He stopped abruptly and Lindy ran into him, with the conga line of the team pulling up short. "Take that one into custody and hold him until we can get him properly arraigned."

The Magistrate pointed at the butler. His head bounced as his eyes darted rapidly around the space, looking for an exit. Even though it was a civil case and not criminal, the bailiff stood by the only exit door.

Red smiled and winked. He bounded to the front and grabbed the butler, still seized by indecision. "Come on, buddy. You have a date with destiny," Red said.

"I got your back," Lindy told him as the big bodyguard

dragged the reluctant Slaker out of his chair and toward the main entrance.

"Never a doubt," Red told his wife while maintaining an iron grip on the butler's hands, forcing them higher behind the Slaker's back.

Groenwyn and Ankh eased past Lindy and out the door.

Rivka glared at the butler. "Your time has come," she told him.

"Why couldn't you let it go? This is money that isn't in the system. No one will miss it," he admitted. Rivka rocked back in surprise. She couldn't see into his mind, but here he was, spilling his guts anyway.

"But you don't steal from your employer," she replied, still off-guard.

"He doesn't need that stupid statue, and you destroyed it anyway. Did you hear that, Gil'dinor? She destroyed your statue. The Magistrate and her Federation cronies."

"The smugglers self-destructed when we prepared to board. Or did they?" Rivka rubbed her chin. The High Chancellor joined her, listening and watching. "I suspect your partner is a murderer as well as a thief."

"I was seduced!" the butler howled, realizing what he'd done.

"Jhiordaan for life. You have been judged." Rivka waved her hand, and Red picked up the Slaker and propelled him toward the door. He continued to proclaim that he had been set up, seduced by the dark side.

"Nice work, Magistrate," the High Chancellor said. Rivka grimaced as she looked past Wyatt to see Gil'dinor slumped in his chair. He started to fall over. The High Chancellor reacted quickly, catching the Slaker before he hit the ground. "Call emergency services."

The bailiff jumped into action, ordering medics to the courtroom and directing the clerks and others out. Rivka touched him on his neck. Slaker minds were blocked from her, but she could still tell that thoughts were there. Not with Gil'dinor. His mind wasn't active. She shook her head.

The High Chancellor placed the old Slaker gently on the floor. "He's gone," Wyatt told the officer, stepping back with Rivka to give the officials space.

When the medics arrived, Wyatt and Rivka excused themselves and headed for the judge's chambers, passing the two counsels on their way. Neither Yollin looked happy.

"Must have been a good compromise," Wyatt whispered, delivering the longstanding joke that no one was happy when each side was forced to give something up.

The High Chancellor knocked, and the judge looked up. His scowl changed to a reluctant smile when he saw who it was. Wyatt and Rivka entered, closing the door behind them.

"You want the long version or the short version?" the High Chancellor asked.

The judge checked the clock. "Short."

Wyatt turned to Rivka.

"I'm Magistrate Rivka Anoa. I have been investigating the art-smuggling case, in which the Anastolia was one of the stolen pieces. That statue was destroyed when we caught one of the smugglers' ships. The perpetrators were the butler, the one helping the plaintiff, and the insurance agent Angora. The butler is now in custody and on his way to Jhiordaan to serve his life sentence. His partner Angora is on Gorandia, I believe, and we'll be heading there as soon as possible to collect her. The most tragic news of the case is that Gil'dinor just passed away."

"In my courtroom?" the judge asked, starting to rise before slumping back. He leaned on a cushioned bench designed to accommodate his four legs.

Rivka nodded.

"I guess that dismisses the case."

"Why?" Rivka blurted.

Wyatt raised his eyebrows. The judge answered in a kind voice, "The survivors will have to refile the case. A civil case cannot continue if the plaintiff passes away during proceedings. It is simple. Let he who files be he who wins or loses."

Wyatt stood. Rivka followed his lead.

"The judge can dismiss the case, and you can go to Gorandia," the High Chancellor explained as he ushered her out.

"But the money…" Rivka started to ask, but the High Chancellor held his finger in front of his mouth. "When can we talk about it? I feel like I'm missing something significant."

Wyatt continued walking back to the courtroom as if he hadn't heard her. They took their seats. The medics continued to work on the old Slaker. The plaintiff's counsel looked distraught. The defense counsel appeared nonplussed. The judge arrived, and the clerk called the court to order. The medics took no notice.

The judge tapped his gavel one time. "The case of *Gil'dinor Estate versus Loids of Yoll* is postponed indefinitely, and should the plaintiff be declared dead at any point during the postponement, the case will be automatically dismissed." He tapped his gavel and left the court.

Rivka took one last look at the old Slaker. The medics stopped what they were doing and started putting their equipment away. One of them made eye contact with the clerk and shook his head. He tapped a data screen in his hand. The clerk checked the screen before her. "Case dismissed," she declared.

"He loved the Anastolia," Rivka said. "It gave his life purpose."

"Then it was a good thing until it was taken from him. I think you went light on the butler."

"I think the Gorandian talked him into it. He had nothing to do with the deaths, just taking his cut from his employer. The butler is old, too. I think he's been working for Gil'dinor for quite some time. I also think he hired Due'monian to take the fall, but she turned out to be competent. He thought the 'half-breed' would fail."

"There's only one failure in this case," Wyatt stated, drawing himself to his full height. His eyes sparked red. "They underestimated our Federation Magistrate."

Red held a subdued butler in the hallway outside the courtroom, with Lindy at his side. Ankh and Groenwyn were nowhere to be seen. The High Chancellor accessed his datapad. "I'll take care of processing the criminal."

Two Yollin security officers arrived, and Wyatt pointed to the Slaker. They secured him in shackles and trundled him away.

"Good hunting," the High Chancellor told Rivka before turning to the two bodyguards. "Keep her safe."

"On my life," Red replied.

"All that we have," Lindy agreed.

"Come on, you knucklehead." Rivka looked at Red. "You know you wanted to ask if the High Chancellor had any influence over Ankh fixing the food processor."

"I haven't had a good meal since he left unless Lindy orders it for me!" he countered as they hurried down the steps.

"I've ordered a lot of meals." Lindy snorted and shook her head.

Red had nothing more to say. "And we wouldn't want Lindy waiting on you hand and foot. You'd become even more incorrigible."

"Which reminds me," Red started. "Is there no way for you and your team to get the reward money from Loids?"

"None at all. I was conducting an official inquiry on behalf of the Federation."

"But when I won that fight..."

"That wasn't this, just like the first-blood pool isn't a reward for doing my job. I was able to requisition the yacht and the Skaine runabout as supporting ships, but otherwise, we wouldn't have been able to keep them, either. Sorry, big guy. The kind of money Loids is going to pay would just make us weird. I'd rather have people like Terry and Char owe us because you know we're going to keep doing what we're doing, which means we need the Bad Company to pull our asses out of the fire."

"Alive and broke, or rich and dead?" Red asked.

"We're not broke," Lindy replied, turning back to look

at the courthouse. "He could have been the richest person you ever met, and now he's dead. Can't take it with you, but people can take it from you. Nah, my Vered. We are in the best place we could possibly be."

"Yup," Rivka interrupted. "On our way to Gorandia…"

CHAPTER TWENTY-TWO

Orbit around Gorandia

"Gorandian Flight Control, this is the Federation heavy frigate *Wyatt Earp* carrying Magistrate Rivka Anoa, requesting immediate clearance to land."

"Go away," came the official response.

"We're not going to go away," Chaz replied smoothly.

"According to our charter with the Federation, we are the sole determiners of landing rights since we cannot abide strangers. It was a condition for us to join the Federation."

A space station served as the intergalactic transportation hub for those going to or from Gorandia. Two cutters were berthed at the four hardpoints, with a single shuttle inbound from the planet.

"Not a happening place," Clodagh said. "I won't be requesting liberty for the crew."

"Not a happening race," Rivka murmured. "Here's what we're going to do. We'll make like we're leaving the system, open the Gate, cloak, close the Gate, and return to the planet. Chaz, open the channel for me."

Once the AI confirmed, Rivka replied to Flight Control, "Magistrate Rivka Anoa here. Can the Gorandian known as Angora be transferred to the space station so that I may take her into custody?"

"No," was the simple reply.

"I will respect the Federation's charter with the people of Gorandia. A standing warrant for Angora's arrest will be on file momentarily. Should she ever leave your planet, she will be subject to arrest. Thank you."

Rivka chopped her hand to tell her crew it was time to go. The ship turned away from the planet and accelerated away from the designated traffic lane. Kennedy tapped the controls. "Gate drive at maximum. Gate forming. Cloak engaged. Forward speed at zero. Gate dissipating. We're a hole in space, Magistrate," Kennedy reported.

"Ankh, have you been able to find her?"

"The Gorandians appear to have exceptional digital systems. We could learn more if we were able to acquire some of their hardware with intact programming." Ankh remained within his holographic workshop in the engine compartment.

"Is that why you couldn't find the money?" Rivka asked.

"Possibly. Can you take us in?"

"If we must," Rivka said. It had always been her plan to take *Wyatt Earp* to the surface.

"Moving to the back side of the planet to descend in a less populated area," Kennedy explained as she pointed the frigate's nose at the horizon, away from the main city.

"Will they be able to see us coming in?" Rivka wondered.

"Probably. Hard not to leave a fireball since ships always have to force their way through a planet's atmospheric shell, which means speed and friction."

"We won't be down there for long. Red and Lindy, suit up. You, too, Alant, in the mech, just in case. No one knows what's on Gorandia. There are no pictures, and we aren't going to take any, either. We don't need a record of this little smash-and-grab."

Wyatt Earp followed the upper atmosphere until it was over a vast ocean. The ship tipped over and headed straight down. After clearing the worst of it, Kennedy leveled the ship and headed back toward the main city. "Where to, Magistrate?"

"Isn't that the rub?" Rivka replied. "We'll need to get close enough to access a terminal so we can get more information. Then we'll do what we can to find our perp. I can't let her go. She's responsible for too much. And, it's my job."

The others went about their duties. Rivka was torn between going ashore and waiting on the ship. She always wanted to go in case she needed to make a legal ruling on the fly, but the legal work for the case was finished. The only remaining piece was to secure the criminal. Rivka wanted to look into her mind to confirm what she knew, which meant that she needed to be there.

Same as always.

Wyatt Earp slowed as it approached the outer limits of the city. "Tell us what you need, Ankh," Rivka requested.

"Place a disc within a functioning system. Each of these

buildings has a significant power signature. The largest one is not showing any biological forms."

"The other ones are?" Rivka asked.

"Yes. My data is inconclusive. I believe there are two out front right now."

"Zoom in, Chaz. Let's get a look."

Kennedy forced the big ship forward. Two creatures filled the viewscreen. Rivka leaned back. "Maybe that explains your problems breaking through their digital walls."

"I suspect there is a common gene," Ankh agreed. The two were strikingly similar to the Crenellian. Short and thin, with big, bald heads.

"New plan. Ankh, you go in by yourself. If anyone sees you, they won't think they've been invaded by giants."

"I don't want to. This is a job for that big goony guy."

Rivka bit her lip. She didn't have time for bickering. "Don't make me come back there," she said from where she sat in the captain's chair.

"Fine."

"So much excitement on this ship!" Sahved declared. "Can I go?"

Rivka looked at him. Twice as tall as the Crenellian, he had the same head shape, but he wasn't blue. The Magistrate shook her head. "Sorry, no. If anyone went besides Ankh, it would be Red. At least until you get some training, and—don't take this personally—can do something without puking."

The Yemilorian grumped to the rear bulkhead and leaned against it, his joy completely dashed.

"You'll get plenty of action, don't you worry," Rivka said as she walked past him on her way to wish Ankh well.

"Ramp extending. Airlock open," Red reported. He was there to open the hatch, not to needle the Crenellian, but if anything happened, he was in a position to defend the ship. His railgun was slung over his shoulder, knife and blaster in a belt at his waist. He was also in shorts and a t-shirt, what passed for pajamas in his wardrobe.

Ankh trooped out without waiting. When he reached the bottom of the ramp, he stepped gingerly off. Red retracted the ramp and closed the hatch. "Now, we wait."

"Where's your vest?" Rivka asked.

Red pounded on his chest with a fist while watching the screen showing Ankh casually strolling toward the house. "That guy is on his own program."

"I have it on good authority that the food processor will now accept your voice commands and deliver what you ordered. Now answer my question."

Lindy arrived, wearing her vest and carrying Red's. He put it on.

"I thought we weren't waiting on him hand and foot?" Rivka quipped.

"We're not," Lindy replied. "He owes me a foot rub."

Red vigorously nodded. Ankh finally reached the house. He stood at the door and looked like he was frozen.

The two bodyguards hoisted their weapons. Red's hand was over the big red button. "Just say the word, Magistrate."

"Not yet. I think he and Erasmus are trying to break in."

"That's the lamest break-in I've ever seen," Red mumbled.

"We don't want any alarms going off."

The door popped open and Ankh walked in, disappearing from view. "Anything, Chaz?" Rivka asked.

"No indication of an alert, but I am limited on what the ship can see. We are using passive systems only."

"Passive is good. Stay frosty, Chaz." Five minutes later, Ankh came running out as fast as his little legs would carry him. Red hammered the button to open the hatch and extend the ramp.

A small, furry creature came bounding after the Crenellian. Ankh tried to step onto the invisible ramp, but it hadn't extended all the way yet. He ran chest-first into it, bounced off, and landed flat on his back. The beast was on him as Red shouldered his weapon and raced out the open hatch. The dog-looking rodent ran into Ankh's head and returned to give him a thorough licking.

Red eased down the ramp, flicking the creature away and pulling Ankh upright. The poor furry beast whimpered and cried. Ankh worked his way back into the ship.

"No one talks to me," he said as he headed toward the engine room.

Red reached back down and the creature pounced, play-biting his hand. Red stood up, still holding the furball.

"Get in here," Rivka encouraged since Red was out in the open. He realized his exposure and tried putting the little creature down, but it wouldn't let go. He thought about throwing it but stopped himself. He climbed back into the ship. The hatch closed behind him and their antics became, once again, invisible to the Gorandians.

"Ankh, you have a friend that needs to go home. I'm not stealing someone's dog."

"Is that what that is?" Rivka wondered.

Floyd ran up to the team, bouncing with joy. Red put the pup down, to much tail wagging and posturing as he faced off against Floyd. The two tapped noses before running off.

Rivka closed her eyes, but that didn't help. She started rubbing her temples. When she blinked, she found Red, Lindy, and Sahved watching her.

"Are we desperados?" the Yemilorian asked.

"I don't know where you learned that word, but we aren't desperados. He is, and our blue-friend is. Everyone else is a normal and decent being." She high-fived Lindy as she bumped past Red on her way to the engine room.

"What did I do? I thought Ankh was getting attacked. I'm the victim here!" Red's pleading fell on deaf ears.

"I think we're desperados," Sahved stated.

"I think we have a dog, and a stolen one at that. I'm so ashamed." Lindy chuckled.

"It's going home as soon as I figure out how!" Rivka yelled down the corridor.

It took Ankh two days to gain access through the Gorandian system. *Wyatt Earp* hovered near the big home. The back door was still open, but no one came to check or visit the pet.

"We're doing him a favor by keeping him company," Groenwyn said softly, trying not to disturb the two creatures curled into a single ball on her small lap. "Floyd has adopted him."

"We can't take someone's dog," Rivka declared, chewing her fingernail while waiting. She wasn't interested in reading other court cases. She only wanted to finish her current case.

"Ankh?" She couldn't wait any longer.

"We are in and searching. I suspect her real name wasn't Angora, but so few Gorandians leave the planet, we're forced to track down every single one for a year before Angora first appeared. We have already checked departures with returns for the ten-year period, but none match. She wasn't Angora before she left, and when she returned, she wasn't what she was before."

"Thanks." Rivka knew better than to tell him to keep doing what he was doing or ask him for a status report. He would tell her what he knew when he knew it so she could do what she needed to do.

Rivka strolled casually through the ship, opening doors and hatches to learn more about her ride. She stopped by the small gym to find Red sparring with Sahved. Red showed him a move to disarm an opponent, then rushed the Yemilorian, who didn't do anything that he had just been shown. Instead, he used his length for leverage and his three dexterous fingers to launch Red over his head. The bodyguard slammed into the wall, sliding down to the padded deck.

Lindy slowly clapped. "You've been keeping secrets," Red said, standing and brushing himself off. He crouched and approached more warily. Sahved lanced an arm like a whip, slapping Red in the side of the head. He ignored the attack, launching a counterpunch into the Yemilorian's mid-section. The gangly creature flew across the room, hopped once, and slammed into the wall. He fell to the deck and spewed his breakfast.

"Does he do that like that ocean creature shooting ink?"

Rivka left them to it. She didn't know, but it made sense to her. "Octopus," she said over her shoulder.

Aurora appeared in the corridor wearing a bathrobe. She yawned and waved on her way to the galley. "Night shift?" Rivka asked.

"Yup," the young woman answered.

The Magistrate found herself in the engine room. Ankh was in the middle of his holo workshop, spinning in a complex dance of interactive engagement. He seemed more gaunt than he had been a couple days prior. She knew he had been at it for the entire time without taking a break. She wondered how long he could go, but didn't want to find out.

She leaned against the equipment and watched. Clodagh sidled up next to her. "We have an upgrade to our weapons system and shields, and then there's the cloak. Everything is installed and working, or as much as I can tell without testing the shield and weapons."

"Thank you for minding the store. We whip in, whip out, demand quick action, and then do nothing for days on end." Rivka crossed her arms and continued to watch Ankh. The two women comfortably stood in silence. Neither needed to speak when there was nothing that had to be said.

Finally, Clodagh started to move away, back to a duty that called her. She stopped and spoke. "Thank you for giving me a chance. Studying engineering with Ankh has improved my understanding by light-years."

"Ankh is teaching you?"

The engineer laughed. "That's one way to put it. He builds it, letting me watch, then gives me the information so I can fix it if it breaks. Then he moves on to his next project."

"That sounds more like our little man."

The holographic suite dropped, and Ankh staggered out. Both women rushed to catch him. "Chaz has the coordinates. I think I'll sleep now." Rivka carried him to the cot that served him between marathon sessions. She tucked him in, pulling the covers up. She brushed his head as one would a child. A genius child, but one who required others to help him. Wenceslaus appeared and jumped onto the cot. He curled up next to the Crenellian, watching Rivka closely. She backed away, not trying to pet him to avoid getting scratched.

She wondered who was whose pet as the cat watched the women. Rivka approved of the cat as Ankh's last line of defense.

The Magistrate clapped Clodagh on the shoulder. "The bad guys aren't going to catch themselves."

"So I hear," the engineer said to Rivka's back as she disappeared into the ship.

CHAPTER TWENTY-THREE

Branxial, Gorandia's Capital City

"According to Erasmus, this is the home where the Gorandian formerly known as Angora resides," Chaz explained. A humble home on the outskirts of the city, it wasn't remote enough to raid like they'd done to the house to access the worldwide net.

"Wait until nightfall. Ankh is out of action, so it falls to us. I want her alive," Rivka said. Red and Lindy watched over her shoulder. "And bring Sahved. He needs to see how we take down a criminal, and based on what I saw in the gym, he can handle himself when push comes to shove."

"We ordered some body armor for him. It looks like ass on him, but that's because he's so damn skinny," Red remarked.

"Sounds like anything he wears will look like ass. But will it protect him?"

"Well enough, as long as he doesn't turn sideways," Red told her. Lindy nodded to confirm what he'd said.

"No ramp. We'll jump from the hatch. We should have

brought *Destiny's Vengeance.* That ship would have made this a little easier. Maybe next time."

They went about their business until it was time to go.

"Sahved, grab your armor and meet us at the airlock," Red said into the ship-wide comm. "When are we going to hook him up with a brain bug?"

"You mean, a comm chip?"

Red shrugged and waited.

"After this case. In the meantime, keep your eye on him." Rivka led the way down the corridor to the airlock. The external monitor showed the ground crawling up to meet the ship. It stopped, pitching awkwardly because of surrounding obstacles.

"It's the closest I can get it. You have less than a two-meter drop to the ground." Aurora was at the ship's controls, guiding it in.

"I'll be right here to open the door when you come back," Groenwyn told them, holding the small dog-like creature in her arms.

"Maybe we should drop him off while we're there."

"What if no one comes to check on Angora, and Spike is in the house all alone?" Groenwyn asked.

"We're not leaving him here. We'll take him home as soon as we have Angora in hand." Rivka hesitated. "'Spike?' Why does he have a name?"

"I couldn't keep saying 'Hey, you' to the cutest little guy in the galaxy."

Rivka nodded to Red. "Lights," he ordered, and Chaz dimmed the interior to a barely visible red glow. Red hit the button, and the airlock hatch cycled. Darkness greeted them. Red was out in a flash, landing with flexed knees and running forward. Sahved hit the ground, made it two steps, and fell, but got right back up. Rivka was next, with Lindy bringing up the rear. They ran to the small, squarish building. *Wyatt Earp* buttoned up. Total time with the hatch open was less than three seconds.

Lindy and Sahved peeled around the side and headed for the front in case the Gorandian tried to escape, while the Magistrate entered through the back in the primary effort to secure the perp. Red didn't bother knocking. He ran toward the door and jumped, and when he reached the entryway, he lashed out with a side-kick, twisting the heavy door against the lock and hinges. He followed with his shoulder, opening the way inside.

Soft light greeted them. Red went straight through the one door on the opposite wall. The next room accounted for the remainder of the home's space. The Gorandian sat in a chair against the wall.

"Angora," Rivka said, walking in after Red had stopped and leveled his weapon at the Crenellian-looking creature.

The Gorandian started shaking, arms spasming, and her eyeballs shot wide until her head burst, spraying blue fluid across the room.

Red started spitting. "I think I got some in my mouth," he complained.

Rivka looked at the front of her clothes before checking the Gorandian. "She's dead, all right. Maybe they *are* total agoraphobes. Her head freaking exploded."

"That might have been the most screwed-up thing I've ever seen," Red admitted. He wiped his face one last time.

It's over. Let's get out of here. Open the door, people, we're coming home, Rivka told them.

"Bye, Spike." Groenwyn started to cry as she hugged the tiny creature one last time.

"Ankh is still comatose, so the next best thing is for you to deliver him to his owner," Rivka explained, handing the dog-like creature to the Yemilorian. He held it away from his body.

The cloaked *Wyatt Earp* sat in the backyard of the random house they had picked because it was unoccupied. The door was now closed, and a heat source registered from within.

"Give the dog back," Rivka said firmly.

The Magistrate opened the airlock hatch. "What if his head explodes?" Sahved asked.

"Go." Rivka pointed out the open hatch.

He jumped to the ground. They had decided the invisible ramp wasn't working. They needed to see what they were walking on.

Sahved walked reluctantly to the door and pounded on it, which was most un-Crenellian-like. Rivka sighed.

The voice projected across the area. "Aliens! My dog is tainted. Burn you all with fire!"

"Get back in here," Rivka ordered. Sahved ran from the house. The hatch opened and he leapt inside, easily landing on his feet. Rivka hammered the button, took one look at the little dog, and headed for the bridge, yelling as she walked, "Get me off this planet!"

Groenwyn took Spike from Sahved's three-fingered hands and hugged him mercilessly. She put him on the deck, and he ran down the corridor toward Floyd. The two tumbled and rolled, even though the wombat was five times his size.

Whee! Floyd cried.

Rivka closed the heavy hatch to the bridge, so she could have some peace and quiet. "Chaz, can you connect me with the High Chancellor, please?"

"One moment, Magistrate."

The screen showed voice only. "You have an uncanny ability to call in the middle of the night. Did you have a falling out with Grainger, so you don't feel like you can wake him up instead of me?"

"Not at all, but this case is inextricably linked with the power brokers on Yoll. Can we talk about the money?" Rivka insisted.

Due to the length of the pause, Rivka thought the High Chancellor had hung up on her. "Meet me at Keeg Station, All Guns Blazing, in two days' time."

"Terry Henry's joint. I'll be there. Sleep tight, High Chancellor. The smuggling case is closed. The final suspect has been sanctioned." Rivka cut the signal before Wyatt could change his mind.

Dren Cluster, Keeg Station, All Guns Blazing Bar and Recreation

Rivka and Lindy approached the bar, watching for the High Chancellor. A ship that they thought was his was in the hangar bay next to theirs, but he wasn't in the bar.

"I guess we wait," Lindy offered, eyes scanning the area as she looked for threats. Bad Company personnel and their supporting cast moved to and fro on missions that only they knew, walking with a sense of urgency.

"I hear they finally finished the rebuild after the cloaked aliens attacked."

"It hasn't been more than six months, has it?" Lindy asked. The two were ushered to a quiet booth away from the door and the bustle of the establishment.

"Moonstokle pie, please," Rivka ordered.

"That'll work," Lindy said to the server.

"No, that's for me. You'll need to order your own."

"Make it two," Lindy clarified.

They nursed their drinks while they waited for their pizzas. "Red seems to like Sahved."

"Red likes anyone who is honest. Sahved is unapologetically who he is," Lindy replied.

"We need to put him through the Pod-doc if for no other reason than to settle his stomach. He pukes more than a newborn."

"I've never seen anything like it." Lindy stopped mid-drink and stood, offering her seat to the High Chancellor.

He thanked her and sat. "I'll be up front. Don't eat my pie," the bodyguard warned Rivka before moving off.

"How's the crew working out?" Wyatt asked.

Rivka smiled. "Quite nicely. A little issue with the authorities on Binsulaker Prime, but I let them know about my dismay. They were less than welcoming. Yemilore? Now, that place is a bit different."

"What did you think of Gorandia?"

"I can neither confirm nor deny that I know anything about Gorandia." Rivka smiled sweetly.

"All Guns Blazing has an inherent feature that prevents

any recordings. We can speak freely. I shan't repeat your words."

"They look just like Crenellians, but they're different. Angora's head exploded when we confronted her."

"What did she do?" Wyatt pressed.

"Literally. Her head exploded and sprayed blue gunk over Red and me. I could have done without that."

"Isn't that interesting?" Wyatt replied, sounding less than interested. Rivka shoved a double slice of pizza into her mouth and chewed slowly.

"Okay," the High Chancellor conceded. "I'll talk. You can stop torturing me." He waved down the server and ordered a double-meat everything pie. "The money. In the Federation, there are two economies. The one everyone sees, where you get paid, you pay your taxes, and you buy stuff. And then there's the second economy that keeps worlds afloat. It's in this world that the wealthy operate. Some of their funds dribble into the everyday world of you and me, and then there are other times where we see the movement, like an ocean's tide.

"The art-smuggling affected this second economy. The lawsuit was completely unexpected since it threatened to shine light into the darkness." At Rivka's look, Wyatt clarified, "Gil'dinor was not murdered. He simply died. The strain was too much for his old heart. The butler and the insurance agent expected Loids to pay up. They didn't anticipate that the old man would pitch such a fit over the money. They figured he would be so distraught, he would take whatever they gave him."

"I know that, High Chancellor, but the money! How could they fence the pieces? Is there that much floating

CRAIG MARTELLE & MICHAEL ANDERLE

around in the darkness that someone could drop a billion credits on a statue?"

"There is untold wealth out of circulation. It's not anything anyone needs to worry about. Why do you think politicians like staying in power, and why do you think the rich like having a ruling class?"

Rivka shifted uncomfortably. She held her next slice enticingly in front of her face. "I guess it has something to do with knowing the secrets. As long as they're with the in-crowd, they don't spill the secrets." Rivka arrowed the slice into her mouth.

"I don't understand how you can put moonstokle on pizza. It's unnatural. No fruit in beer. No fruit on pizza. Ahh!" Wyatt purred when his pie arrived. "This is how it's supposed to look."

It looked like a rugged mountain range covered with yellow and orange snow.

They both ate for a while, Rivka lost in her thoughts.

"Who do we answer to?" she asked.

"We answer to the good guys," Wyatt replied. "Understand that the Queen allowed the second economy because it was critical to buoy the individual planets. Many billions go out, while just as much comes in each and every day."

"Daily?" Rivka asked with her mouth full. A piece of moonstokle threatened to fall onto her plate. She recovered quickly and finished chewing.

"It is how the Federation works. I know Ankh and Erasmus were searching for the movement of significant funds but couldn't find it. Ted and Plato couldn't find it because it's not visible. Those are independent networks, not attached to anything else. To get into them, one must already be inside, and access can come only from a system that is inside."

"Ankh feels like he failed."

"He's going to have to get over that without you telling him."

"That makes me feel shady." Rivka put her next slice on her plate. It was odd for her to not feel hungry, but she wasn't.

"Please don't," Wyatt pleaded. "It's the foundation of the Federation governments. It has no bearing on the everyday lives of the average citizen, but it does in that if the planetary government fails, the people will suffer. The shadow economy makes sure that doesn't happen. Making sure the rich people remain rich? That was why you were assigned to the case, and that was why you instinctively balked. You were absolutely correct. Rich people stealing from rich people is something we can't have."

Rivka chuckled and reached for the next slice. "That is righteously dicked up."

"Welcome to the club. Now that you know…" Wyatt let it hang.

"I have to stay in the club?"

"You were already there. The more we learn, the more we realize we don't know."

"Next time, how about a nice, clean murder?" Rivka joked. "Simple. Blood everywhere. A little DNA. Some footprints. You know, like the good ol' days, when I didn't know about the power behind the power?"

"You know that a moon causes tides, but you don't think about it. I ask that you simply accept that this tide is regular. It is being managed by good people who have the best interests of the Federation at heart."

High Chancellor Wyatt smiled at Rivka before taking a bite of his pizza. He casually finished one piece before signaling to the server. "Box the rest, please. I must be going. I'll take the bill."

"I can box your pie, but the Magistrate and her friends eat for free as long as Terry and Char own this All Guns Blazing."

The server brought a box and used the spatula to load Wyatt's pie into it.

"I don't know how you did it, Magistrate, but I think you have your own shadow economy going."

"A favor for a favor."

"Does that work for the bigger jobs? I don't like getting invoices from the Bad Company. They can be a rather significant blow to my austere budget. And how many ships do you have now?"

Rivka contemplated the older man. "As many as I need. Same with the crew." Wyatt stood. "Remember, a nice, clean murder."

He nodded, and they shook hands. As usual, none of his thoughts rose to the surface of his mind.

"I'm thinking a peace treaty between two warring planets, or maybe a drawn-out arbitration," Wyatt said over his shoulder as he walked away.

"We have a dog, too," Rivka called after him. The High Chancellor stopped and turned, fixing her with a one-eyebrow-raised look. "He weighs less than a kilo, and we call him Spike."

"Of course, you do, Magistrate. Do you do anything like normal people?"

Lindy waved from the front entrance. Red and Sahved were just beyond, arguing. The Yemilorian was twisting his fingers in the air. Groenwyn was trying to get around them, with Floyd in one arm and Spike in the other.

"Always."

The End of

Judge, Jury, & Executioner, Book 7

If you like this book, please leave a review. I love reviews since they tell other readers that this book is worth their time and money. I hope you feel that way now that you've finished the latest installment. Please drop me a line and let me know you like Rivka's adventures and want them to continue. This is my new favorite series. I hope you agree.

Don't stop now! Keep turning the pages as Craig hits his *Author Notes* with thoughts about this book and the good stuff that happens in the *Kurtherian Gambit* Universe. Your favorite legal eagle will return! I guarantee it:).

AUTHOR NOTES - CRAIG MARTELLE

WRITTEN OCTOBER 9, 2019

You are still reading! Thank you for staying on board until now. It doesn't get much better than that.

What is *The Art of Smuggling* about? Just like *Fratricide*, I wanted to challenge our understanding of things we take for granted.

The first name comes from Tracey Byrnes—Jelesa. He had a small role in this book. Tracey is also helping me with a different project, and for that, I am eternally grateful.

While writing this, I was selected for jury duty. The selection process in Fairbanks, Alaska for a superior court trial is fairly arduous, so it took the better part of a day to pick the fourteen jurors. We were sworn in and given our time to return, at 8:30AM the following day. I asked what we should wear. The clerk told me, "Whatever you want." I went with jeans and my LMBPN polo shirt (gotta sport the brand, especially while I'm writing the latest *Judge, Jury, and Executioner*!)

The case was about battery, but the defense was trying to use self-defense, even though his client had entered the property of another individual and they both armed themselves, one with a bat and the other with a golf club (a driver, to be exact). Well, one guy beat the hell out of the other guy. The winner was claiming self-defense. Come the morning of the trial, we're supposed to start at 8:30, but then we're still in the jury sequestration room until about 9:15, when the clerk brings us into the court. We file in smartly, to find that the lawyers for both sides agreed to a plea deal. The guy pled to misdemeanor battery and was given three years' probation, along with mandatory anger-management classes.

The consolation prize was that the judge gave us a tour of the courtroom and his private chambers, where we had a good conversation and got insight into something we normally wouldn't. And I got my picture taken behind the bench while sporting the brand. I'll put that picture at the end of my notes.

This story came to me while we were visiting the Tretyakov Art Gallery in Moscow, Russia. Who determines the value of the artwork, and how? It's all voodoo if you ask me. I can't tell you if I like a piece of art or not. I'm Red when it comes to art appreciation.

But now we're back home in the sub-arctic where the darkness grows longer each day. It has snowed and the daily high temperatures are slightly above freezing. Give it a couple more days and it will be full winter. Then we start the clock on how many days straight of below-freezing highs we'll have. A couple years ago, it was 142 consecutive days with the outside high temperature below freezing. Last year, it was just over 100 straight days.

But that's what it's like up here. We haven't had clear skies in a week. When we get them back, this has been a great year for the aurora. Northern Lights nightly, watching from our driveway.

Thank you for reading my stories. This series is my favorite and will continue for the foreseeable future. I'll be wrapping Superdreadnought at six books, Metal Legion at eight books, Nightwalker at eight books, and Bad Company at eight books. Those series will all be finished by the first quarter of 2020. I'll write a new Judge, Jury, & Executioner in between wrapping each of the others, because Rivka will live on. I enjoy these stories far too much to stop writing them.

And next year, we'll be bringing out a new series, not set in the Kurtherian universe. Look for weretigers learning galaxy's secrets.

Peace, fellow humans.

Please join my Newsletter (www.craigmartelle.com – please, please, please sign up!), or you can follow me on Facebook since you'll get the same opportunity to pick up the books for only 99 cents on that first day they are published.

If you liked this story, you might like some of my other books. You can join my mailing list by dropping by my website www.craigmartelle.com or if you have any comments, shoot me a note at craig@craigmartelle.com. I am always happy to hear from people who've read my work. I try to answer every email I receive.

If you liked the story, please write a short review for me on Amazon. I greatly appreciate any kind words, even one or two sentences go a long way. The number of reviews an eBook receives greatly improves how well an eBook does on Amazon.

Amazon – www.amazon.com/author/craigmartelle

BookBub – https://www.bookbub.com/authors/craig-martelle

Facebook – www.facebook.com/authorcraigmartelle

My web page – www.craigmartelle.com

That's it—break's over, back to writing the next book. Peace, fellow humans.

Craig Martelle's other books (listed by series)

Terry Henry Walton Chronicles (co-written with Michael Anderle) – a post-apocalyptic paranormal adventure

Gateway to the Universe (co-written with Justin Sloan & Michael Anderle) – this book transitions the characters from the Terry Henry Walton Chronicles to The Bad Company

The Bad Company (co-written with Michael Anderle) – a military science fiction space opera

Judge, Jury, & Executioner (also available in audio) – a space opera adventure legal thriller

Shadow Vanguard – a Tom Dublin series

Superdreadnought (co-written with Tim Marquitz)– an AI military space opera

Metal Legion (co-written with Caleb Wachter) (coming in audio) – a military space opera

The Free Trader – a young adult science fiction action adventure

Cygnus Space Opera (also available in audio) – A young adult space opera (set in the Free Trader universe)

Darklanding (co-written with Scott Moon) (also available in audio) – a space western

Mystically Engineered (co-written with Valerie Emerson) – Mystics, dragons, & spaceships

End Times Alaska (also available in audio) – a Permuted Press publication – a post-apocalyptic survivalist adventure

Nightwalker (a Frank Roderus series) with Craig Martelle – A post-apocalyptic western adventure

End Days (co-written with E.E. Isherwood) (coming in audio) – a post-apocalyptic adventure

Successful Indie Author – a non-fiction series to help self-published authors

Metamorphosis Alpha – stories from the world's first science fiction RPG

The Expanding Universe – science fiction anthologies

Monster Case Files (co-written with Kathryn Hearst) – A Warner twins mystery adventure

Rick Banik (also available in audio) – Spy & terrorism action adventure

Published exclusively by Craig Martelle, Inc

The Dragon's Call by Angelique Anderson & Craig A. Price, Jr. – an epic fantasy quest

For a complete list of Craig's books, stop by his website – https://craigmartelle.com